"Is something wrong, Mom?"

She ought to tell him she didn't expect to see Joe ever again. But she couldn't. Not at Christmas. "No," she said shakily.

Mark nodded, apparently satisfied.

"You really like Joe, don't you?" Teresa asked.

Mark stopped playing with his Christmas gift from Joe. He lifted his head. Joe was the first man Mark had really cared about since his father's death. Losing Joe, too, would devastate her son. *Her* heart wouldn't be the only one breaking.

"Yeah," Mark said carefully, "he's really cool. I was thinking—I mean, wondering...well, do you think you might marry him?" The last came out in a rush.

She couldn't seem to speak, didn't know what to say.

The truth, she thought. Tell him as much of the truth as you can bear.

"If he ever asks me to marry him, I'd say yes."

Mark studied her for a long moment, his eyes serious, then gave another decisive nod. "Good."

ABOUT THE AUTHOR

Janice Kay Johnson is the bestselling author of twenty-eight books, and her deeply emotional and involving stories have enthralled readers around the world. It will come as no surprise to her many fans that Janice is the mother of two daughters, or that her home is filled with animals—one dog and ten cats, at the last count.

Books by Janice Kay Johnson

HARLEQUIN SUPERROMANCE

483—SEIZE THE DAY
561—HOME AGAIN
627—HER SISTER'S BABY
648—IN THE DARK OF THE NIGHT
677—HIS FRIEND'S WIFE

Janice Kay Johnson

WHAT SHE WANTS FOR CHRISTMAS

Harlequin Books

TORONTO • NEW YORK • LONDON
AMSTERDAM • PARIS • SYDNEY • HAMBURG
STOCKHOLM • ATHENS • TOKYO • MILAN
MADRID • WARSAW • BUDAPEST • AUCKLAND

ISBN 0-373-70720-7

WHAT SHE WANTS FOR CHRISTMAS

This edition published by arrangement with Harlequin Books S.A.

Printed in U.S.A.

WHAT SHE WANTS FOR CHRISTMAS

CHAPTER ONE

"CAN'T WE GO shopping?"

Thirty seconds after walking in the front door from a lousy day at work, these were not the first words Teresa Burkett wanted to hear from her daughter.

"Don't whine," she said automatically. "I didn't let you whine when you were two, and I'm not going to start now."

Nicole dumped a cat off her lap and rose from her slouch on the sofa. Sounding teenage indignant, she said, "Can't I ask a perfectly reasonable question?"

"Certainly." Teresa headed for the kitchen. "Go right ahead."

Mark was already there. A typical ten-going-on-eleven-year-old boy, he was eating. String cheese, a bowl of some sugary cereal and a pop. Teresa shuddered.

She opened the fridge and grabbed a cola. Caffeine. She needed it quick. One long swallow later, she noticed the casserole dish, still covered with aluminum foil, reposing on the refrigerator shelf.

Stay calm. "You didn't put dinner on like I asked."

"Mo-om." Her pretty dark-haired daughter looked at her as if she were an idiot. "It isn't *time* to put dinner on. You're home early."

Teresa sighed. "I'm sorry. I forgot."

Mouth full, Mark asked, "How was your day?"

"Crummy." She made a face. "I did three spays, wormed two horses and treated a few miscellaneous cats and dogs. Otherwise, I hung around the clinic hopefully and helped Eric load his truck."

The dairy farmers had decided their animals could afford to wait until the vet they knew—a man—could get around to them. They were a conservative lot, these farmers. Their daughters and wives might get their hands dirty helping out, but they didn't make the major decisions and they didn't become veterinarians.

A couple of the farmers had checked Teresa out by bringing their cats or dogs in for treatment. She had to assume that her appearance was part of the problem. Maybe if she'd been a big strapping gal, they would have accepted her gender philosophically. Instead, she was a slender five foot four when she stretched. Her wiry strength didn't show. She looked petite and elegant, ornamental instead of useful.

Only, if they wouldn't give her a chance, how the hell did she demonstrate her competence? A wave of panic washed over her. Financially and legally, she was Dr. Eric Bergstrom's partner now; she'd bought into the practice. But she wouldn't blame him if he got damn tired of doing all the work while she loitered around the clinic.

"Dr. Craig said you could come back to your old job any time." Nicole was trying hard not to sound hopeful. "It's not too late. The sale on this... house hasn't even closed." The pause was calculated; the three-bedroom farmhouse on the edge of town was not, in Nicole's opinion, a suitable residence for a sophisticated teenager. *She* belonged back in the oversize, ostentatious, French-provincial style home they'd

left behind in Bellevue, an increasingly ritzy community across Lake Washington from Seattle. Teresa was trying very hard to be patient. Fifteen was a tough age at which to have to move, but Nicole would adjust.

Assuming, Teresa thought ruefully, that her mother didn't end up tucking her tail between her legs and running.

"Actually, I signed the papers today. It's all ours. Give up, kiddo," she said lightly, then groaned when the dogs leapt to their feet and raced, barking, to the front door. A second later the doorbell rang. "Are either of you expecting a friend?"

"Friend?" Nicole struck an astonished pose. "Who has a friend?"

Nonetheless, she trailed her mother to the door. Presumably even some hick neighbor would be a diversion in this outpost of civilization.

"Quiet!" Teresa snapped at the dogs. Golda and Serena quit barking and looked sheepish. She opened the door and gaped. If the man on her porch was a hick, might she never find civilization again.

He actually wore overalls and muddy work boots, as most of the farmers around here seemed to, but this guy was built. Muscles, shoulders wide enough to shelter a woman from a cold wind, long legs... He had to be at least six foot two. His straight dark hair looked silky, his lean face was tanned, his wide mouth set in the kind of grim line that served as a challenge to any self-respecting woman. But it was his eyes that riveted her. In that dark face, they were a vivid electric blue.

"May I help you?" Thank God, she didn't sound quite as dumbstruck as she felt.

He moved his shoulders, as though uncomfortably aware of what had been going through her mind. "Dr. Burkett?"

"Yes?" A client?

"My sister suggested I stop by. Jess Kerrigan. She said you wanted some trees taken down."

Trees? Jess Kerrigan? Teresa snapped out of it. Jess was the nice owner of those show-quality Arabians. She had actually agreed cheerfully to let the new vet treat one of them. And the conversation with her had even been useful. During a discussion of Teresa's old farmhouse—Jess knew the previous owners—Teresa had asked about tree-toppers. Her client had remarked that her brother was a logging contractor.

"He'll give you a good price," she'd announced. "I'll tell him to."

"Oh, you don't need—"

"We like to welcome newcomers to White Horse."

If only the dairy farmers felt the same.

The man was still standing there on her doorstep waiting. Teresa pulled herself together. "Bless you. I'd forgotten to get your name or phone number from her. Why don't you come in?"

He glanced down at his boots. "I'd better not. If you could just show me the trees . . ."

"Sure." She stepped out and let the dogs slip through. Closing the door in her astonished daughter's face, she smiled. "Around the house."

She was conscious of him behind her in a way she couldn't ever remember being. She couldn't remember, either, the last time she'd hoped so fervently that a man had noticed her, as well. Unless... Oh, no—had Jess Kerrigan said anything about a sister-in-law? But of course he'd be married. Any man this beautiful had

to be. In fact, any man over thirty with a half-decent character was married, never mind what he looked like.

The front lawn was springy under her feet. Too springy; it was half moss, shaded by the stand of mixed cedar and hemlocks to the south of the house.

"These," she said simply, standing aside. "The realtor said one of them came down last year on the roof, which is why the house has a new one. I don't want to take a chance on a repeat. Besides, I'd like a little more sun. The closets are mildewing."

He nodded and rubbed his chin reflectively as he stood contemplating the fifteen or so trees, tilting his head back to gaze up, then glancing around as though her yard told him something.

"I thought I might leave the big cedar," Teresa said, feeling the need to fill the silence. "It's pretty."

Without a word, he went to the tree. From a pocket in his overalls, he pulled a screwdriver and poked it into the trunk. "Rotten. Better take it out, too."

"Rotten? Oh, what a shame."

"Are you thinking you might get much for these trees?"

"Get much?" She blinked, then realized she didn't even know the man's name. When she asked, he looked surprised.

"Sorry. I guess I figured Jess would have mentioned it. Joe Hughes." He held out one large hand.

It completely engulfed hers. She liked the feeling, which took her aback. She'd spent most of her life trying to overcome the handicap of her size. Now she wanted to be overwhelmed by some primitive hunk of masculinity?

There was no denying it. That was exactly what she wanted. Their clasped hands brought other visions to her mind: his head bent over hers, his body pressing hers down, his— She firmly put the brakes on her imagination. He was married, she reminded herself. He must be. Besides, he hadn't demonstrated any great interest in *her*. Maybe his tastes ran to six-foot Nordic goddesses.

But, no. He hadn't let her hand go, and when she lifted her gaze to his, it was to catch a flicker of something in those eyes that sped up her pulse more than her first chance at surgery had. Were his cheeks tinged with red as he finally released her hand?

"Jess always says I have no manners," he said ruefully. "I guess she's right."

"What do sisters know?" Teresa said, grinning at him.

He lifted one dark brow. Didn't it figure he could. "You have some, too?"

"Two. I'm the middle child. I'm sure that's why my psyche is so fragile."

For a moment he studied her as gravely as he had the stand of trees. Then he smiled, slow and heart-stoppingly sexy. "You look fragile all right, but my mama always taught me appearances are deceiving."

"Smart woman."

His eyes lingered on her face as the smile faded. She felt flushed and dizzy.

"Five hundred dollars," he said.

"What?" She stared at him.

"For your stumpage. The trees aren't big enough to be worth much, but I can get them out easy enough—the truck can back right down your driveway. Pulp

mill'll take 'em. You'll be rid of the trees and have a little cash."

Thank heavens for his speech, the longest out of his mouth yet. It had given her time to realize he wasn't offering five hundred dollars for her body.

"Does that include your taking the stumps out, not just grinding them down?"

"Yup. And burning the stumps and slash."

"You're on," she said.

That eyebrow rose again. "Don't you want to get other bids?"

"I already have. Two. One of the guys wanted to charge me two thousand dollars. Said the trees weren't worth anything. He was going to buck them into firewood length and leave them for me. I'd have been stacking them for the rest of my life. The other fellow didn't do stumps. He gave me the names of a couple of places that grind them down. I'm thinking of putting the vegetable garden there. How can I if the ground is full of roots?"

Joe Hughes nodded. "I don't think anybody would beat my price, anyway."

"Your sister guaranteed you."

"Sisters are good for something," he said, straight-faced.

"Yours seemed like a nice woman. She let me touch her horses."

He heard the flash of bitterness, because those disconcerting eyes fixed themselves on her face again. "You're a vet."

"I'm a woman."

His gaze flicked downward, then back to her face. "I noticed," he said in a voice that had roughened just enough to be a compliment.

"Women are apparently competent to treat a five-pound cat. A thousand-pound Jersey cow is another story."

He frowned. "Guess we're a little backward in White Horse."

"Eric—Eric Bergstrom, that is—warned me, but he thought the farmers would get over it. Judging from my first few weeks, they're not in any hurry to."

"We'll have to see what we can do about that," Joe said.

She made a face. "Don't tell me you're a dairy farmer on the side."

"Nope. Hardly know one end of a cow from another. But I have friends who are."

"Ah. You're going to tell them what a sweet girl I am."

He apparently didn't mind her sarcasm, because one corner of his mouth twitched. "I'm going to tell them which end of their cow not to be."

A cow's ass. She liked it.

"Might come better from you than me," she conceded. Her basically cheerful nature triumphed and she laughed. "When can you take out my trees?"

"Next week. Say, Monday."

Monday was one of her days off. She could watch. She didn't kid herself about what—or who—she'd be watching.

She smiled and held out her hand. "See you then."

He glanced down at her hand and seemed to deliberate for a moment before he took it. His grip sent a shiver through her. When he released her, he flexed his fingers before balling them into a fist. Unfortunately his face told her remarkably little.

"Monday," he repeated, gave a brief nod and headed for his huge shiny blue pickup without a backward glance.

Teresa wandered into the house. Both kids were waiting for her.

"Who," her daughter demanded, enunciating carefully, "was *he?*"

"A hunk, wasn't he?"

Nicole's lip curled. "He was *dirty!*"

Teresa was in just the mood to provoke a little outrage. Musingly she said, "There's something about a sweaty man . . . a day's growth of beard . . . a little dirt under his fingernails . . ."

"But, Mom!" Mark stared at her as if she'd gone stark-raving mad. "Then how come you won't let *me* go to school dirty? How come I have to wash my hands before we eat? How come—?"

"You're not a man, stupid." His sister didn't even glance at him. "You're a boy. A little kid. A—"

"You think you're so grown-up? Then how come the *men* aren't all lined up outside?"

"There isn't anyone in this nowhere place I'd *want* lined up!" Nicole flared. "And can't you tell when Mom is putting you on?"

"Actually, I wasn't," Teresa said calmly. "He's a very handsome man. Now, can we quit bickering? He's also a logger who is going to take those wretched trees out for us. Monday."

"Cool," Mark declared. "Can I watch?"

"Nope. You'll be in school by then, remember? Registration tomorrow."

"School!" Nicole collapsed on a kitchen chair. "Mom, what am I going to wear?"

"How about leggings and a sweater?"

"How about overalls and work boots?" her fifteen-year-old retorted bitterly.

"Seems to me a pair of sacky overalls is one of your standards," Teresa agreed. "Good idea."

"Please, please, please, can we go shopping?"

"Nope."

"Why?" Nicole wailed.

"Because I don't want to," Teresa said reasonably. "And you have a perfectly adequate wardrobe. Now, can I turn the oven on?"

"Why didn't you let me move in with Jayne?" Nicole jumped to her feet. "This place stinks!" She ran from the room and a moment later Teresa heard her feet thundering up the stairs.

She'd probably spend the rest of the evening on the telephone with her friends in Bellevue. The long-distance charges would have to become an issue eventually, but for now Teresa figured they were a small price to pay. She sighed and saw Mark staring after his sister with almost as much bewilderment as his mother felt.

"Like Bellevue was so great." He stuffed some string cheese in his mouth. "What's for dinner, Mom?"

Thank God for one cheerful member of her family. "Chicken and artichoke hearts."

"Cool," he said again. He even submitted to a hug, though he didn't have a clue why she felt compelled to give it.

"YOU SHOULD HAVE seen this guy." Nicole flopped back against her pillow and rolled her eyes, even though Jayne couldn't see. "I swear he had size-twelve feet, and these clumps of mud were sticking to his

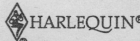

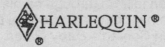

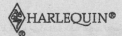

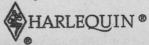

boots, and he wore *overalls*. I wouldn't have been surprised if he'd been chewing on a piece of straw."

"He's your neighbor?" Jayne sounded properly horrified.

"No, he's some kind of logger. Mom's having some trees taken out."

"Well, then, you'll probably never see him again."

"Everybody here looks like that," Nicole said gloomily. "They're all farmers or loggers or something. I heard these two girls talking the other day, and one of them is competing to become Dairy Princess at the fair next year. Can you imagine? The crown probably has horns on it!"

Nicole wasn't sure why, but she didn't tell Jayne her mother had thought the logger was a hunk. No, that wasn't true; she did know why. She was embarrassed. Her own mother, for crying out loud!

"Listen," Jayne said, "I gotta go. Maddy and Kelly and I are going to a film festival tonight. They're running a bunch of foreign films. I don't like subtitles, but Maddy says some of the guys are going, including—get this—Russell Harlan, so I'm wearing that red dress—you know, that one you helped me pick out and my hair on top of my head in a scrunchy, and he can't miss me, right?"

Talking to her best friend hadn't helped, Nicole thought a moment later, hanging up. Now she was more depressed. *She* was the one who'd liked Russ Harlan, not Jayne. He had these really dark eyes and he wore an earring and he was super intense about things. She'd wanted him intense about her. She was the one he was supposed to be noticing, not Jayne.

"I feel like I've been sent to prison," she said aloud to her empty room. *Her* room. Yeah, right. Her bedroom had had blue plush carpet and a cushioned window seat and its own bathroom. This room had peeling wallpaper, which her mother said they'd replace, and bare wood floors. Her gilt-trimmed bedroom set looked about as out of place as Nicole felt.

They couldn't stay in this dump. They just couldn't. Things were great in Bellevue. Nicole wished she'd paid more attention to all Mom's talk about buying into a veterinary practice somewhere. She'd been looking for so long Nicole quit listening when Mom talked about why she liked or didn't like this town or that vet or whatever. Big mistake. She should have listened carefully. Instead, first thing she knew, her mother had gone ahead and **done** it. A For Sale sign appeared in their front yard, and they all drove up here one Saturday to look at houses.

The sight of White Horse had put Nicole in shock. It had a whole two streets of businesses. One pizza parlor that she could see. One! The movie theater was this run-down little place that played a single movie at a time, a month or more after it'd opened in Seattle and Bellevue and even Everett. The high school was this huge ugly stucco building that must have been built fifty years ago. Mom thought it was great that you could walk anywhere in town. Great. Where were you supposed to go? The library? The bowling alley? Who bowled?

And she had to register for school tomorrow and start the next day. Mom insisted that moving during the summer was easiest, so she wouldn't be the only kid whose first day it was. Nicole had believed her then, but that was before she'd seen White Horse. How many new kids were there likely to be in the high school? Two? Three? She could just see it now: heads turning as she walked into each class, the stares as she went down the hall.

Well, she didn't care what a bunch of farmers thought, anyway. What she had to do was figure out how to get her mother to change her mind and move back to Bellevue.

At first she'd thought it was hopeless, but lately she'd begun to wonder. The farmers around here didn't want a woman vet, which Nicole thought sucked, except for the fact that her mom was looking more discouraged every day. Her mom had figured White Horse was some kind of rural paradise; she'd given Nicole and Mark all these lectures about how the move was as much for them as for her, because in a small town like this they were getting away from drugs and crime and gangs. So everything was supposed to be perfect, right?

The first glimmerings of an idea brought creases to Nicole's brow. Wait a minute—Mom was catching the drift, but too slowly. Dr. Craig would hire someone to take her place at the animal hospital in Bellevue; then, even if they left White Horse, they might have to go somewhere else. What if Nicole could speed up the process? *Show* her mother all the crummy parts of life in this cow town? She could mount a campaign. She wouldn't want to be obvious; that would make Mom mad. No, she could be really subtle, just sort of coax Mom to really look around.

Surely that was all it would take.

By this time, Nicole was sitting bolt upright, legs crossed. Like tomorrow. She wouldn't let her mother stop at the school office. No, she'd insist that someone give them a tour, show them the lab facilities—did this school know what a lab was?—and the library. Another of the things Mom went on and on about was how important a good education was. Nicole smiled. If her mother thought they wouldn't get a good education here, they were gone.

Back to Bellevue. *Yes.*

JOE GLANCED at his watch. Noon. "Take an hour," he called, and the two men he'd brought out on this job nodded and carried their chain saws to the open back of his pickup.

They consulted briefly and then Brad Mauser said, "We're going to run into town and get some burgers. Want to come?"

Joe's glance strayed to the kitchen window of the farmhouse, where he could see the blur of a white face and dark hair. "Nah." He shrugged. "I brought a sandwich."

Though he was used to the scream of chain saws and the thunder of falling trees, the silence after the men left was welcome. Autumn sunshine warm on his back, he looked around at their morning's work.

A dozen trees lay on the ground between the house and fence, lined up as neatly as pick-up sticks pulled from the pile. Most of the downed trees had already been shaved of their limbs and were ready for loading. If all went well, they'd have the other half down this afternoon. Come morning, they could get the timber out of here and clean up. Give the slash a few weeks to dry and he'd come back and burn it. If he was smart, he'd come back on a day when Dr. Teresa Burkett was working and therefore not home.

The jolt he'd felt in his gut when she opened the door that day last week had scared him a little. She was out of his league. He was lucky to have a high-school diploma. She'd finished God knows how many years of college. He was a small-town boy with no ambition to leave his home. She was a big-city professional woman who probably thought White Horse was pretty and peaceful. It was. But, unlike him, she'd be heading for Seattle every time she got bored.

He couldn't afford to acknowledge his attraction to her or the spark of interest he'd seen in her dark eyes.

Sandwich, he reminded himself, before his glance strayed again to her kitchen window. He grunted and turned toward the driveway where his pickup was parked. Rounding the house, he walked right into her.

Joe reached out and grabbed her before she went tumbling. Eyes wide, she looked up at him. "I'm sorry! That was dumb. I wasn't watching—"

"I don't know who was dumb," he interrupted. "I'm the one who almost ran you down." Reluctantly he let her go. Her shoulders felt as fragile under his hands as she'd declared her psyche to be. "Did you come out to see our progress?"

"Well, actually—" her tongue touched her lips "—I came out to invite you and your men in for lunch."

He had trouble not staring at her mouth. "They went into town."

Damn, she was beautiful, tiny, with these huge brown eyes and delicate features emphasized by the severity of the French braid that confined her dark hair. But it was neither the tiny nor the beautiful that got to him; it was the defiance in her eyes, coupled with the smile that played most of the time at one corner of her mouth.

"Well, then." She met his gaze boldly, though now her cheeks were touched with pink. "Can I talk *you* into lunch?"

"You don't need to cook—"

"I already did. Homemade minestrone soup and fresh-baked bread."

"I'm too dirty to come in."

"You can take your boots off."

What could he say? A moment later he padded in stocking feet into her bathroom to wash his hands. Waiting for the water to warm up, he frowned at his image in the mirror. What the hell did she see in him? All that met his eyes were dirty denim, callused hands and a haircut that was long on function and short on style. She'd discover soon enough that his conversation could be summed up about the same way.

But, by God, at least he was clean when he returned to the kitchen. She'd set the table there: two quilted place mats, a glass jar of spiky asters and late daisies, stemmed water glasses, silverware laid out properly, with an extra fork for some unseen dessert. It was pretty—and made him feel awkward. Only the sight of her black Labrador lying under the table belied the formality.

Her eyes touched his face and shied away. "You're my first guest in this house. I thought I'd celebrate."

He nodded and sat down while she ladled steaming fragrant soup into his bowl and offered him slices of crusty warm bread.

"Would you like a beer?" she asked, and he relaxed a little. At least she wasn't pouring French wine.

"No, thanks. I don't drink when I'm going to operate a chain saw or heavy equipment."

"Oh. No, of course not."

"I haven't seen a woman blush in a long time," he heard himself say.

That did it. Her cheeks were now as rosy as though a winter freeze were biting at them. But she also laughed.

"I don't usually blush. I think it must be you."

Him? What was she saying? If she'd been any other woman, he would have known, but her? Why him?

"I'm sorry if I'm making you uncomfortable," he said clumsily.

He almost thought he heard her sigh. "Are you married?" she asked.

His heart did a peculiar heavy-footed dance in his chest. "No."

Her cheeks hadn't faded one iota. "Engaged or...or..."

He helped her out. "No."

"Oh."

A slow smile was growing on his face. "Are you going somewhere with this, ma'am?"

"I'm just curious," she said with dignity.

He laid down his butter knife and said quietly, "Good."

Their eyes met and held for a long quivering moment. The breath of air he sucked in seared his chest.

"I know you're not married," he said. "Are you divorced?"

"Widowed." Pain, or at least regret, twisted her mouth. "Five years ago. My husband was an idiot. He made an ultralight from a kit. He was flying it when it drifted into some electrical wires. The day was windy—" She snorted. "But he had to go up."

"You didn't approve of his hobby, I take it."

"I hated it!" He felt her tension. "I haven't forgiven him yet."

"I don't blame you," Joe admitted. "I've never understood why someone would risk losing everything—" *a woman like you* "—for some kind of momentary thrill."

"It was what he did to the kids." Her eyes appealed to him for understanding.

"Tell me about them."

She did, while Joe had three bowls of soup and more slabs of bread than he wanted to count. The woman was not only beautiful, she could cook. And he'd better quit thinking this way.

Mark, he heard, was almost eleven, a fifth grader who'd taken the move philosophically and had already signed up for soccer.

"Boys," she said, with an expressive shrug. "They always seem to play in mobs and accept one more kid without question. Girls, now..."

Her fifteen-year-old, whom Joe had seen over Teresa's shoulder last week, was another story. When he asked about her, an odd expression crossed her face, half amusement, half exasperation.

"She had friends—although I didn't like them very much. Moving is a lot harder at her age. I just wish she'd *try.*"

"With her looks, she won't have any trouble getting dates."

"Thank you." Teresa flashed him a grateful smile. "She is pretty, isn't she?"

"Looks a lot like her mother."

A shadow crossed Teresa's face. "I don't know if that's a blessing or a curse."

He heard a car out in the driveway and assumed his men were back, but she didn't seem to notice. "Because you have trouble being taken seriously?" he asked.

"Uh-huh." Her faraway expression faded and she jumped to her feet. "Listen to me. And I tell my kids not to whine. Will you have some apple pie, Joe?"

He ran an internal check and decided he could squeeze in a slice.

While she cut it, she chattered some more. "We have four cats and the two dogs—you've met them. Most vets have even more animals than that. It's an occupational hazard. I keep encountering ones that need homes. At least *they're* happy here." She set two plates of pie on the table.

"From our own trees," she said with satisfaction, lifting a forkful to her mouth. "This is the life."

For how long? he wondered. About as long as he'd interest her? Or was he misjudging her?

If he was smart, he wouldn't bother finding out. But he'd never been accused of belonging in any program for the intellectually gifted, now had he? He told himself he'd hurt her feelings if he didn't ask her out. They'd made too many spoken and unspoken acknowledgments to each other for him to drop it here.

He insisted on carrying his dishes to the sink. There, he turned to face her. "Any chance you'd have dinner with me Friday night?" he asked casually enough that she wouldn't feel pressured if he was reading her wrong.

She smiled saucily. "I'd say there's a chance."

"You remind me of my sister," he said without thinking.

"Jess?"

"No, the other one. Rebecca."

"Looks? Or because we're both mouthy?"

He hesitated a little too long. Sooner or later she'd meet Rebecca and discover they didn't look anything alike. Sure enough, it was the smart mouths they had in common.

Apparently unoffended, Teresa laughed. "I'll look forward to meeting her. Tell me her husband is a dairy farmer."

"Nope. Owns a string of rental stores."

"I've been in the one here in town. His?"

"Mmm."

"Is there any pie your family doesn't have its finger in?"

"Not many," Joe admitted. "My brother, Lee, owns an auto-body repair place on Third. Rebecca sells wallpaper and blinds out of Browder's Flooring. Jess—but you know her. Her firm cleans the veterinary clinic, as I recall. Our father sold insurance until his heart attack a few years back."

"You must have a heck of a grapevine."

He grimaced. "You have no idea."

"Your men are peering in the windows," she said suddenly.

He turned and waved, hoping he wasn't blushing. He could imagine how they'd razz him if they got a good look at his stocking feet and the pretty table set for two.

"Six o'clock?" he said.

She blinked. "Why does that remind me of five hundred dollars?"

He stared at her. "I have no idea."

"Six," she agreed, and he nodded.

"Thanks for lunch."

He got another one of those impish grins. "Thanks for not dropping a tree on my house."

"Bad for the insurance rates," he said laconically, and let the screen door slam behind him while he sat down on the porch to lace up his boots.

CHAPTER TWO

WHEN JOE HAD ASKED about Nicole, the very mention of her name had been enough to prick Teresa with exasperation, amusement, puzzlement, frustration and even reluctant admiration. She'd no doubt gotten an odd look on her face. There was a good reason for it. In the past week, Nicole had obviously changed her tactics. Teresa wasn't foolish enough to think she'd given up.

For example, last Wednesday Nicole had gone along sweetly and willingly to register at the high school. When Teresa stared doubtfully up at the building and said, "Gee, it's kinda ugly, isn't it?" Nicole didn't jump right on her mother's minor criticism and try to make something major out of it.

Instead, she gave a dainty shrug and said, "It probably doesn't matter, as long as the district has spent their money where it counts."

What kid ever thought of a school district in terms of a limited budget and priorities? Not Nicole, that was for sure. Wary, Teresa trailed her up the wide stairs and in the double doors.

Sounding sanctimonious, her daughter whispered, "Don't they have handicapped access?"

"I'm sure they do," Teresa returned dryly.

The guidance counselor in the office was friendly. She agreed to put Nicole in third year French even though the class was technically full. Nicole's face fell with exaggerated disappointment as she examined the offerings.

"Oh, I was really looking forward to taking song writing this year."

"Maybe you should worry about bringing your algebra grade up, instead," her mother suggested.

The counselor had a twinkle in her eye. "Perhaps you'd like to try drama, Nicole. You look like acting might come naturally."

"Only if it's in the form of melodrama," Teresa muttered.

Her daughter gave her a glare. "Yeah, okay," she said to the counselor. "Why not? There isn't anything else."

"It's too bad you missed new-student orientation," the counselor concluded brightly, "but there's no reason you and your mother can't wander around the building right now. Here's a map, so you can find your classrooms—"

"Are the rooms unlocked?" Nicole sounded so earnest Teresa was immediately suspicious.

"Why, yes, I think so. You'll probably find some of the teachers—getting ready for the onslaught tomorrow."

"*Can* we look around?" Nicole asked when they left the office.

"Well, of course." Teresa nodded at the map and schedule Nicole carried. "What's your first class?"

"Um . . . algebra. Room 233." She peered around doubtfully. "Are we *on* the second floor here, do you think?"

They were; 233 was just down the hall. Nicole insisted on glancing in. It looked like any other classroom to Teresa, if a little old-fashioned. The ceilings were high, the woodwork dark, and a smell of floor polish was underlaid with that of chalk and the pages of new textbooks, piled on a table by the door.

The chemistry lab looked perfectly adequate to Teresa, as well; Nicole critiqued it as they wandered between high black-topped tables furnished with microscopes and glass beakers and petri dishes. Teresa, filled with nostalgia for her own high-school days, was able to tune her daughter out. She'd had a mad crush on her biology/chemistry teacher, in part because he inspired her with his own passionate interest in the unseen organisms that cause disease or well-being. It had taken her a while to realize she was more excited by cell division than she was by him.

They progressed to the library, where Nicole prowled the shelves, returning to announce, "This collection is *ancient!* How does anybody do any research here?"

"Fortunately White Horse belongs to an excellent public library system," Teresa reminded her. "In fact, the local branch isn't two blocks from here. You can go over there on your way home from school."

Her daughter frowned at her. "Don't you think they *ought* to have a better school library?"

"Yep. I'll join the PTA and campaign for a bigger book budget."

"Fat lot of good that'll do me," Nicole muttered.

"Probably not," Teresa admitted, "but it might achieve something before Mark gets to high school."

"I suppose you think *his* education is more important than mine!"

Teresa gave an inward sigh. "You know that isn't true. But I see no reason you won't get a perfectly adequate education here. Let's face it, at this level it's the teacher that counts. The teacher, and the effort *you* are willing to expend." She added some briskness to her voice. "If you get bored, next year you can start taking some classes at the community college in Everett."

"I'm supposed to be happy when you pulled me out of a great high school—"

"Rife with drugs and gangs."

"—and moved me *here.*" Examining a banner decorating the wall above a bank of metal lockers, Nicole curled her lip. "This one is full of Future Farmers of America." Every word was a sneer. "What am I supposed to do, learn how to milk a cow?"

"Wouldn't hurt. *I* had to," Teresa said unsympathetically. "Have you seen enough? Shall we go find Mark?"

Rolled eyes. "Yeah, I've seen enough."

Outside they found Mark involved in an impromptu soccer game with a bunch of boys who ranged from third or fourth grade on up to middle-school age. He trotted over.

"Can I stay awhile, Mom? For an hour or two?"

"You bet." She cuffed him lightly on the shoulder. "Have fun."

Nicole turned the full battery of entreaty on her from wide brown eyes. "Since we have an hour, can we go shopping, Mom? Please?"

Teresa hated to shop. She didn't care about clothes, seldom bothered with makeup, couldn't remember the last time she'd worn a dress. How she'd given birth to a child obsessed with appearances would forever remain a mystery to her.

But this struck her as an intelligent moment to compromise. "Fine. We'll see what the town has to offer."

A smug smile curled her daughter's pale mouth. Because she'd won? Or because she figured she had a chance to show her mother how inadequate White Horse was? Self-absorbed as she was, she probably hadn't noticed that Teresa visited malls only under duress.

Teresa decided the answer was the latter when she shocked Nicole out of her socks by actually finding an outfit she liked. White Horse only had two clothing stores. One of them had beautiful, high-quality casual clothes for women. Teresa looked around happily. "I'll never have to hit the mall again. I'll just come in here and snap something up."

"But this is old-lady stuff!"

"You mean, it's not teenage stuff. *I* am not a teenager, believe it or not." She headed for a display of cotton sweaters.

"Mo-om."

She waved Nicole off. "Let me try these things on."

Twenty minutes later, she paid for a pair of slim-fitting pants, a tunic-length sweater and a chunky silver necklace to wear over it.

A very sulky teenager followed her out onto the sidewalk. "Where am *I* supposed to shop?"

"The Everett Mall is only forty-five minutes away."

"Everett!"

"Bellevue Square isn't much over an hour. Surely some of those friends who used to pick you up every morning will come up here and get you once in a while."

"Oh, right." Nicole flung herself into the passenger seat of the car and slumped down, her expression tight. "They're supposed to drive for almost four hours just to see me."

Once behind the wheel, Teresa studied her daughter. She looked and sounded so unhappy Teresa reached out and stroked her hair. "Sweetheart—"

Nicole averted her face. "Oh, please. Spare me the lecture about making the best of it."

Teresa hesitated, then started the car. Maybe, determined that her children be as happy about the move as she'd been, she *had* been insensitive to Nicole's misery. On one level, she understood it; on another, she didn't at all. She hadn't been as social a creature as her daughter was. At that age, she'd been absorbed in her books and her studies and her ambition for the future. She'd had friends of course, but she didn't remember missing them all that much when she went off to college. Probably she wouldn't have missed them any more if her family had moved.

And here she'd been accusing Nicole of being self-absorbed. Maybe, Teresa thought ruefully, *she* was the selfish one. She'd convinced herself that the kids would be better off in small-town America because this was what she wanted for herself. She still thought this was a better place to raise children—but maybe Nicole was already too formed by her environment to adjust. Maybe, along with the veterinary practice and the farmhouse, Teresa had bought her daughter unhappiness.

The thought was an unsettling one.

IT WAS STILL on her mind on Friday as she dressed for her date with Joe Hughes. Nicole hadn't been happy to hear that her mother was going out with the logger and that she was condemned to baby-sit her little brother. It didn't help when Teresa pointed out that Nicole would have been sitting home, anyway.

Realizing her mistake immediately, Teresa tried to amend it. "You haven't picked up any baby-sitting clientele yet—"

"How can I? I don't *know* anybody."

"Why don't I put up a notice for you at the clinic?"

Nicole lifted one finger and traced a dispirited circle in the air. "Wow."

"Joe mentioned brothers and sisters. Maybe they have kids."

"Mom." Nicole waited until her mother turned to look at her. "I don't *care* if I baby-sit. I don't need the money. There's nowhere to shop, remember? Nobody to shop with? Okay?"

Teresa gritted her teeth at the snotty tone, but decided to let it pass. This time.

She ended up wearing the outfit she'd bought in town that day with Nicole. If Joe showed up in a suit and tie, she'd whisk back into the bedroom and exchange the leggings for a calf-length gauzy skirt.

As it turned out, he wore jeans and a plaid sports shirt that echoed the extraordinary blue of his eyes. His eyes took in her appearance with one swift assessing glance and returned, obviously approving, to her face.

"Do you like Mexican food? I thought we'd go to La Hacienda here in town."

"Love it," she assured him, standing aside. "Joe, I'd like you to meet my kids. Nicole, Mark, come here."

He shook hands solemnly with both, didn't remark on Nicole's teenage sulkiness and agreed with Mark that soccer was a popular sport in White Horse.

"One of my nieces plays select soccer," Joe said. "She's darn good. They go to tournaments all over the state."

"That'd be cool." Mark's eyes were wide.

Briskly Teresa ended the preliminaries. "See you, guys. I don't know what time I'll be home."

In the pickup, Joe said, "I feel a little guilty leaving them behind. I could feed them, too—"

"No!" she exclaimed, then saw his surprise and amusement. She made a face. "Nicole's driving me nuts," she admitted. "I need a break." There was more, of course. The moment she'd answered the door, she'd remembered why she'd wanted so badly to go out with this man. The fantasies she'd indulged in this past week had *not* included her children.

"You ought to talk to Jess. Her oldest is, uh—" he obviously had to calculate "—twelve going on thirteen. She's been a pain in the butt lately."

"Maybe I will. Tell me, how many nieces and nephews do you have?"

"Uh..." More calculations. "Seven. Lee has four, Jess two and Rebecca one. Although she's expecting another."

"And you *all* live here in town?"

He offered her that heart-stopping grin. "Pretty overwhelming, huh?"

Had she sounded rude? She would have liked to see her own sisters and their families more often, but...

"My younger sister was so *nosy*," she said. "Still is."

"My mother is the nosy one." His big shoulders moved. "I ignore her."

Teresa could imagine that. His rock-solid steadiness was part of what attracted her, but it wouldn't make him a flexible man. So to speak.

"You don't have any kids?" She hoped her question sounded casual.

"Never been married." The statement so carefully held no inflection it should have stopped her from commenting. It didn't.

"You're kidding."

Joe shot her a glance. "Why's that so surprising?"

"Because you're, ah..." Fumbling for words, she settled for the truth. "You're a hunk. I can't believe some woman didn't snap you up."

"Like a tasty fly?" he asked wryly.

Teresa couldn't resist it. She chanted, "There was a young woman who swallowed a fly..."

"And now she'll die?" he concluded.

Of happiness, maybe, Teresa thought, but had the sense not to say.

"I guess the whole analogy is a little—" she grinned "—distasteful."

He groaned. "Oh, God, a woman who likes puns."

"Didn't someone say it's the highest form of humor?"

"Are you sure it wasn't the lowest?"

"You should have heard us in vet school," Teresa said cheerfully. "We were bad."

"Question is, are you hungry?"

She blinked and looked around. Heavens, they were parked in front of the restaurant. How long had they been here while she blathered?

"Starved," she admitted. "A day of standing around always makes me think about food."

He started to circle the truck, presumably to get the door for her; she didn't wait. If he wanted a lady, he could look elsewhere. But all he said was, "Things no better at work?"

"Heck no." Teresa sighed. "Let's talk about something else."

Over enchiladas, they did. She chattered on about her years of school; he merely shook his head when she asked if he'd gone to college.

"How'd you get started in logging?"

"Summer jobs," he said easily. "By the time I got out of high school, I was already a cutter—I was the one who climbed the trees to top 'em, or take some limbs out. Pay was too good for me to bother looking around for any other line of work. My boss encouraged me to learn to cruise—that's estimating what a stand of timber is worth, so you can make a realistic bid on it. I always had a head for math." He shrugged. "Got some money put away, went into business for myself. Now I keep six other men working."

"You're a family of entrepreneurs."

"Who wants to work for someone else?" His gaze was shrewd. "Isn't that why you bought into a practice?"

She paused in the midst of cutting her enchilada. "I suppose so. Well, partly. It's not the money-making side of being a vet that interests me. I wanted more responsibility. In Bellevue I worked at this big clinic with half a dozen vets. It was like I just put in my time—I didn't make the overall decisions, which sometimes bothered me. For example, I thought our charges were too high. Especially for preventative medicine. I wanted us to keep neutering and vaccination costs to the very minimum. The partners smiled and told me I wasn't looking at the big picture."

"You're an idealist." The faintest of smiles lurked in his eyes.

Teresa wrinkled her nose. "I suppose so. But partly I was being selfish, too. I was bored. In vet school I especially enjoyed the large-animal work, and we didn't do any of that where I worked. I was hoping for a mix."

"Which you found."

"In theory."

"They'll come around," he said quietly.

"Damn straight they will." She frowned at him. "I'm going to get every one of those farmers to admit I'm the best vet they've ever had!"

"You show 'em." His smile seemed a bit rueful, and she wondered why.

"Do *you* think a man could do a better job?" She tilted her chin up in challenge. "Come on. Be honest. What if you needed a mechanic to fix that...that hundred-thousand-dollar monster you had out at my place the other day. Would you hire a woman?"

"Skidder. And it cost a hell of a lot more than a hundred thousand." Joe set down his fork. "Yeah, I'd hire a woman if I thought she was the best mechanic. You can't outmuscle a machine that size, *or* a horse or a cow. You need to outthink 'em. I've seen Jess with those horses of hers. She's a small woman. Those Arabs would do damn near anything for her."

A sigh escaped Teresa, leaving her deflated. "Sorry. I get worked up."

"It's your livelihood."

"I don't like injustice."

"Prejudice of any kind isn't pretty."

She almost asked what he knew about it. A handsome white male—he had it made, right? But she'd be a fool to leap to that kind of easy assumption. A kid could be the odd one out for any number of reasons. A teacher friend had once told Teresa there was a "leper" in every class, as if the group as a whole could only bond through rejecting someone who didn't fit. Teresa had memories of some kids she'd gone to school with who didn't fit. Looking back, she couldn't even remember why. Maybe they gave off the wrong pheromones or something.

Not that there was anything wrong with Joe Hughes's pheromones.

Figuring she'd pushed the limit on sensitive subjects, Teresa backed off over coffee. "Since clients won't let me treat their animals," she said, "I've been doing most of the billing and follow-ups. Do you ever have trouble collecting debts?"

His mouth curled. "I just tell 'em I'll be back with the skidder and take their roof off in pieces. Check is usually in the mail."

She laughed. "Okay. So we should get a rabid Doberman and plan to turn it loose on anyone over thirty days late?"

"There you go." The smiling intimacy in his eyes was enough to make her think about other even more intimate expressions—and about the approaching end to the evening.

Surely he would kiss her. She hadn't been on a date where the man didn't at least give her a peck on the lips. Although truth to tell, she hadn't been on that many dates. After Tom's death, she had gone into shock. It must have been a year or more before the numbness began to wear off, letting her be mad as hell at him. And miss him.

She was embarrassed to remember her astonishment when a fellow vet asked her out to dinner and to the symphony. She'd almost blurted, "Me? You want *me* to go with you? Why?" Then a vague memory of such rituals had clicked in, and she'd realized that, yes, he was a man and, yes, she was woman. Both single. Good Lord, he was interested in her!

She'd gone; why not? She knew him, if not well. It seemed an easy reintroduction to the world of dating. She wasn't all that impressed, either with that date or the scattered few that followed. She never had liked groping for conversation or realizing halfway through dinner that she didn't want that wet mouth to cover hers.

No such problem tonight. Obviously she'd been celibate too long. That had to be the explanation for why she kept staring at Joe's hands, big and tanned and callused, and imagining how those calluses would feel against her skin. Tom had been an airline pilot. Smooth well-kept hands. Nothing like this man's.

And that mouth, tight and controlled. He tilted it into a smile from time to time, even grinned roguishly, but somehow she never had the sense he was really relaxing. Oh, yes, she'd like to see him lose control.

At this point in her speculation, of course, she realized that he was watching her with interest, one eyebrow raised, and that *she* must have been staring, her expression giving away God knew what. She'd never been accused of being poker-faced.

Damned if she didn't blush. "Sorry. I, uh..."

"You were thinking," he said tactfully. Then a grin twitched the corner of his mouth. "Not that I wouldn't be interested in knowing *what* you were thinking, but to get back to your question, actually I don't have too many problems with debt collection. As you know, I get half up front, which is enough to pay the men. A lot of my work is on a larger scale than your job. I log land that's going to be developed, for example. I suspect it's the smaller bills people put off paying."

"I hate dunning people." Teresa made a face. "But then, that's what I let myself in for when I insisted on a partnership."

"In a perfect world—"

"In a perfect world, everybody would have plenty of money to pay their bills. And my daughter would be eagerly making new friends. And the woman you take out on a first date wouldn't spend it whining."

"You haven't whined. You've talked about your problems. I don't mind."

"You haven't talked about yours," she said.

His lean dark face went expressionless again. "I guess I don't have any pressing ones at the moment."

If he'd just quirked an eyebrow or smiled apologetically or done anything else, she'd have believed him. As it was, she had the feeling she'd just walked up against an electric fence: invisible but powerful.

The waiter presented the bill; Joe paid. Outside, the sun was sinking in the west over Puget Sound and the hazy line of the Olympic Mountains. It must be eight-thirty, but days were still long at this time of year. Teresa didn't protest when Joe used his hand on the small of her back to steer her toward his pickup. As if she didn't know where it was.

"Sure you don't want to go to a movie?" Joe asked.

"I wish I could," she said, meaning it. "But I'd better not. I have to be at work awfully early tomorrow."

He nodded, and she wished she could tell if he had asked again only to be polite. The short drive to her house was mostly silent. She wondered what he was thinking, anticipated that moment when he'd turn toward her, hoped her children would be tactful enough not to dash out to meet her when they heard the engine. She should have rented them a video, something engrossing. Next time...

The pickup pulled into her long driveway. She needed to mow again, she noticed, with one tiny corner of her consciousness. The rest of it was occupied with agonizing. What if he *didn't* kiss her? Maybe he'd invited her out because he'd felt cornered; she'd been obvious enough, coming right out and asking if he was married. Maybe he didn't like direct women.

Then they might as well forget the whole thing right now, she admitted.

The pickup slowed, stopped. No dogs; the kids must have let them in the house. He killed the engine. The front door of her house didn't fly open. He turned toward her.

Teresa took a deep breath and smiled. "Thanks for dinner, Joe. I enjoyed myself."

"Me, too." His voice had roughened slightly. With surprising awkwardness, he said, "I don't suppose we have an awful lot in common, but... maybe we could do it again."

Was that a brush-off? Good Lord, why was she panicking? This was a first date! If it worked, it worked. If it didn't, it didn't.

"Sure," she murmured.

He reached out more tentatively than she might have expected, although his hand was solid and warm on the back of her neck. His thumb traced a circle around the bump of her vertebra, which had the effect of tapping a Morse code directly into her spinal cord. *This feels good. More. More.*

He bent his head as though giving her time to withdraw. Fat chance. His lips were soft and dry and as warm as that big hand, gently massaging her neck. Their mouths brushed together, once, twice, before his settled more firmly on hers and nudged her lips apart. By that time, she was enthusiastically participating.

If he minded her leaning into him and nibbling at his lower lip, his groan wasn't a good way of telling her. His other hand gripped her upper arm and tugged her even closer. Somehow his mouth was hot and damp now, and his tongue had touched hers, circled it just like his thumb was circling on her nape. She felt as mindless as a teenager making out with the object of her first crush.

More. More.

Joe was the one to pull back a little and let out a shaky breath. "I think," he said huskily, "we'd better say good-night."

"Good-night?"

"Isn't that the appropriate way to bid someone farewell in the evening?"

Consciousness was returning. She tried to straighten with dignity. "I knew what you meant."

"Good." The trace of amusement in his voice didn't show in the molten blue of his eyes. His hand tightened on her neck, then released her. "How about a movie next week? I'd suggest tomorrow night, except..."

When he hesitated, she finished, "I might have a rebellion on my hands. Next week sounds good."

He muttered something inarticulate, gave her a quick hard kiss, then got out. She was dazed enough to wait until he came around and opened her door, offering a hand to the little lady so she could hop down from the high seat. He walked her to the door, smiled, his eyes intense, touched her cheek and left her there.

It was the first time since her husband's death she'd gone out with a man she wished wasn't leaving.

CHAPTER THREE

NICOLE WAS DISCOURAGED, but she wasn't about to give up. This was her *life* she was talking about!

Mom didn't even listen when she tried to tell her about her day at school.

"The bathrooms are *gross,*" she said. "And the girls are all ignoring me. It's like I don't even exist."

"Are you sure you're not ignoring them, too?" her mother asked, handing her a cookie and a glass of milk, as if she were five years old, home from a day at kindergarten.

"I'm not walking around grinning like some idiot, saying, 'Hi, I'm new!' if that's what you mean," Nicole said disagreeably. She bit into the cookie, which was still warm.

"How about the boys?"

She shrugged. "Oh, some of them are coming on to me. Like I'd be interested in any of *them.* But I guess *you* wouldn't understand that, would you?"

Mom's eyes narrowed and she held up one hand. "Okay, that's it. Time for a little chat."

"Little chats" were lectures. Nicole wasn't going to argue during this one. She shouldn't have said that; Mom didn't date very often, even though she was still pretty, and it wasn't like she was *marrying* the guy. The dig had just slipped out.

Mom put her hands on her hips. "*A*. I will not put up with any more snotty remarks. I know you're unhappy, but you don't have to make everyone else unhappy, too. *B*. I will have no sympathy for your unhappiness until you start making some effort to adjust to the move. You'd decided you were going to hate this place before you even saw it. Why not give it a chance?"

Tears came in a rush and Nicole wailed, "Because I was happy before! What was so wrong with that?"

"Absolutcly nothing," her mother said gently. "But you can be happy again. Happiness is inside *you,* not a place."

Nicole took a deep breath, sniffed and wiped at her tears. "Jeez, Mom, you ought to write greeting cards."

Her mother gave her a mock frown. "Okay, it sounds sappy, but it's true, believe it or not."

"Are *you* happy?"

One of the nice things about her mother was that she really thought about questions like that before she gave an answer. It would have been easy to snap, "Of course I'm happy!" whcther she was or not. But she frowned a little and finally said, "Yes, I think I am." She actually sounded surprised. "This move is something I've wanted to do for a long time. Our house in Bellevue fit your dad better than it did me. I like small towns, I like Eric, I like this house." She wrinkled her nose. "I guess I like a challenge. And I've certainly bought into one, haven't I?"

The screen door banged and both Nicole and her mother looked up. Mark kicked the kitchen door shut, dropped his backpack on a chair and headed straight for the fridge.

Mom's face brightened. "How was *your* day?"

Nicole knew what he was going to say even before he said it.

"Cool! Can I have this chocolate milk?"

"Sure. Still liking your teacher?"

"Yeah, she's okay." He'd found the cookies. "She's into astronomy. I like stuff like that."

"Make some friends?" Mom asked casually, as if it was that easy.

He shrugged and shoved a whole cookie into his mouth. Around it, he mumbled, "I hung around with a couple of guys all day. Can I watch TV?"

"Yes, you *may* watch TV. For half an hour."

"Gol, I don't have any homework or anything." He grabbed three more cookies and his chocolate milk and headed for the living room.

Nicole blew her nose. Her own brother hadn't even noticed she'd been crying. "How come it's so easy for him?" she asked.

Her mother kissed the top of her head. It felt good. Comforting. "Maybe because his personality is different. He's always been cheerful and outgoing, uncomplicated. Maybe because he's a boy, and boys accept newcomers more readily. Maybe just his age. It's harder to leave your friends when you're a teenager."

"Then...why wouldn't you let me stay in Bellevue? I could have finished school there."

Brown eyes serious, her mother faced her. "For lots of reasons. I might have considered it if you'd been a senior, but you have three more years of high school. I don't think Jayne's parents were really prepared to finish raising you, and I didn't want to let them. I'm already in shock at how fast you and Mark are growing up. You'll be gone before I know it. But I'm not ready yet, and neither are you. You're still a kid, and you're *mine.*"

She hardly ever sounded that firm. Secretly Nicole didn't mind. She'd wanted to stay in Bellevue, but the idea of becoming part of her friend's family had been a little scary. She hadn't wanted to lose her mother or even Mark, brat though he was. She just didn't want to move.

Now she nodded. But she wasn't going to pretend she was Mark, either. "I still hate it here."

"I know." Her mother gave her an odd twisted smile. "But I hope, after a while, that you won't. Think about getting a horse. That might be some consolation."

Nicole had always wanted a horse more than almost anything else in the world. But she wasn't about to let her mother *buy* her cooperation. She shrugged sulkily. "I'm not a little kid anymore."

"Well, then," Mom sounded as tart as a green apple, "don't act like one."

Nicole stomped off to her bedroom.

LEAVING NICOLE sulking in her bedroom and Mark in front of the TV, Teresa went to town. The farmhouse needed remodeling, starting with the basics, and she might as well take advantage of the rest of her day off. She hadn't forgotten Joe's sister worked at Browder's Flooring, but Teresa told herself curiosity wasn't why she'd chosen to start there.

A woman named Carol offered to help her, then let her browse in peace among the carpet and vinyl samples. Almost immediately she realized she'd better choose kitchen and bathroom countertops before the flooring.

The back of the store was a veritable treasure trove, if you liked redoing houses. Shelf after slanted shelf held tiles in a mouth-watering selection of colors and textures. Blinds in colors equally rich covered mock windows on the wall and were topped by calico and satin and wood valances.

Teresa headed straight for a lacy pleated blind that would be perfect for her old house.

At her murmured "ooh" of pleasure, an amused voice from behind her said, "A woman of taste, I can tell. I put that one in my own living room." When Teresa turned, the woman held out one hand. "Hi, I'm Rebecca Ballard."

Joe's sister-with-a-big-mouth. In her mid to late thirties, she had little in common with him physically except the blue eyes. Her curly brown hair brushed her shoulders, her smile was as warm as a cup of hot chocolate, and she was just a little plump—and undeniably pregnant. Teresa liked her on sight.

"Teresa Burkett," she introduced herself.

"The new vet."

"Yes," she said a little warily.

"Jess told me about you. Jess Kerrigan. She's my sister. She said you were dating Joe." Rebecca clapped her hand over her mouth. "And I was to pretend I don't know," she said sheepishly.

Teresa grinned. "He did mention the family grapevine."

"More like a patch of blackberries. You know how fast *they* spread."

Teresa's laugh felt good. "Yes, we had dinner. Your brother seems nice. He took out some trees for me and gave me a good deal."

"Oh, he's nice." Rebecca shook her head. "A little hard to get to know, but don't let that stop you."

She wanted badly to ask *why* he was so guarded, but refrained. This was, after all, a complete stranger. Her struggle must have showed, though.

His sister tilted her head to one side. "I'd love to tell you his life history, but I have a suspicion he'd be annoyed at me." She thought about it for a moment. "Well, probably not annoyed. Mad as hell. I'd better let him tell you in his own good time."

"You're probably right," Teresa said. "What I'm really here for is help picking out some tile. And window covers. And, heck, I even need a new kitchen sink. You don't happen to sell those, do you?"

"Nope, but I keep some catalogs on hand, so you can match colors if you're not planning to go with plain white or stainless steel. The hardware store sells Kohler and a couple of other brands. Shall I dig the catalogs out?"

Teresa spent a happy couple of hours poring over the tiles, carrying them to the vinyl, discussing how best to get the hardwood floors refinished.

"My daughter's room first," she said. "Nicole's miserably unhappy about the move. She keeps bemoaning her old bedroom's built-in vanity and window seat. Maybe I can shut her up by making her new one equally charming."

"How old is she?" Rebecca asked.

"Fifteen."

"You have my sympathy. My son, Alan, was barely sixteen when I met my current husband. Alan didn't think he liked him, and you wouldn't believe the stunts he pulled."

"Oh, I'd believe them," Teresa said grimly.

Rebecca tilted her head to one side again. "I don't suppose your daughter is petite, dark-haired and takes French III?"

"That's her."

"Ah. Alan's mentioned her." Rebecca heaved a wallpaper book onto the counter. "He thinks she's, uh, pretty."

"I don't suppose that's the word he used."

Joe's sister gave her a wry look. "I don't want to sully your ears with current teenage-boy terminology."

"Probably no worse than 'chick' or 'babe' or 'fox.'" Teresa contemplated briefly. "'Babe' and 'baby' were always my personal pet peeves. They're so...so..."

"Belittling?" Rebecca asked. "Sort of like going through life as 'Becky'?"

"Exactly!" Teresa raised her eyebrows. "You didn't start that way, did you?"

"No. Sam, my husband, asked once if I liked to be called Becky. I told him only if he wanted to be Sammy. That nipped it in the bud."

"I can see why," Teresa agreed, amused.

She borrowed samples of tiles, wallpaper and vinyl, then made an appointment for Rebecca to come to the house and take measurements. She'd let Nicole pick out her own wallpaper and window coverings—within reason.

Lugging the wallpaper books, she came in the back door to hear the phone ringing. Both the kids were upstairs. She dropped the books on the table and grabbed the receiver on the fifth ring.

"Hello?"

"Teresa, this is Joe. Joe Hughes."

"You're the only Joe I know," she said. "Hey, a poem."

He groaned. "Just don't add another line, okay?"

"All right. I can't think of anything that rhymes, anyway. Except toe. And no. Neither of which are fraught with possibilities. Unless you want to get kinky."

Silence. Then, "I won't answer that one."

"Very wise." She leaned against the counter. "So, uh, what can I do for you?"

His voice was low and amused. "Do *you* want to get kinky?"

She chuckled. "I set myself up for that one, didn't I?"

"Yup." She could hear his smile, which sent a flood of warmth through her. "Actually," he went on, "what I called for was to ask if you'd like to have dinner again."

"I'd love to," she said promptly. "If we can make it Saturday night, I could even stay out later than nine o'clock. I don't work Sunday. It's Eric's turn to be on call."

"Saturday sounds good," Joe agreed. "How about a movie, too?"

"As long as it's not too gory."

"You're a vet. You're used to blood and guts."

"Not human blood."

"You'd faint if I cut myself?"

"Probably," she said cheerfully. "There's a reason I didn't become an M.D."

"Why don't I believe you?"

"I don't know. Why don't you?"

He only laughed. She loved his laugh, a husky rumble that sounded just a little rusty, as if he didn't laugh often enough. Well, he lived alone, so he probably didn't. To keep their sense of humor intact, adults required children. Or maybe it worked the other way around: you required a sense of humor to *stand* your children.

THE WEEK SEEMED LONG without seeing Joe. It was funny, considering she hardly knew him. She watched for him in the grocery store and at stoplights. Logging trucks, a common sight in a town with two lumber mills, reminded her of him. She did see his sister, Jess, once to wave to, and Rebecca came out and took measurements. Teresa craned her neck every time she drove past the auto-body-repair place on Third. She felt like a teenage girl with her first crush. It *felt* like a first crush; falling in love with Tom had happened an eternity ago. The first flush of romantic feelings were unfamiliar but absurdly sweet.

The saving grace was that she was busy at work. Not doing farm calls; of necessity, Eric handled all of them. Which meant that the clients who arrived with a sick cat or an injured dog had to accept her or go to the other animal hospital in town, where, Eric had told her, the vets seemed to rotate more often than a horse threw shoes. Teresa was accepted. She brought an epileptic spaniel out of a prolonged seizure with phenobarbital, stitched up a Lab that had argued with a car, catheterized a cat with a blocked urethra and removed a fish hook from a dog's lip. He'd apparently tried to snap up the fly when the owner was practicing casting.

As she calmly handled one emergency after another, it seemed to her that the staff was warming to her. They'd been pleasant but distant thus far: she was their employer, but that didn't mean they had to like or respect her. She began to hope that they'd decided to do both.

On Friday morning, she had to put down a puppy with parvo. She comforted the owner, thanked the technician who was disposing of the body, then walked into the office and started to cry.

"Dr. Burkett?" someone said uncertainly.

She snatched a tissue and looked up.

Marilyn, the younger of the two technicians on duty, stood in the doorway. "I'm sorry. There's a phone call—"

"That's okay." Teresa gave a wavery smile. "I just hate doing that. I should be colder, shouldn't I?"

"No." Marilyn's smile trembled, too. Her own eyes, now that Teresa looked, were red.

Teresa took the call and saw another client a few minutes later. The routine marched on. But something had changed; for the first time, Marilyn and Libby, the other veterinary technician working that day, invited her to join them for lunch. It felt like a victory.

When Saturday night finally rolled around, Nicole whined only halfheartedly about having to baby-sit her little brother, who made only the obligatory objection to the words "little" and "baby-sit." Joe knocked on the door promptly at seven, Teresa called goodbye to her kids and whisked out onto the porch.

Joe's smile was the deliciously slow lazy one that muddled her insides. "Cabin fever?" he asked.

"Kid fever." She smiled back. "Actually, they're being good. Amazingly good. I figure if I make a quick escape, it might stay that way."

Belatedly it occurred to her that, if she was imagining Joe as husband material, she ought to quit complaining about her children. After all, husband also meant stepfather. The way she'd been talking, he must think her kids were hell on wheels.

She made a point over dinner of bragging about them. Which, she realized in amusement, must mean she was thinking about him as a potential husband.

"Mark never seems to lift a finger, but he gets perfect grades. He'll be starting in the gifted program, which I'm excited about. I know he gets bored sometimes."

Joe only nodded. His face was annoyingly expressionless. She couldn't decide whether she was boring him or whether he was only waiting for her to go on. Well, if he was bored—tough. She came as a package with her kids.

"Nicole's a good student, too, but what she loves—besides boys, of course—is to dance. Ballet and jazz both."

"There's a dance school in White Horse, you know."

"Is there?" She set down her fork. They were eating at a waterfront restaurant on Marine View Drive in Everett. Boats at a marina just below the big windows bobbed gently on quiet shimmering swells. "I hadn't checked into it yet. I ought to get her started."

"Two of my nieces dance." Joe grinned ruefully. "I get to see the recital every year. Thank God they've progressed from the junior recital to the senior one. The first year, I thought the three-year-olds in their pink tutus were cute. By the second year, I was wondering why the hell their parents were paying for dance lessons when they were obviously too young even to learn how to stay in line, never mind how to pirouette."

"I remember those days." Oh, boy, did she. "Ragged rows of little girls—and an occasional boy whose friends hadn't yet persuaded him it was unmanly to dance. Usually there'd be a couple who had some vague idea what to do, and one or two sucking their thumbs, frozen in terror. The rest would just kind of wander around."

"One of my nieces was a thumb sucker. We have it captured for all time on videotape."

"You sound like a fond uncle."

His big shoulders moved uneasily, as though he didn't know how to take compliments. "Yeah, I guess so. Tell you the truth, I've tried to stand in for Rebecca's first husband and Jess's ex. Neither of them was any great shakes as a parent. Alan especially—Rebecca's boy—needed a man around sometimes. Before Rebecca remarried of course. I, uh, didn't mind."

Okay, so he hadn't been bored; he *liked* kids. Definitely husband material. Except that he couldn't be as good as he looked. Otherwise, why wasn't he married? Teresa didn't believe in that "waiting for the right woman" stuff. Just like animals, humans reached an age when they were ready to mate. Occasionally that urge got sidetracked—it often happened to vet students, because they were too busy and too tired for the dating rounds. But Joe must be in his mid-thirties at least. So what had he been doing, instead of marrying?

"How old are you?" she asked.

He looked startled, but answered willingly enough. "Thirty-six. You?"

"Thirty-five. And yes, before you count back, I had Nicole before I started veterinary school. I must have been nuts. Fortunately, while Tom may have had his flaws, he was a great father. We did wait to have Mark until I was done with my schooling, though."

"Does Mark even remember his father?"

"Yes, but his memories are fading," she said with sharp regret. "He was in his second day of kindergarten when I had to meet him at the bus with the news that his dad was dead. It's natural that he'll forget him. I mean, all you have to do is think back. If you're like me, you can hardly remember your kindergarten days."

"I remember them." Before she could begin to speculate about what his flat tone meant, he added, "That must mean you just passed the anniversary of your husband's death. Does it still hit you hard?"

"It has before, but not so much this year." She made a face. "I was so damned mad at a farmer who decided he didn't really need a vet when he saw me get out of the car, it carried me through the day."

His mouth had an odd twist. "Anger is a useful emotion."

"Mmm." All she had to do was remember the days after Tom's death. "Very."

Joe glanced at his watch. "Still in the mood for a movie?"

"You bet. I even looked at the listings in the paper. I don't suppose you like sword and sorcery?"

He lifted an eyebrow. "Swordplay usually leads to some blood and gore. Don't I remember that being forbidden?"

"It's different from a contemporary shoot 'em up," she tried to explain. "Less realistic. In a fantasy, the blood doesn't count."

He loomed above her as he helped her out of her chair. More of that sense of being fragile and feminine that she usually hated. "I think you're splitting hairs," he said in amusement.

"Swirling capes and galloping horses are romantic."

"The truth comes out! All women want is romance."

She had to ask. "Is there something wrong with romance?"

Their eyes met, held. Her skin tingled. "No," he said quietly. "There's nothing wrong with romance."

The other patrons and the hovering waitress blurred; for a heartbeat, only the two of them existed. Then she blinked, or he did, and the moment passed. He was laying some bills on the table, thanking the waitress, holding out Teresa's sweater for her. Slipping her arms into it, Teresa gave her head a small shake. Had she imagined the intensity of that look?

Then Joe's eyes met hers again, and she thought, *No. I didn't imagine it.* Why else was he so wary now?

Her dates in recent years had taken her to French restaurants and the symphony and the opera. When half an hour later she settled into the plush seat at the movie theater, her upper arm just brushing Joe's, Teresa decided this was more romantic, no matter what movie was projected onto the big screen.

The lights were already dimming; she was very conscious of the man so close beside her. She felt his every breath, knew when he glanced at her, even though she pretended to watch the previews. Would he put his arm around her? She would have liked to lay her hand on his thigh. Her eyes and the nearly forgotten recesses of her memory told her it would be solid, bulky. The muscles might ripple under her touch.

She swallowed hard, disconcerted by the strength of her longing. What was wrong with her?

Joe reached out and took her hand. She jumped, and he whispered, "Sorry," and started to let her go.

She grabbed his hand and held on. His went still for a surprised moment, then relaxed and returned her clasp. He exhaled what might have been a chuckle.

Then he lifted their clasped hands and laid them on his thigh. Oh God, had he read her mind? He shifted in his seat, and the muscles under the fabric of his pants bunched. Teresa sat motionless, taking in every sensation. Heaven.

It wasn't Joe in particular, she told herself in panic; it couldn't be, not so quickly. He must just represent something to her—solidity, masculinity, a calm reassuring presence. A sexy body, honesty made her add; a sensual mouth, hands that knew how to touch a woman. In other words, a man. She'd turned into that pathetic creature, a sex-starved widow who'd take whatever she could get.

Well, no. She'd had other chances to take, and turned them down. This was the first time she'd been tempted to grab and hold on. Literally and figuratively. So maybe it *was* Joe. Maybe him in particular, or because he represented whatever she'd been looking for when she bought into the White Horse Animal Hospital and practice.

It might be fun to find out.

Eventually Joe let her hand go, and she made a tiny noise of disappointment she prayed he hadn't heard. But apparently he'd only released her so that he could put his arm around her shoulders. Now he tugged her closer to his warmth. Of course, the arm of the theater seat dug into her rib cage, but who was noticing? The feel of his mouth against her hair was far too tantalizing.

After a while, he murmured, "Ever necked in a movie theater?"

She sneaked a glance around to make sure no one had sat near them. Only a few others were scattered throughout the theater. The movie had been out for weeks and was probably about ready to disappear from Everett. Nobody was nearby at all.

"Not since I was young enough for a curfew."

"Me, neither. Want to pretend we're too young and horny to wait until we can find a deserted side road?"

Pretend. Oh, sure. She could do that. "Why not?" she whispered, and turned her head to meet his mouth. Pure excitement shot through her. It added eagerness and urgency to their kiss from the moment his lips claimed hers.

They kept it discreet. Nobody moaned or whimpered. Joe didn't rip her clothes off or throw her down onto the sloping aisle. Not, as far as she was concerned, for lack of wanting. After the first few seconds, pretty much anything would have been fine with her. Which was, when she thought about it for a fleeting moment, alarming. What was *happening* to her?

Whatever it was, it felt good. His hand brushed her breast, cupped it. His teeth grazed her neck. She nipped the lobe of his ear. She tasted the skin at the base of his strong brown throat. She kneaded the muscles on his shoulders and neck. She hadn't the slightest idea what happened to the sorceress in distress up on the movie screen. She didn't care.

When the credits rolled, they rearranged their clothing to leave. Teresa was very careful not to look at anyone else, just in case they'd glanced over their shoulders and noticed the couple in back. She didn't want to face a knowing smile or disapproving frown. Blast it, she was blushing again!

Thank God, she thought suddenly, that Nicole hadn't made any friends! What if one of them had seen her mother carry on this way? Nicole would have run away from home.

Teresa wasn't eager to meet Joe's eyes, either. They passed through the lobby and out into the night. A mist scented the air and glistened off the pavement and car windshields under the yellow sodium lamps. Joe unlocked the passenger door first and held it open for her. Inside, she stared straight ahead while he circled the pickup and climbed in behind the wheel. He didn't start the engine. She felt his gaze.

"I don't suppose you want to find that deserted road."

"I, uh, don't think that'd be such a good idea."

"Are you embarrassed or mad?"

She appreciated his bluntness. It made it easier to turn toward him. "Embarrassed," she admitted. "I don't usually act like a randy teenager."

"I didn't do any better."

"I enjoyed it," he confessed.

"Me, too."

"Then?" He waited.

"Oh, heck." She fidgeted with the seat belt. "I just don't want you to think—"

"I don't."

"Oh, well, since we've settled that..."

He must have liked her sarcasm, because he laughed. "I'll give you a chaste good-night kiss. On the cheek."

"Something to live for."

He laughed again, the sound less rusty than the first time she'd heard it. She had *some* use in life.

The good-night kiss wasn't all that chaste. But this time, there wasn't any potential audience, either. Her legs felt a little shaky when Joe walked her to the front door. She didn't want him to go tonight, either, which made her wonder with renewed panic where, and how quickly, this relationship was headed. How long would he—would *she*—be content with kisses? Was she really ready to have an affair with a man she hadn't met three weeks ago?

And in all honesty she had to admit she didn't know him very well. They talked, they laughed, but he hadn't let her see below the surface. Maybe he had no profound secrets, but everyone had a darker side. Every time she edged too close to a truly personal issue, his face went expressionless. Even kissing her, he hadn't yet reached the edge of control. How could she make love with a man she'd never seen angry, despairing, laughing helplessly? She wanted to know that he went deeper than amusement, amiable charm, lazy sensuality.

Maybe she was expecting too much after two dates—well, counting the lunch, two and a half. It wasn't as if she'd done anything to goad him to anger or despair, or that she was all that funny.

But then, she shouldn't be thinking about making love with him, either. It was too soon.

Oh, how she wished it wasn't.

CHAPTER FOUR

"DAMN IT, WE'LL JUST send you, anyway." Eric dropped his scalpel and reached for a handful of gauze sponges. He was working on a shepherd with an ear hematoma. Teresa had anesthetized the dog and now stood watching her partner. It was a pleasure—in more ways than one. He worked quickly and neatly. He also looked damned good while he was doing it. Tall and rangy, he had close-cropped blond hair, a narrow intelligent face and gray-green eyes that could be as sharp as his scalpel. He didn't stir up her hormones, though, and she couldn't figure out why. In his own way, he was as sexy as Joe Hughes.

"What can they say?" Eric continued. "Even if you were incompetent, it's not as though you could do any damage on a preg check."

"Except be wrong," she said. Knowing as early as possible that a breeding had taken was critical to the dairy farmers—thus the monthly pregnancy checks.

He grunted and clipped off a piece of suture material. "You know, we've been letting a few of the old farts keep you from doing farm calls. Truth is, plenty of the younger dairy farmers wouldn't mind a woman. Some of them have wives who are darn near equal partners. All they care is whether you can do the job."

"I can do it."

"Then you take the farm calls today." He nodded toward the office. "It'll be a hell of a day. Ten farms, I think. You'll be shoulder deep in—"

She didn't need him to tell her what she'd be shoulder deep in. Cows—especially dairy cows—made a toddler with diarrhea seem like a poor producer. "I don't mind," she said.

Eric flashed her a quick grin. "Have fun."

"And if we make someone mad?"

"We can afford to lose some customers. They get damned good service from us. If they go with another veterinarian, so be it. Their loss."

"You're a prince," Teresa told him, and headed off to finish loading up the truck.

An hour later, she was driving through one of the mountain valleys, where an early snowfall already gleamed on the peaks. She found the first farm with no problem. A Dairy of Merit sign hung proudly out front. Long low red barns and green fenced pastures beyond made a postcard-pretty scene.

Teresa parked in front of the nearest barn and climbed out. She already wore rubber boots and overalls over a heavy flannel shirt. She was shrugging into the vinyl vest and reaching for a plastic sleeve to cover her arm when the farmer appeared in the barn door.

"Hi," she said, holding out a hand. "Eric was tied up today. I'm Dr. Burkett, his new partner."

The middle-aged man in the dairyman's customary costume of jeans and high rubber boots shook her hand without noticeable enthusiasm. "Know dairy cows?"

"You bet." She'd done some reading to update her knowledge, acquired during an internship in Minnesota. After that year, she'd looked forward to working in a warm clinic on animals she outweighed. But the cold stinky physical parts of the job had faded quickly from her memory, leaving the good parts: the satisfaction of helping with a difficult birth, of curing instantly a cow down with milk fever, the relationships with farmers. She'd come to miss the Jerseys and Holsteins, with their generally good natures and soft brown eyes.

This farmer jerked his head toward the open double doors. "I have the first batch locked in."

Figuring he'd prefer someone laconic, she only nodded and grabbed her tray of syringes, prepared with anything she might need.

They passed the milking parlor, spotlessly clean. A dozen black-and-white Holsteins were lined up, heads locked into stanchions, in a concrete holding area. Teresa breathed in the odors, which she'd never found objectionable. Setting down the tray, she went straight to work.

"Number 23," she said, peering at the ear tag.

The farmer nodded and referred to his clipboard. "Bred September 5."

Teresa inserted her hand into the cow's rectum and began cleaning it out. Green manure splashed at her feet. Eventually, concentrating, she reached in deep, feeling through the wall of the rectum for the uterus and the pea-size growth of a new calf. She smiled when she found it.

"Pregnant."

The farmer nodded and made a check on his list.

"Number 138," she said, moving on to the next cow. The rump shifted away and she grabbed the tail.

"September 10."

"Nope," she concluded at last.

They fell into a rhythm that she remembered and enjoyed; few words were exchanged, and those were to the point. Along with the pregnancy checks, she examined the cows that had recently given birth, treating a few for infections.

When she finished the first batch, the farmer released the metal stanchions and waved the animals out into a loafing area. Another man chased the next ten in. Grain lured them to thrust their heads through the locking mechanism. Teresa shook liquid manure off her arm, clad in clear plastic, and called out the first number.

When she was done, she threw away her plastic sleeve and hosed herself down. Manure sluiced off her boots and overalls.

The farmer asked if she wanted to look around, and she agreed. In a separate barn, she paused, gazing down at the calves. She scratched a snowy white soft head, and lips nuzzled her hand.

"Daughter takes care of those," the farmer said.

Teresa nodded. Bottle-feeding the calves was often a woman's job on a dairy farm. Typically the newborn calves were allowed to nurse for the first three to four days, for the sake of the health-giving colostrum, then bottle-raised on a milk replacer so the more valuable milk could be sold. By the time they were a month old, the calves were weaned even from that.

"Do you raise your own heifers?" Teresa asked.

He shook his head. "We send ours at three or four months to a farm in eastern Washington to be raised. Don't have enough pasture here."

That, too, she'd gathered, was typical of dairies on this side of the mountains. This farmer had a dairy herd of perhaps 160 cows, and as little as fifty or sixty acres. He wouldn't be growing his own hay, either, as a larger farm might. Yet she was impressed with the cleanliness of the barns and the condition of the herd. The pregnancy rate was high, too, a sign that everything else was going well.

The tour over, the farmer walked her out to her truck. "Eric be back next month?"

Her heart sank at the question. "Probably," she said, "although eventually we'd like me to be handling half the calls."

"You're quicker at the preg checks than he is," the dairyman said unexpectedly.

A compliment? Or was he implying that she'd gone so fast as to seem careless?

"I always had a knack."

"Either of you want to handle calls here, that's fine."

She felt like babbling gratefully. Instead, she nodded and offered him a smile with enough wattage to hint that he'd given her a gift. "You have a nice place. I look forward to working with you."

He nodded now; she climbed into the truck, waved and drove away. Barely out of his sight, she began caroling, "Oh, what a beautiful morning!"

Of course, her whole day couldn't be that easy. Three of the remaining farmers greeted her matter-of-factly. Three were wary and noncommittal. Two refused to let her do the preg checks. The last grudgingly let her into the barn only because he had two cases of milk fever and desperately needed her to wield the syringe that would have his cows leaping to their feet and strolling off to the loafing shed as though nothing had ever been wrong.

He watched them go suspiciously, as though she might somehow have tricked both the cows and him. After a moment he grunted. "Since you're already here..."

She was tempted to try to work even faster to impress him. She curtailed the temptation. A mistake would kill her reputation for good. Instead, she worked deliberately, calling out numbers, wrestling with recalcitrant cow butts, confirming and denying pregnancy.

She was examining a pretty little Jersey when the farmer said gruffly, "That one has a blocked teat. Feels like a pea in there."

"I'll take a look when I'm done," she said.

They herded the Jersey into a station in the milking parlor, where Teresa could stand in the center aisle, three feet below the stall level. As the cow shifted restlessly, she manipulated the long pale teat.

"Let me tranquilize her," Teresa said after a moment. She chose the base of the tail for the injection and waited until the cow swayed. Then she pulled out her forceps and probed inside. It took only a moment to remove the hard whitish blob.

She showed it to the farmer. "Scar tissue. Probably left over from mastitis."

He grunted. "Snipped the teat, did you? I suppose we'd better treat her for mastitis now."

"I didn't have to cut it," Teresa said. "Just keep an eye on her."

"Ah." The look he gave Teresa wasn't warm, but it had thawed. Treating for mastitis meant the cow's milk was unusable. She'd just saved him some bucks.

He, too, walked her out to the truck. "So you're the new partner."

"That's right." She unbuckled the rubber overalls and peeled them down.

"I suppose I'll be seeing you again."

"We'll try to accommodate preferences," she said evenly. "But that may not always be possible."

He nodded, which could have meant anything from understanding to acquiescence. Teresa chose to take it as the latter. She'd done well.

Eric agreed when she got back to the hospital. "Two phone calls saying they liked you," he informed her when she'd tracked him down to the kennel. Their resident cat, a huge fat tortoiseshell, sat slavishly at his feet. He was petting the still-groggy shepherd, who now had one floppy ear.

She crossed her arms. "And the two who wouldn't let me in their barns?"

"One wants to know when I can come. The other says he's changing services."

"Oh, for Pete's sake!" She stomped across the room, then swung around violently. "If they'd just give me a chance..."

Eric closed the cage door and rose to his feet, a smile playing at the corners of his mouth. "Ol' Man Eide says he did only because he couldn't wait. He sounded grudging, but he's willing to concede you're okay."

"Eide? That was my last call."

"Yup."

"And he phoned you to praise me?"

"I think 'okay' is praise in his book."

Teresa pumped her fist. "Yes!"

Eric slapped her on the back. "You'll win 'em over."

Already, she reflected as she unloaded the truck, it felt as if she and Eric had worked together forever. As if they were best friends. It was a good thing they *didn't* stir each other's hormones.

"*HE'S* HERE AGAIN," Nicole said into the telephone to her best friend from Bellevue. "He didn't even make an excuse for stopping by this time!"

"He?" Jayne echoed. "Oh. You mean that guy. The one your mom is seeing."

"If she marries him, we'll be stuck here forever!" Nicole said hopelessly.

"Hold on. My call waiting is beeping."

While Nicole sat listening to silence, she brooded. Couldn't Jayne tell how upset she was? Like some other phone call was so important.

Leaning against her bed, her door shut, she could still hear voices drifting up the stairs. Laughter. She felt...shut out. Even though she knew she wasn't really. Mark was down there in the kitchen with them. But she didn't belong.

Five minutes must have passed before her friend came back on the line with a rush. "That was *him,*" she said dramatically.

"Him?" But Nicole knew.

"Russ Harlan. He wanted to know if I'm going to a party tomorrow night. As if I'm going to say no."

Nicole's chest burned with envy and hurt. She struggled to say something. *Cool. I hope he asks you out.* Something. But she couldn't. It was a relief to hear a beep in her ear.

"My call waiting," she said. "Just a sec."

The voice was hesitant and male. "Can I talk to Nicole?"

"Speaking," she said coolly.

"Hi. This is Bill Nelson. I'm, uh, I sit next to you in English." He waited for her to agree that she knew who he was. When she didn't, he stumbled on, "I have brown hair. I play football. I'm, you know, a linebacker. We...we talked yesterday. After class."

She could hear him sweating. Bill Nelson was an okay guy, just kind of big and dumb. But she didn't care right now. Did he really think she'd go out with him?

"What do you want?"

He swallowed, making a gulping sound. "I...well, there's this movie in town. Steven Seagal. I thought... that is, I hoped... Would you go with me?"

She felt mean suddenly. "You're joking."

Pause. His voice got a lot quieter. "No."

He must be the tenth guy to hit on her since school started. She'd been nicer to the others. They were all such hicks they didn't deserve it. Hicks, like the one sitting at her kitchen table right now.

"I have a boyfriend. In Bellevue. I'm really not interested."

"Oh." Bill cleared his throat. "Okay. I, uh... Sorry. I didn't know."

"No big deal," she said ungraciously. "See ya." She pushed the button to cut him off and bring Jayne back onto the line.

"Who was that?" Jayne asked.

"Some guy." Nicole felt a little sick. She shouldn't have been so hateful. It wasn't Bill Nelson's fault that her best friend in the whole world had just snatched the coolest guy she knew away from her.

"Are the guys all lame?" Jayne sounded pitying.

Nicole gritted her teeth. "Of course not. You ought to see the quarterback of the football team. He's really fine. If I can just figure out how to meet a senior..."

"How hard can it be in a school that small?" Jayne didn't let her answer. "Well, listen, I gotta go. I'm supposed to help Mom with dinner. Then I need to call Kelly and Roz and tell them all about Russ."

"Sure."

"Wow, I wish you were here like you used to be."

Nicole strained to decide if Jayne meant it or not. "Yeah," she said slowly. "Me, too."

She had other friends she could have called, but they'd been sounding distant, too. It just wasn't the same, when she hadn't been there at school to see Liza tell off her boyfriend, or hear the new government teacher make an ass of himself, or watch Coach Murphy get a speeding ticket right in front of the high school. Everything was different. One-sided. They told her all the latest, and she grumbled about being stuck in this backwater town. But life hadn't changed for *them*.

The kitchen door slammed. Nicole lifted her head. Was he leaving? But she could hear Mark talking excitedly and a low calm counterpoint. Careful not to be seen, she went to the window. Sure enough, Mark the traitor was taking a football out onto the lawn with Joe Hughes. They started throwing it, Mark's passes wobbling, Joe's perfect spirals.

Like Joe was his dad or something. Didn't Mark have *any* discrimination?

What made her maddest was that she was jealous. He never offered to do stuff with *her*. Actually, she thought she made him uncomfortable. Well, that was how he made *her* feel. Like neither of them belonged when the other one was around.

But watching her brother and him through the window, Mark chattering, Joe not saying much but making every catch look easy, as though her little brother had a great arm, she had this flash of déjà vu. Their yard in Bellevue hadn't been very big, but she remembered looking out from her bedroom window seat because she heard her father's voice out there and seeing him and Mark throwing a football. In her memory, it was bright blue—probably a Nerf ball. But there'd been some connection between them, a closeness that had made her feel jealous for a moment, before she'd heard footsteps on the stairs and her mother's voice calling her. She'd jumped off the window seat and run to her bedroom door—

She shook her head, jolted out of the dream remembrance. *Had* she heard her mother calling? But the house was silent. And when she looked out again, standing to one side of her window, she saw that her mother sat on the back porch steps, arms wrapped around her knees, watching Mark and that guy. Why would she bother calling her, Nicole?

Nicole yanked the ugly curtains closed and threw herself facedown on her bed. She told herself she was crying because she missed her father. Sometimes it was hard even to picture him. But she'd just now seen him so vividly, as though it was Dad down there right now, not that redneck logger. She remembered stuff they'd done together, like the time he'd taught her ballroom dancing. Sometimes while Mom was cooking dinner, her father would put on a CD, a waltz, maybe, and bow to her. He was a really good dancer. She could almost forget he was her father. They'd twirl and twirl and twirl, perfectly in time. She guessed that was his way of throwing a ball with her. Maybe that was why she loved to dance so much.

Angrily she wiped away the tears and dug in her closet for her ballet slippers. She hadn't worn them in weeks. Scrambling to her feet, she straightened in first position. She wouldn't hear the voices from outside. She wouldn't.

Instead, she concentrated on the arch of her back, the strain on her thigh muscles, the curl of even her smallest finger as she slid into second position, then plié, third position, a reach for the ground, fourth position. Her routine caught her up, mindlessly, in its demands.

OUT ON THE STEP her mother brooded. What was Nicole doing up in her room all the time? They'd once been friends. They could talk. Now all Nicole did was sulk and slam her bedroom door.

Teresa could guess part of why her daughter was hiding up there. Nicole didn't like Joe, who had taken to stopping by a couple of times a week after work. Sometimes he stayed for dinner, sometimes not. It had started when he came back two days running to burn the pile of slash. She'd said something casual about seeing him tomorrow, and he'd turned up. They had continued to date, too, going out to dinner or to a movie on the weekend, but in a way she was happiest when he was here at her house.

Once he'd taken her to watch an afternoon of cow penning, a genuinely comic sport—when done by amateurs—where middle-aged men and women tried to stay on horses that had a better idea of what they were doing than the riders did. Joe had gone flying off once. He'd gotten up dusty, then grinned and slapped his hat against his thigh and set it back on his head. The others razzed him, but he took it well, which Teresa figured was a mark in his favor.

Anyway, Nicole got sulkier the more often Joe came by. Since Teresa refused to forget she was a woman until her children had grown and gone, understanding her daughter's resentment didn't help much.

"Watch out, this is going to be a long one," Joe called.

Teresa blinked and came out of her reverie to see her son taking off across the lawn—which still needed one more mow. The dogs, barking, chased him. Joe let loose a bomb that arced across the late-afternoon sky before it settled neatly into Mark's outstretched hands. Her son yanked it in, staggered two or three feet, then hit the ground rolling.

"Touchdown!" he yelled, jumping up to spike the ball.

Teresa had to smile at his playacting. Nicole wasn't the only melodramatic one around here.

Man and boy were coming toward her across the lawn, Mark laughing and Joe tousling the boy's hair. Teresa's heart gave a painful squeeze at the sight. Both kids had missed having a father, but especially Mark, as sports-minded as he was. She hardly knew a third down from a strike. He'd had to depend on his friends' fathers for coaching and encouragement. It would mean so much to him to have someone all his own—

Whoa! She almost gave herself whiplash yanking in the reins so hard.

The fact that Joe had agreed to throw a football with her son did *not* mean a marriage proposal was in the near future. In fact, instead of sitting here daydreaming, she should be worrying. Mark could get hurt if he started to count on Joe. What if her romance with Joe foundered? Maybe she should discourage him from hanging around. Keep their dating formal. Even if she did like having him here and guessed that he was lonely.

She still wanted to know *why* he was lonely.

"Hey, Mom, can we get a pizza tonight?" Mark asked eagerly.

"I already defrosted the hamburger..." she began, then threw up her hands. "I didn't feel like cooking, anyway."

"Yes!" Mark shuffled his feet in a bizarre spastic war dance that involved, once again, slamming the football to the ground. "I want pepperoni."

"Whatever you say. Just don't dislocate anything." She smiled at Joe. "Will you join us?"

"How about if I take you out, instead?" He lifted one dark eyebrow in that way he had. "You tried Mitchelli's Pizzeria yet? Best-kept secret in town."

"No. I'd been meaning to ask someone."

"Where's Nicole?"

Teresa nodded upward. Joe glanced at her daughter's bedroom window, then met her eyes again. "If it's awkward having me, I don't mind skipping it."

So he, too, had guessed why Nicole was being such a brat.

"I would," Teresa said decisively. "Mark, go get your sister. I'm starved."

Nicole tried to pretend she wasn't hungry. Teresa insisted she come, anyway. The girl managed to drop back on the sidewalk so that she entered the hole-in-the-wall restaurant far enough behind them to suggest she was on her own. When she discovered that not a soul within fell between ten and twenty-five years of age, she rolled her eyes and sat at the booth with them.

"Can we play video games?" Mark asked, bouncing.

Joe tried to look offended. "Video games? Hey, do you see any?"

Mark's eyes widened as he scanned the long narrow room. "But it's a pizza place. Pizza places always have video games."

Joe leaned forward. "This one specializes in pizza. Wait'll you taste it."

Nicole curled her lip. "I don't suppose they have a salad bar, either."

"You don't like pizza?"

"It's okay," she said shortly.

Joe didn't appear perturbed, Teresa thought. He had to be used to teenagers. He only smiled and laid an arm across the back of the booth behind Teresa's shoulders. "I tell you, just wait."

Nicole rolled her eyes again. Mark whined, "But what are we supposed to *do* while we wait?"

"Conversation is always nice," Teresa said briskly. She'd kill them later, when she didn't have an audience. Joe must think she'd raised them with no manners whatsoever. Maybe she had. For a single parent, it was often easiest to please the kids. Two against one. Oh, Lord, had she spoiled them rotten?

"Nicole, Joe tells me there's a dance school here in town," she said. "I left a message yesterday asking them to call me. I figured we'd go talk to them."

"It can't be very good," Nicole said sullenly.

Voice quiet, Joe said, "Actually, it is. A couple of my nieces dance. I think you'd be surprised."

"I doubt it," her charming daughter mumbled.

"Nicole!" Teresa snapped.

"Sorry." She gave an exaggerated shrug. "I just meant that I'm probably farther along than they are."

"Maybe so," Joe said equably, "but some of the senior dancers have been winning prizes in state competitions. They're pretty serious about what they do."

Peace might have been restored if Mark hadn't felt the need to get a jab in. "But just think," he taunted Nicole, "you'd finally be better than everyone else. You could be a star. Isn't that what you always wanted?"

She turned on him. "No, that's not what I wanted! I wanted to be good! Is that too much for you to understand?"

"Jeez!" He shrank back against the wall. "All I said was—"

"That I just want to look better than everyone else!"

"Well, don't you?"

"You little brat—"

Teresa raised her voice. "Enough already!" Thank heavens, here came the drinks. She didn't give the kids a chance to get going again. The second the waitress left after promising that the pizza would be along before they knew it, Teresa asked Joe what he was working on right then.

In his calm deliberate way, he took a sip of his drink. "I have a crew over on 205th, where they're punching the new road through. Today I looked over twenty acres of woods up toward Orr. We're going to high-grade it—that is, selectively log it."

"What did looking at it tell you?" Teresa asked.

"There're some formulas for estimating how much the timber will be worth. Height and girth of the average tree of course, but you have to think about how easy it'll be to fell and get out. Say it's on a steep hillside. It'll be hard to drop a tree without breaking it. Same's true if the ground is rocky or there are too many old stumps and snags around. I'm looking for defective trees, storm damage..." He shrugged.

"Is logging dangerous?" Mark's expression was avid.

"Can be." Joe didn't sound very concerned. "I'm careful. I don't let anybody take chances. If I get a young buck who's looking for a stretcher ride, he doesn't keep working for me."

"Have you ever seen anyone crushed by a tree?" Mark looked as if he wished he had. Were males born bloodthirsty?

Joe glanced at Teresa, one brow raised in silent inquiry. She shrugged resignedly. Maybe a gory anecdote would scare her son off any desire to top trees for a living.

"Once," Joe said, "I put in a couple of summers working logging camps in British Columbia. Good money." He was silent for a moment, gazing at the past. "The second year we had a new kid. Cocky. We'd been working a hillside in the rain that day. Someone was supposed to count noses when we got on the crummy—the bus—for our ride back to camp at the end of the day, but he fouled up. Wasn't until we sat down to dinner we realized Rod was missing."

The waitress plopped the fattest cheesiest pizza Teresa had ever seen down on the table along with a stack of plates. "Enjoy your meal!" she chirped.

Nobody else even glanced at the pizza.

"So you went hunting for him?" Mark urged.

"Yeah, we loaded back onto the crummy. Up on the mountain we spread out, most of us with flashlights. Slash everywhere, trees down we hadn't bucked to length yet, visibility lousy. We yelled his name every so often, poked through every heap of slash for something that looked like a rag." He paused. "I stepped right on his face with my caulk boots. Not that he noticed."

Even Nicole shuddered.

"Yeah," Joe said thoughtfully, "logging can be dangerous. But we take every precaution and then some."

"Can we eat?" Mark said brightly.

His sister looked at him. "You're sick."

"You mean, you don't want any?"

"Yes," Teresa interrupted, "you may eat. Nicole, do you want pepperoni or veggie?"

Her reaction to a long-ago death wasn't enough to make her fast. "Veggie, I guess."

Everyone was served when Mark swallowed a bite. "Hey, Joe?"

"Mmm?"

"After you found that guy's body? Did you all go down and eat dinner anyway?"

"You *are* sick," Nicole declared.

"Funny you should ask." Joe set his slice back on his plate. "Yeah, we ate dinner. We were even hungrier by that time."

"I thought so," Mark said with satisfaction.

Joe gave Teresa a rueful glance. "Sorry."

She wondered if her own appetite would desert her, but, no, it was alive and well. As usual. She could perform open heart surgery and enjoy a rare roast-beef sandwich right afterward.

"He asked," she said, and took a bite.

"You're *all* sick!" Nicole leapt up.

"Oh, for crying out loud." Teresa gave her daughter a meaningful look. "It was history. You don't get squeamish studying the American Revolution."

She sounded close to tears. "But he stepped on his face!"

Joe said quietly, "It still gives me nightmares sometimes. But as far as eating dinner goes...we were starved. We'd worked hard from dawn until well after dark. We were alive. I won't apologize."

His steady gaze held Nicole's. Her lip quivered, but after a moment she threw herself back into the booth. Teresa chattered about something that had happened at work that day—something that didn't involve blood—and when she sneaked a peek, it was to see that Nicole was downing her piece of pizza with every sign of enthusiasm. So much for teenage angst. Unless Joe couldn't stomach it.

Back at her house, he shook his head when she suggested he come in. The kids had already jumped out of the car.

"Nicole and Mark might like to see just you sometime today."

"You mean, you can't stand their bickering for another second."

"Bickering?" He looked surprised.

"You're used to it?" she asked incredulously.

"I come from a big family. We still bicker." His mouth curled into a faint smile. "My brother has four kids. You ought to hear them."

"Are you trying to tell me mine aren't any worse than most?"

"Pretty average," he said, straight-faced.

"And Mark's no more ghoulish than average?"

"Nah." Now he did grin. "Your kids are okay. Takes more than that to scare me off."

Did it really? Something had kept him from commitment all these years. If two kids, one a snotty teenager, couldn't do that, what had?

Even as Joe bent his head to kiss her, Teresa had the gut feeling she'd find out.

CHAPTER FIVE

"YOU DID *WHAT*?" One eye on the pot simmering on the stove, Joe had only been listening with half an ear to his sister's voice on the phone. He'd been wondering why the hell she'd called when they were to see each other in less than an hour. Now that she'd dropped her bombshell, he knew.

"I invited Teresa and her kids to our Sunday dinner," Jess repeated blithely. "I thought it would be neighborly."

"Neighborly?" he growled. "Not a one of us lives anywhere near her."

"She's treated my horses. Rebecca and I like her."

"You like half the people in town. You haven't invited them to a family dinner." Could she hear his gritted teeth? He was clenching them to hold in the panic.

He could see it already. Lee and his wife and brood would be there. Jess and her kids. Rebecca and her new husband and her son. Mom, benevolently seated at the head of the table. And Joe and Teresa and *her* kids.

No, the invitation was not an innocent gesture of friendship. The Hughes family had traditionally gathered once a month for Sunday dinner. Sometimes the kids brought friends. But for an adult, or even a teenager, to bring someone of the opposite sex was tantamount to announcing a wedding date.

And now Jess wanted him to bring Teresa and her kids. Just to be sure everyone knew whose guest she *really* was. Oh, yeah, Jess knew damn well what she was doing.

"Tell me again why you can't pick her up."

"John Peters just called," his sister repeated, parrotlike. "He's mad. My crew cleaned last night, and he claims they didn't lock up and he had a robbery. He wants me down there right now. It shouldn't take long."

Joe knew the owner of Peters' Furniture. He could skin Jess alive in five minutes. No, it shouldn't take long.

"Well, then?"

"But I don't want to be late picking Teresa up. I told her eleven."

"Call her. Tell her you're delayed." God. He was sweating. To bring Teresa to his sister's house. Introduce her to his mother. Have everyone smile knowingly, fall under her spell. Give her the seal of approval.

He wasn't ready. Sure, he liked her. She kissed like a teenage boy's erotic dream. But she was a doctor of veterinary medicine and he'd scraped through high school on grades given out of pity. Wedding bells were not in their future.

"You're being a jerk," Jess told him. "Teresa's place is barely out of your way. You're dating the woman, for crying out loud! You can't take an extra five minutes and give her a lift?"

He knew when he was beaten. "I'll do it," he said, "but one of these days, I'll get you for this." He slammed down the phone, trying to cut off the smile he knew would be growing on her face.

Joe transferred the spaghetti sauce to a Crockpot and wedged it behind the seat in his pickup truck. The kids would have to ride in back, he realized. Which was technically illegal. He could have used that as an excuse. Hell, some idiot might run a stop sign and barrel right into his Chevy somewhere during the half-mile drive through the placid small-town streets to Rebecca's place.

Before he left, he went back inside and shaved and changed shirts. To make his mother happy, he told himself, not acknowledging the fact that ten minutes ago he'd intended to go in stubble and a sweatshirt.

Another ten minutes later he pulled into the now familiar gravel driveway leading to Teresa's white farmhouse. The dogs raced to meet him, barking joyously as they escorted him down the driveway. The whole neighborhood knew when visitors arrived at the Burketts'.

Alerted by the dogs, Mark burst out the front door. "Wow, are you gonna give us a ride, instead of your sister? Are there any boys my age?"

"Yes, I'm giving you a ride, and, uh..." He had to think. His nieces and nephews were growing up with such alarming speed it was hard to keep track. "The closest is twelve," he decided. "My brother Lee's next-to-youngest. But Jess has a ten-year-old daughter."

The boy's face screwed up. "You mean, a *girl?*"

Joe scratched the head of the black Lab. "Yeah, daughters usually are."

"I don't like girls."

Mildly Joe said, "Sarah's okay. Give her a chance."

Nicole was next out the door. A ridiculously short tight denim skirt displayed spectacular legs, and a snug little ribbed shirt showed . . . Hell, she was fifteen. He felt like a lecher for even noticing. But damn it, with makeup even he could tell was expertly applied and wavy dark hair twisted into two rolls that met and mingled on the back of her neck, she could have been twenty.

He nodded. "Hi."

She gave him a cool smile, the princess greeting a footman. "Hi."

Teresa locked her front door and came down the porch steps with a wrapped dish in one hand. Her daughter's prettiness suddenly looked unfinished, like a tightly closed bud next to petals unfurled. Teresa Burkett showed what her daughter might be lucky enough to look like in fifteen years.

Black leggings revealed legs even longer than Nicole's. The flame red turtleneck was tunic length, but it clung in enough places to make Joe's mouth water. Today her hair was braided in coronets around her head, leaving a few wispy tendrils curling on her forehead and long graceful neck. How she could be elegant and sexy at the same time, he didn't know, but she managed.

"Hi," he said again, and heard how his voice had roughened.

"Hi." Her smile was at least fifty degrees warmer than Nicole's. "We were expecting Jess."

"She got held up. I was deputized."

"I'm sorry."

"Don't be. I should have thought of inviting you myself." Sooner or later he would have thought of it. And rejected the idea just as quickly.

Her smile turned saucy. "But your mother might have misunderstood that."

His mother was going to misunderstand this, too, he thought grimly. All he said was, "I warn you, in the crowd you might get lost."

"That big a family, huh?"

"We're a mob." He opened the tailgate. "Nicole, Mark, you're going to have to ride back here."

"Really? Wow." Mark vaulted in, followed by one of the dogs. Teresa sternly ordered it out again.

Nicole looked incredulous. "How am I supposed to get up there in this skirt?"

"Joe could turn his back while you shinnied it to your waist," her mother suggested.

"Which isn't far," he muttered, earning a flash of amusement from Teresa and a dirty look from Nicole.

The dirty look went double for her mother.

"Oh, heck, we'll be there in five minutes, won't we?" Teresa hopped up without even giving him a chance to take her hand. "I'll ride back here. Nicole, you can sit in front with Joe."

Lucky Joe. He closed the canopied back of the pickup and courteously held open the passenger door for the teenager.

She climbed into the high cab as gingerly as a cat ascending the staircase in an unfamiliar house.

She did put on the seat belt without his having to say anything, which would have gotten them off on the wrong foot, but then she sat rigid, staring out the windshield, while he started the engine and wheeled the pickup out of the driveway. She looked snotty as hell, but he'd been around enough teenagers to recognize well-disguised shyness. He hoped.

Conversationally he said, "We're going to my sister Rebecca's. She's fixing up an old house that's about the era of yours. She's a gardener, too. Grows old roses and lavender and that kind of thing. She got married a second time about a year ago. Has a son who's a senior in high school and she's pregnant with another one."

"I've met her," Nicole said stiffly. "She came out to our house and measured our windows and floors and stuff."

"Maybe you know her son, Alan, too."

"I doubt it." Good manners, presumably, inspired her to add a grudging, "I'm only a sophomore."

Having braked for a red light, Joe drummed his fingers on his thigh. "You started your dance class yet?"

"I'm taking two." And sounding superior. "Jazz and ballet."

"How do you like them?"

A shrug. "They're okay."

This was tough going, but he was stubborn. "Is there a Stephanie in either of your classes? Dark and skinny, except for..." He restrained his hands from sketching a bosom.

For the first time Nicole showed some animation. "Yeah, there's a Steph in both my classes. She's, like, twelve or thirteen?"

"Probably her. She'll be here today. Unless she's with her dad."

"Are they...divorced?"

"Yeah." Silently he added, *Thank God.* He'd never liked Roy, and he had an unpleasant feeling that Jess's ex had sometimes crossed the line from uncouth into abusive. She'd never said so, but Joe had seen fear in her eyes a few times.

Half-a-dozen cars were already parked in the driveway and along the curb, starting with Alan's beater. Joe parked behind his mother's Honda. "This is it," he said unnecessarily.

By the time he'd opened the tailgate and let Teresa and Mark out, Nicole was standing on the cracked sidewalk looking apprehensively at the house. He actually felt a twinge of sympathy. He remembered that age when you want so badly to be unshakably poised and, instead, you're quaking.

Teresa looked at the house, too. "Oh, it's gorgeous! I've just been converted. White is boring."

Rebecca had thought so, too. Her old house was painted a muted deep teal now, with pale seafoam trim. Roses in a last autumn flush of bloom climbed the porch rails, the heads heavy with white and pink petals. A herringbone brick walk led to the porch. Even Joe, who preferred modern, had to admit that his sister's place had charm.

What looked like a dozen teenage boys were sitting and leaning on the porch rail. In reality, there were only four. Alan, two of Lee's boys, and Carl, a buddy of Alan's.

Ron, the college freshman, caught sight of Teresa. "Uncle Joe brought a girl!" He let out a long low whistle.

Joe glared. Alan leapt over the railing and landed on the grass, making it look easy. He was a hell of an athlete. He was also showing off, Joe realized, as the boy swaggered toward them. And it wasn't Teresa he was openly giving the eye to.

"Hey, I've seen you at school."

Nicole's cheeks, Joe was interested to see, flushed. "Maybe," she said. "I'm a sophomore."

"I know. We're in French III together."

"Are we?" She batted her eyes and tried to look surprised. Neither Joe nor Teresa, who hid a smile, were fooled.

"Come on, I'll introduce you to everyone," Alan suggested. "You're Nicole, right? This your brother?"

"That's Mark," she said offhandedly.

Her brother had turned small and shy around the big broad-shouldered teenager. Fortunately Alan had a kind heart. He cuffed the kid lightly and said, "I'm Alan. Come on. Sarah's about your age."

Mark didn't say anything about *girls*. He went, meekly.

"Well," Teresa said, watching Alan put a hand on Nicole's back to steer her up the stairs, "my heart's fluttering in alarm."

"Alan's a good kid."

"Rebecca's?"

"Yep."

"Mmm." She pursed her mouth. "I hear he's noticed Nicole already. Is he, um..."

"Trustworthy?"

"You took the word out of my mouth."

"Up to a point," Joe said, secretly amused. "I wouldn't altogether trust any seventeen-year-old boy with a pretty girl."

"Gee, you make me feel lots better."

"You shouldn't trust me, either."

Her eyes widened at something she saw in his. Damn, he'd have liked to kiss her. Right now, right here. He *needed* a kiss to give him the courage to walk in that house with her.

Maybe it'd be easier if appearances were truth. He wouldn't mind being engaged to her.

Yeah, well, life was never simple. He couldn't ignore the chasm between them. One misstep and he'd plunge right in.

"Lead on," she said, waving her hand as though she was shooing a goat. Her daughter might be nervous, but she wasn't. He wondered if Teresa Burkett was ever anything but supremely confident. And why shouldn't she be, with her brains and beauty?

Lee and his wife, Janine, were waiting to pounce right inside the front door. This was the moment for a cowardly man to utter his disclaimer: *I didn't invite her. Jess did.* Of course, he couldn't say any such thing if he ever wanted to kiss Teresa again. All he could do was introduce her and let the inquisition begin.

"How nice to meet you, Teresa." All solicitude, Janine reached for the plate Teresa carried. "Why don't we go on into the kitchen and you can meet everyone else? On the way, you can tell me about yourself. Do you live here in White Horse?"

Feeling helpless, Joe watched his sister-in-law usher Teresa toward the kitchen, where the other women would be lying in wait. Lee grinned and slapped him on the back.

"Pretty."

"She's Jess's guest. Not mine."

"But you're seeing her, aren't you?"

"Yeah," he admitted.

"Seriously?" his big brother asked.

He wished. "Oh, hell, I don't know!" he snapped. "Excuse me."

He pushed open the swinging door to the kitchen. The first voice he heard was his mother's, steely beneath the courtesy. "And where are you from originally?"

Margaret Hughes didn't look a day over fifty, although her sixty-third birthday was only four months away. Some of it was grooming and makeup: her russet hair was short and stylish, the silver streaks adding distinction rather than age. She'd kept her figure and wouldn't be caught dead in the jeans and sweatshirts her four grown children favored. Today she wore a turquoise silk blouse with pleated wool slacks.

"The Midwest actually," Teresa answered, sounding unperturbed. "My parents have retired in Arkansas now—they've got a place on a lake. My two sisters and I are spread across the country, so it's a good thing Arkansas is nice and central."

"Are your sisters married? Do you have nieces and nephews?"

Teresa peeled the clear plastic cover from her vegetable-and-dip plate. "One of my sisters has two kids, four and seven. The other one is pregnant for the first time." She smiled at Rebecca, who was just closing the refrigerator door. "Annie must be due about the same time you are. The first of January, I think."

"I'm due January twenty-third." Rebecca made a face. "With my luck, I'll be three weeks late. I can hardly get out of a chair now."

"Don't you think you should quit working?" Joe's mother fussed, her spotlight momentarily leaving Teresa. Which was probably exactly what Rebecca had intended. "You shouldn't be on your feet so much."

"The doctor says I'm fine. If I do nothing but sit around, I'll get fat."

"How much have you gained, dear?"

"Mother!"

She blinked in surprise. "Why, it's just family, Rebecca. Well—" she smiled at Teresa "—almost."

Damn it, his mother had him married already. He'd known this would happen. What surprised him was the sudden sharp pain under his breastbone. Stronger than an ache, a knife thrust of longing for what might have been, what he wished could be. If he weren't who he was.

His mother was already going at Teresa again. Oh, she was a veterinarian, was she? Weren't the hours awfully long? What did her poor children do while she was working? Her husband had died? Oh, dear, how long ago?

When Rebecca had introduced Sam to the family a year and a half ago, Joe had sympathized. But he hadn't really understood until now how excruciating it could be.

Rescue for Teresa—or was he the one being rescued?—came from a quiet deep voice at Joc's shoulder. "Introduce me."

"Sam." Joc had scldom felt fonder of his taciturn brother-in-law. "Sure. Teresa?"

She came with a quick smile, the gold bangles on her wrist clinking. "You must be Rebecca's husband."

Sam lifted an eyebrow. "How'd you know?"

"Oh, Rebecca said you were tall, dark and handsome." Teresa waved one hand airily. "And, of course, there's the process of elimination. Jess isn't married, and I've already met Lee."

"Ah." His gray eyes rested warmly on his wife, bent over the open oven door. "Rebecca's biased."

"You complaining?" Joe asked sardonically.

"Are you kidding?" Something about the words seemed to amuse Sam. "I still think she's graceful, too."

Joe slanted an incredulous glance at his sister. She didn't look like a whale yet, but at five months pregnant she couldn't be mistaken for a prima ballerina, either. She moved slowly, awkwardly, pressing her hand occasionally to her back.

He had a quick flash of imagining Teresa pregnant. Not ten years ago, but now. With his child. She'd stay graceful and quick moving, losing none of the impatient energy that made him feel so alive. Maybe if the woman you loved was carrying your baby, you saw her differently.

The woman you loved. Shock slammed in the pit of his stomach. He didn't love her. He couldn't afford to. He wanted her. He liked her. Neither emotion was love.

He tuned back in to find that she and Sam were laughing about something, surprising in itself since Sam was a reserved man who sometimes unbent to give a dry chuckle. Of course, Rebecca had softened him up some. He and Joe's mother had even developed a relationship of grudging respect, if not affection. His role in providing another grandchild would probably remold that relationship into something a little stronger, more permanent. Children did that.

Teresa smiled at Rebecca. "Shall I put this out on the coffee table?"

"That's a good idea." His sister made a face. "Maybe the kids will accidentally grab a carrot stick, instead of a handful of potato chips."

Teresa touched Joe's arm. "Speaking of kids, I'd like to find mine after I put this out. I don't want them to feel abandoned."

His mother smiled benignly after them. That was just what he needed: to have his family believing in the impossible. Damn it, he thought viciously, they of all people ought to understand that she was out of his reach.

He hated knowing that. He hated being made to feel inadequate. It brought back memories of his school years. He'd had a long struggle to accept his limitations and know his strengths. He was an idiot for having let his hormones tempt him into wanting things to be different.

No, not things. *Himself* to be different.

NICOLE SAT on the hood of an old wreck of a car and watched the boys and Jess's two girls shooting baskets through the hoop attached to the garage. Beside her, Alan leaned one hip on the fender. She could feel his gaze.

"You always this quiet?" he asked at last.

He was better-looking than Russ Harlan, which made her shy. Knowing he was two years older made her even more uncomfortable.

She shrugged. "I guess I don't have anything to say."

"Have you made friends at school yet?"

She shrugged again, like she didn't care. "Not really."

"Steph says you never talk to the other girls in your dance class."

"I have friends." She wouldn't look at him. "At home."

"You mean, where you came from?"

"Bellevue. That's where my friends live."

"But you don't anymore."

"Like I need you to tell me," she snapped.

His brows drew together. "I take it you didn't want to move."

She didn't dignify that with an answer.

"I guess it's hard." He almost sounded sympathetic. "I'd have hated to move last year when Mom married Sam."

Irrationally Nicole resented the suggestion of fellowship. As if they had anything in common. He was a star jock, and cute, besides. If he'd gone to a new high school, he'd have been mobbed the first day, not ignored.

Sarah, the cousin who was Mark's age, finally missed a shot. Looking smug, she rebounded and bounced the ball to Mark. He grabbed it and dribbled almost to the bumper of the cars. Then he turned and let it go. The ball whispered through the net and he pumped his fist in triumph.

Great. Another sport he was good at. It figured. Sometimes she just wished he'd screw up. She was sick of having a perfect brother. It'd serve him right if Sarah beat the pants off him.

Alan's gaze was still on her face. She knew her tone was surly and didn't care. "I wanted to stay in Bellevue and finish high school. Mom wouldn't let me."

"What was so great about Bellevue?" he asked, as though he couldn't imagine.

"Everything!" Was she supposed to itemize it? "We had a really great house and I had friends and there was stuff to do there."

Alan didn't appear impressed. "White Horse isn't so bad."

She leveled a look at him. "Have you ever lived anywhere else?"

He shrugged. "No, but I go down to see my dad in Seattle. It's cool, but I wouldn't want to live there."

"You've got to be joking," Nicole said incredulously.

"I don't like crowds." He shrugged again. "And it's noisy. I have trouble sleeping."

Her lip curled. "Yeah, well, I guess if quiet is all you want out of life..."

He shook his head and pushed off from the car. She could tell he was going to walk away. "Jeez, you have a real chip on your shoulder."

To his back Nicole said, "You mean, because I don't like living in a dump in some little burg that stinks of manure all the time? Well, excuse me."

He whirled around, eyes narrowed. "You've made up your mind to hate it here, haven't you?"

Her mother had said the same thing. Remembering made her tone more pugnacious. "I didn't make up my mind. I *do* hate it here."

"How much of White Horse have you seen?"

"How much is there to see?"

"You been down to the river yet? Horseback riding? Hiking? Wait'll Christmas. And our Fourth of July parade. We know how to do holidays. And the movie theater. It isn't fancy, but it's a lot cheaper than the big cinemas. And people are really friendly."

Hot blood surged to her cheeks. She refused to decipher why. It was okay to be angry. She didn't want to feel ashamed.

"Right," she sneered.

Sounding disgusted, he added, "People are friendly if you're friendly back."

Her cheeks burned hotter. "So it's my fault?"

"It might be." His gaze challenged her. "If it's not your fault, prove it."

Out of her peripheral vision, she was vaguely aware that the basketball game had ended and everyone had turned to watch them. Suspicious, she asked, "What do you mean, prove it?"

"Give me a chance to show you that White Horse isn't so bad." When her mouth opened, Alan held up one hand. "A *fair* chance. You can't go at it expecting to hate everything before we get there."

Nicole's mouth was still open, but she didn't know what she'd intended to say. Forget it? Ask him if he was suggesting a date? A real boy/girl date, with him a senior and her only a sophomore?

She must look like an idiot. She snapped her mouth shut. After a minute she shrugged. "Why not?"

It wasn't like she had anything better to do with her time. And he was cute.

Besides, with luck he'd provide her with some ammunition to use on her mother.

Alan smiled, but his eyes still held a challenge. "Then you're on."

CHAPTER SIX

NICOLE WAS CAREFUL not to look toward Alan even once during French class. When the bell rang, she grabbed her binder and books and hurried out.

But his voice chased her down the hall. "Hey, Nicole!"

Already blushing, she stopped and turned. The current of bodies sweeping by parted to go around her, only jostling her a few times while she waited.

Alan gave a high five to some other guy, then grabbed Nicole's arm and pulled her to one side. "What's your rush?"

"I have to go to my locker." Her arm tingled where he'd touched it.

"Oh." He ran his fingers through his hair, and her stomach did a little dip. "Well, I just wanted to tell you that we can't start our tour until Saturday. I have football practice every day after school."

"And a game Friday," she blurted.

"Yeah. You coming?"

If she'd had a friend to go with, Nicole would have liked to see the game. She'd always gone to football games in Bellevue. And she would have liked to find out whether Alan was any good. But she'd feel really stupid sitting all by herself in the bleachers.

"I doubt it," she said coolly.

"Why doesn't that surprise me?"

Something in his tone made her feel as if she should apologize. A little awkwardly she said, "I'm not a big football fan."

He propped one shoulder on a locker and grinned lazily. "Maybe we can change that."

Was he flirting with her? she wondered in shock. Her stomach had recovered from the dip and was climbing into her throat.

She tried to sound sophisticated. "Who knows?"

His smile faded. What was he thinking? She made a production out of adjusting the books in her arms so she didn't have to meet his eyes.

"Is Saturday okay?"

"Only if you don't mind Mark coming along. Mom works every Saturday, and I get stuck baby-sitting."

In her heart, she was hoping his face would fall and he'd say something like, "But I wanted to be alone with you."

It stung when all he did was shrug. "That's okay. He's a nice kid."

Alan would probably spend the whole day talking to Mark. She wanted to say, "Then why don't you take just him?"

Of course, she couldn't admit Alan had deflated her ego.

She started backing away. "I've got to go." She bumped into someone and mumbled an apology. To Alan she called, "Do you know where I live?"

"Yeah, I remember when the house was for sale. See you at ten Saturday?"

She agreed and sprinted for her locker.

In her very next class the girl who sat in front of her turned around and said, "I saw you talking to Alan

Harstead. Are you going out with him or something?"

Nicole flipped open her binder. "Or something."

The girl's brown eyes were avid. "He's never even noticed I exist. You're really lucky."

"His uncle and my mother are friends. Probably his uncle asked him to be nice to me." The words just popped out, but the minute they did, she realized they might well be true. Nicole hated the disappointment that burned in her chest.

"You're still lucky," the girl whispered.

"Why, because *I* exist now that he's noticed me?"

Her nastiness earned her a narrow-eyed look. As the girl whirled to face the front, she tossed over her shoulder, "I said hello the first day."

Nicole stared at the back of her head. As if one transparency had been laid over another, she saw herself sitting down that first day and the girl turning around to smile.

"Hi, you're new, aren't you? My name's Ariana."

She'd said something sullen. She knew she had. She was so resentful at being here she'd felt like taking it out on other people. Not just Ariana. Bill Nelson, too.

The teacher came into the room and raised his voice. "Okay, class, settle down. Let's get started."

Nicole leaned forward and whispered, "I'm sorry." She didn't know if Ariana heard her.

But after class, when Nicole was gathering her books, Ariana turned around again. She looked a little wary, but she said, "It's okay. Moving when you're in high school must be a bummer."

"I miss my friends," Nicole admitted.

"You'll make new ones." Ariana stood up. "Come on, it's lunchtime. I'll introduce you around."

People are friendly if you're friendly back. She could hear Alan's voice.

She still hoped she could persuade her mother to return to Bellevue. But it wouldn't hurt to make new friends in the meantime, would it?

"Thanks," she said shyly, and stood up, too. "Do you live here in town?"

NATURALLY, MARK THOUGHT the dirt-bike track was cool. Nicole added it to her list of places to show Mom. Although she might not have to bother. Mark was stupid enough to go home chattering about it and about how much he wanted his own dirt bike. Mom wouldn't like the idea of Mark's tearing around on a motorcycle. On this course, it'd be easy to break a leg at the very least.

And if Alan had thought to impress her by borrowing a friend's bike and taking a couple of circuits in a cloud of dust and roar of the engine, using his feet to keep him from going over on tight turns, flying off bumps like an idiot, he failed. This was just about what she'd figured people did for fun around here.

But then he slapped the dust off and suggested lunch in Mt. Vernon and some shopping at the discount mall.

"Mall?" she echoed hopefully.

"Yeah, haven't you been there?"

"What is it, like K-Mart's rejects?" Discount meant cheap, right?

Alan grinned. "You'll see."

The drive north took about half an hour. Nicole sat in front with Alan and her brother took the back. At first she felt shy, but Alan was easy to talk to. He answered questions and told her about some of the teachers and kids she'd met.

"Next year you'll have Walker for advanced algebra. He's a real crack-up. If you know what you're doing, you can get him going and he'll forget about whatever he was going to teach that day. You can't pull it off too often, but once in a while, when you really don't want homework..."

"I'll remember that."

He turned into a parking lot, and her heart almost stopped. Jordache, Izod, Gitano. There was a whole *store* of Jordache clothes. Discounted.

"The café here is pretty good," Alan said offhandedly. "Then maybe you guys can help me pick out something for my mother's birthday."

Nicole waited for Mark to whine, "Shopping!" but apparently he was too much in awe of Alan to complain.

"When is it?" Nicole asked.

"Next week. She's down about it. She's been going around mumbling that she's too old to be pregnant. She swears she keeps finding gray hairs. She claims she pulls 'em out every morning, which is why no one else ever sees one."

From the back seat, Mark contributed, "Mom doesn't have any, but she's always saying that I'm going to give 'em to her."

Alan didn't bother locking the car. Nobody would want to steal it. In a daze of wonder Nicole followed him as he wended his way through the parked cars. This whole place was made up of designer outlets. Jayne would have a cow!

But Nicole was just as stunned by the way Alan talked about his mother with such obvious affection.

Most kids pretended they didn't like their parents. And she remembered when Cathy's mother had gotten pregnant last year. Cathy was utterly humiliated. It was like her mother was telling the whole world that she still had sex. And to be pregnant, when she was at least thirty-five!

But here was Alan, enthused about having a brother or sister. "I almost wish I wasn't going away to college next year. I'll miss so much." He held open the café door for her and Mark. Good smells drifted out. "But I'll be home for vacations," Alan finished more cheerfully.

The lunch wasn't half bad. When Nicole offered to pay, Alan pulled out his wallet. "Nah, I make plenty working for my aunt. I clean offices and stores after they're closed. It's okay, as jobs go. Aunt Jess is a cool boss."

"Usually I just baby-sit." Nicole made a face. "But I don't know anybody here yet."

"Have you put up notices? I'll tell Mom to hire you once she's had the baby."

Nicole hunched her shoulders and mumbled, "Thanks."

Bored, Mark trailed Alan and Nicole around the shopping center. Nicole kept darting off to look at clothes, but mostly she concentrated on helping Alan pick out a gift for his mom. If she'd had more money with her, she might have started thinking about Christmas presents. Jayne would like *everything* here.

Alan said, "I thought I'd get something pretty. You know, since she's pregnant and keeps saying she looks like a hippo. I mean, if I bought clothes, they'd have to be shaped like a tent. And it'll be a while before she gets back to her regular size."

"Yes, but she might like to be reminded she'll get there."

He looked dissatisfied. "Yeah, I guess. But if it was something that would make her feel pretty now—"

"Jewelry," Nicole suggested. "Or, um, perfume, maybe?"

His face brightened. "Hey, cool! Will you help me choose one?"

"Sure," she agreed.

Under the suspicious scrutiny of a clerk, they sprayed and sniffed their way through a store that carried every brand of perfume, bath oil and powder known to women.

Even Mark offered opinions, wrinkling his nose at scents he thought were gross and declaring, "It's okay," to ones he liked.

Of course, Alan had no idea whether his mother ever wore perfume or what she smelled like. Nicole rolled her eyes. Men.

But maybe subconsciously he did know, because he rejected strong perfumes like musk, and they finally settled on a delicate floral scent that, discounted or not, still cost a fortune. He bought both bath oil and powder.

It was late enough that they had to go straight home. In their driveway, Mark leapt out. "The dirt bikes were cool!" he told Alan, and slammed his door.

Nicole put her hand on the latch. "I had fun."

"Yeah, me, too." His smile was friendly enough to make her heart beat faster. "Thanks for helping me get my mother's present."

"Uh, sure, no problem." Nicole hesitated a second longer, then felt like an idiot. Did she think he was going to kiss her or something? On that thought, she jumped out of the car before he could see her blush. "Bye."

"See you in French." He waved, then laid his arm on the back of the seat where she'd just been sitting. Looking over his shoulder, he backed around, then accelerated down her driveway with a burst of gray exhaust and a roar that suggested his muffler was history.

Nicole stood there a moment longer, the dogs gamboling about her, watching him go, a funny tightness in her chest. What if he *had* kissed her?

Shock made her suck in her breath. Oh, no! She couldn't be falling for him, could she?

Alan probably thought of her as some little sophomore he had to be nice to. For all she knew, he had a girlfriend.

But even if he didn't, even if he liked her, even if he *was* sexy and a football star, Alan Harstead thought she was nuts for preferring Bellevue to this backwater town. He enjoyed dirt bikes. He wished he wasn't going away to college, for crying out loud!

He and she had nothing in common. Nothing. Anyway, Nicole bet that her mother had told Joe to ask his nephew to be nice to her. It was all a plot. They were trying to weaken her, and she wouldn't let them. Nothing would make her like it here.

JOE TUGGED uncomfortably at his collar. He wore a tie so seldom it chafed when he did. He'd gotten to the point where he felt almost at ease at Teresa's house. It must be the tie and slacks that made him want to bolt.

Teresa hadn't quite been ready for their big date when he'd arrived, so he was waiting in the kitchen. Nicole sat at the round oak table doing homework and ignoring him. The obese tabby who was draped across the top of the refrigerator wasn't interested in him, either. If Mark hadn't had a friend here, Joe would have joined him in the living room where he was battling evil foes on his Nintendo. As it was, all Joe could do was sit here and twitch.

He wished he'd had the guts to refuse Teresa's suggestion for tonight. He was a logger, not a lawyer. He didn't belong in some fancy French restaurant in Seattle. But when he'd tried to demur, Teresa had given him a quick kiss on the cheek and said breezily, "Oh, come on, it'll be fun. We do local all the time. Let's go yuppie for once."

It was true that he'd decided all their destinations thus far. And, hell, it wasn't as though he hadn't known it would come to this. A woman like Teresa wasn't going to be content dining out in White Horse or munching popcorn at the movie theater in Everett. His idea of variety was hitting a few balls at the batting cage or penning cows on his quarter horse. Hers was the Seattle opera or traveling Broadway shows. Their tastes were bound to collide eventually.

He was roused from his brooding by Nicole, who was scowling at a paper covered with red scrawl.

"I don't know why this is wrong," she muttered. "Who cares whether you say which or that?"

He sure as hell didn't. Assuming her question had been rhetorical, he didn't comment. But he made the mistake of moving restlessly, and she looked up, fixing him with pleading eyes.

"Do *you* understand the difference? Can you explain it to me?"

That was all it took for a lead weight to settle in his stomach. Every time he'd imagined having children, he'd known it would come to this sooner or later: they'd want help with their homework. Help he couldn't give.

His wry smile hurt. "You're asking the wrong person, kiddo. It was a miracle I graduated from high school."

Her eyes widened in shock. Most of her mother's friends were probably doctors and lawyers and vice presidents of companies like Microsoft and Nordstrom. They were the kind Dr. Teresa Burkett belonged with. Not him.

"Damn," he mumbled, and lurched to his feet. Nicole kept staring. The weight in his stomach ballooned until it filled his chest, too, and almost choked him. His voice was thick when he said, "Tell your mother—"

"Tell me what?" her mother asked from the doorway.

He swung to face her like a trapped animal. God, she was beautiful, a movie star sweeping into the Academy Awards, not anybody he could know. Her black pants were made of nubby silk and were so full that at first he'd thought skirt. Above, a snug lacy black top bared the pale curves and shadowy cleavage of her breasts. Over it, a red silk jacket clung at hips and waist. Exotic gold earrings and choker emphasized the slender grace of her neck, otherwise bare because her dark hair was wound into an intricate knot on the crown.

"Somebody steal your tongue?" she asked pertly.

"I . . . You look great."

A smug mischievous smile dawned. "Ah, poetry," she breathed, then twirled so he could see the full effect. He almost groaned. What would it feel like to slip his hand inside the lace and cup her breast? And that smile. He could see her lying with her hair frothing over his pillow, laughing up at him.

"Tell me what?" she asked again, still smiling.

"Never mind." He had to clear his throat. "I was going to make a phone call."

She waved toward the kitchen counter. "The telephone is right there. There's another in the living room if you want privacy." She cocked her head. "No, forget privacy. Mark and Colin are out there."

"That's okay."

She kissed the top of Nicole's head. Her gaze lit on the paper covered with red marks. "Having trouble in English?"

"No," her daughter said, lower lip sticking out. Then, "Yes. Who cares about who and whom?"

"Or—" Teresa read over her shoulder "—that and which."

"It's stupid!" Nicole burst out. "Why do we have to learn junk we're never going to use?"

"For starters," Teresa said mildly, "you might use it. There are lots of professions where you need to write grammatically. Second, every adult should be fluent in his or her own language. That's all the school is trying to accomplish."

"Can *you* explain?" The teenager flicked what he saw as a disparaging glance at him. "Joe—Mr. Hughes—couldn't."

He felt himself flush, but Teresa only laughed. "Maybe not, but I'll bet he could help you with the algebra I've long since forgotten."

Yeah, but he knew which was the more important.

"Really?" Nicole's voice sounded hopeful and she reached for her backpack.

"But not now," her mother said firmly. "We're going out to light up the town."

"A forty-watt bulb would do that," Nicole muttered.

"Not this town. The city. I left phone numbers on the fridge. Don't forget to feed the animals." Teresa kissed Nicole's head again. "We're going into Pioneer Square. I imagine we'll be late. You get Mark to bed by ten."

"Can I kick Colin out right now?"

"No, you may not. His dad's picking him up at eight." She grabbed a tiny beaded purse and looked expectantly at Joe. "Shall we go?"

"Why not?" He could think of plenty of reasons why not, but wasn't about to articulate them. Number one would be *because I'll feel like a mutt at a dog show.*

He relaxed marginally during the drive. She was easy to talk to. She actually seemed interested in his day, which never failed to surprise him. Sooner or later she'd figure out that his kind of logging was all sweat, risk and numbers, and she'd lose interest. In the meantime, she asked questions: Why is fir worth more than hemlock? How do you calculate how many board feet of lumber you'll get out of a certain tree? Why not selectively log, instead of clear-cut?

In turn, he listened as she told him about her day, half of it in surgery and the other half seeing clients for routine vaccinations and minor problems.

"Which part do you enjoy the most?" he asked.

"Umm..." Teresa wrinkled her nose as she thought. "Surgery, I'd have to say. I was so excited in vet school to get my hands on those instruments and do something *real.* We had partners—mine was a guy named

George. That first time—" she laughed "—we had to administer a preanesthetic and then insert a catheter into the vein. It was a nightmare. We stabbed and stabbed, and those damn veins kept disappearing. I was convinced a vampire had sucked that dog dry just to spite us. I swear it took us an hour to prepare that poor animal. Then we had to scrub. *That* took forever—you have to wipe every side of every finger ten times with an antiseptic." She gave him a sidelong glance. "You may have noticed the skin on my hands isn't magnolia soft."

He hadn't. His own were so callused and rough he could have snagged silk with one pass. He grunted some response, and she chattered on, but he was left imagining again that he was cupping her breast, only this time she was wincing away from his touch. Her husband had probably had smooth manicured hands.

Joe tuned back into her story at the point where she was all "prepped"—wearing surgical gloves to be completely sterile—and was draping the dog.

"That's when I had this terrible itch. I didn't even think. I scratched my nose. I could see this horror in George's eyes and feel a tingle on my nose, and it dawned—I had to start all over. It took three hours before we even opened the dog up. I was ready to quit."

He had to laugh. "How long does it take you now?"

"Fifteen minutes." Her chuckle danced over him like teasing fingers. "No vet in the world would have hired me as an assistant if it had taken me three hours to prep for every surgical procedure."

He found parking space along the waterfront. Dusk had brought a misty fog, out of which floated the plaintive horn of a docking ferry. Seattle's Pioneer Square was an odd hybrid: chic shops sat cheek by jowl with missions that fed the homeless. During the day, the dozen blocks were crowded with tourists, and cars lined up to take the ferry to Bainbridge Island and other points. By this time in the evening, winos slumped in dark doorways and staked out park benches in the cobbled square. This wasn't a place for a woman to come alone at night.

He survived the French restaurant by letting Teresa order for him. He glanced at the menu, but he couldn't decipher a word on it and wouldn't have known what it was if he could have. The food was good, if rich for his tastes, and he liked to look at her face in the candlelight, which added mystery to the shadows beneath her high cheekbones and the dark cloud of her hair. Her laugh seemed less earthy now, more knowing, cosmopolitan. And as though inspired by her surroundings, Teresa's conversation ranged from concerts and gallery openings she'd attended to books she'd read. He had never felt more like a blockhead.

Only once did she pause and look quizzical. "You're awfully quiet tonight."

"I enjoy listening to you," he said only half-truthfully.

"In other words, I'm letting my mouth run away with me." She laughed at him. "Stop me. Say something."

Was he capable of being witty? No. Woodenly he said, "Are you ready to go?"

"Go? What time is it? Oh! Yes, of course." They'd argued earlier over who would pay the bill, and he'd won by a nose. In his world, women didn't take a man out for dinner. Another sign, he realized, that he was a foreigner in a strange land.

The wail of a saxophone drifted from a doorway several steps down from the street. They followed its cry into a small club with an exorbitant cover charge and drinks that had fancy names and prices. The music almost made it worth both, however, and he began to relax. His radio was usually tuned to a country station, but this music played by black musicians from New Orleans was as emotional as a woman crying or a man sighing with bitterness when life had screwed him over.

Several of the men were young, too young to grieve so powerfully or laugh so joyously. But the saxophonist had cheeks puffed out by an eternity spent playing his horn, and seams across his forehead had been stitched by the years. Joe guessed the music was his, as was the crying voice of the sax.

He and Teresa were both silent when they left the club. The music followed them down the street as it had lured them in. A wino thrust out a hand and whined, "Spare a little change?" and sudden pity at the desperation in those rheumy eyes made Joe thrust out a ten.

Teresa squeezed his arm and said softly, "That was nice."

They were within a block of his pickup when Teresa exclaimed, "Oh, look, Elliott Bay is open!"

Joe's tension had been easing; he'd survived the evening without making a fool of himself. Now his muscles tightened. What the hell was Elliott Bay? A brightly lit doorway and display windows ahead were answer enough. A bookstore.

Panic grabbed him, but he had to say something. "They can't get much business at this time of night."

But as they paused on the sidewalk in front of the store, he saw that he was wrong. The dozen or more fine restaurants, the Comedy Club, the Jazz Club and even the regularly arriving and departing ferry meant the sidewalks were almost as crowded as they were in the daytime. Half the couples having a romantic evening out apparently stopped to pick out a good book on their way home.

"Come on," Teresa urged. "Let's go in."

"I'm not much of a reader."

She squeezed his arm again. "We can cure you of that. It'll be fun."

Fun. Damnation. Reluctantly he let himself be towed through the narrow doorway. He hated bookstores, and a single glance told him this was worse than most. Tables were stacked high with books he supposed were literary; the covers weren't as familiar as the bestsellers he'd noticed face out in front of the chain stores at the mall. A balcony that looked down on a coffee shop below was lined with shelves packed with more books. Aside from audiocassettes, he couldn't see a thing for sale that wasn't between two covers. No cards, no novelties, nothing he could pretend interest in.

It didn't get any better: past the registers, another doorway opened onto a maze of shelves and nooks and crannies, all lined and stacked with books.

"Oh, I love this one!" Teresa pounced. "Have you read it?"

He stared blindly at the cover. "I don't think so."

"Oh, you should. Here, take a look." She shoved it into his hands. "Oh, and Roger Caras has another book about cats. He always makes me look at my own pets with a new eye."

He'd flipped open the one in his hands, feeling clumsy. It was something about firefighting, he got that much, although he didn't even try to decipher the jacket copy. If he looked engrossed enough, maybe she'd wander away without noticing what he was doing.

But no, she kept exclaiming with wonder and delight and pressing new books on him that "you have to try." The panic was nearly suffocating him. He was rescued only by anger that grew from roots planted in his past. Damn it, hadn't she listened to him? He wasn't a reader. He wasn't going to become one because Dr. Teresa Burkett kept pushing books at him.

He put each one back down where it had come from. She ruminated over one after the other and decided to buy half a dozen. They all looked dense to him—thick weighty volumes on obscure subjects by writers he'd never heard of. Her choices emphasized the chasm between them, as if the sun was slanting in just the right way to deepen the shadows in the depths.

He was sweating when at last she declared herself satisfied. For the first time since they'd walked in the door, Teresa really focused on him. Her gaze moved from his face to his empty hands and back again.

"You're not buying anything?" She sounded disappointed.

"I told you, I'm not a reader."

"But if you tried the right books..."

His face felt numb after an hour of keeping it wiped clean of expression. Thank God, the line ahead of them moved forward just then.

"There's a clerk free." He nudged her. "Let me pay for those."

"Don't be silly." She gave him a severe frown. "If you want, buy me flowers. I'll pay for my own reading material, thank you."

"But you like books better than flowers."

"And I can afford them. I buy 'em all the time. I never buy myself a corsage." She slapped the pile on the counter.

He should have been amused by the picture of an orchid corsage pinned to the baggy sweaters she usually wore, but he wasn't. Oh, hell, he could pretend. He'd been doing a lot of that with her.

"They need chaperons for the high-school prom. You could wear a corsage there. I can volunteer us to Alan, if you want."

As if from a distance, Joe saw her come-hither smile. "You're on, just so I get that corsage. Make it something fragrant."

The next few minutes, she was occupied paying for her stack of books and thanking the clerk. Joe waited, concentrating with every fiber on the clear path to the door. It was like felling a tree; you always chose an exit route, in case things went wrong.

Tonight, at last, he was able to take it. The minute they walked out the door, he could breathe again.

He was mostly silent on the way home, preoccupied with a vision so clear he knew it was real: the end of this mismatched romance. He had tailored a life that suited him, one where he felt competent and content. But it wouldn't suit Teresa. No sense kidding himself. She'd keep dragging him out of his comfort zone. Pretty soon she'd notice that he was sweating, and then he'd be an embarrassment. Worse yet, he'd see himself through her eyes and he might start to despise himself. He'd gone that route before. He didn't want to head down it all over again.

End this, his instinct for survival told him. *Now.*

From the darkness in the pickup cab, Teresa asked softly, "Why so quiet?"

"Nothing to say."

That's a lie, the inner voice told him. *Do it.*

But Joe discovered that he couldn't be blunt enough to tell her he wouldn't be calling again. God help him, he would be. He didn't have the guts to keep his hand away from the phone. He wanted her. He wanted to be a different man.

Well, then, make her end it. Show her what you see. She'll drop you like an old hemlock in a windstorm. You don't have to worry.

Joe felt a twinge of reluctant amusement. *Thanks,* he told himself. *You're a real comfort.*

You've always been honest with yourself before. Don't be a fool now.

His fingers tightened on the wheel. Yeah, okay, he was being a fool. He never should have asked out a woman like her.

But that was his fault, not Teresa's. Now he had to figure out a way to turn her off. A way that would spare her from being the rejected one.

If his good-night kiss had an edge to it that night, a shot of desperation, she didn't seem to notice. Her arms just tightened, and she murmured in that way she had of driving him crazy. Her tongue met his in a sensual dance. She was the only woman he'd ever known who gave as good as she got, who had the confidence to let him know what she wanted. Damn, how he liked that. If she did the same in bed, she'd be every man's dream come true.

But you, that brutal voice in his head whispered, *will never find out.*

CHAPTER SEVEN

JOE WAS OBVIOUSLY in a bad mood, which made Teresa wonder why he'd asked her out in the first place. It wasn't as though they'd planned this a week ago and he'd felt as if he couldn't get out of it. Actually, he'd called just this afternoon. Nor was he drinking heavily, although they were at a tavern.

In fact, when she thought about it, he'd been a little surly on the phone, too.

"I spend a lot of Friday nights at the tavern shooting pool," he'd told her brusquely, as though he thought she might sneer. "You want to discover what a thrill White Horse is at night?"

"Why not?" she'd said. "I'm a mean hand with a pool cue."

And she was, too. A hole-in-the-wall dive a few blocks from the campus had been a popular hangout for vet students because it had boasted a battered pool table. When she and Tom could afford a baby-sitter, they'd joined them. Some of the others had helped make money for their living expenses by looking sophomoric enough to suck in unwary patrons who then got skinned.

White Horse Tavern was a step up from her graduate-school hangout, although still dark, smoky and loud. Here, the music that blasted from the jukebox was all country-western: George Strait whining and steel guitars twanging. Fortunately she liked country music, just as she liked playing pool and drinking beer foaming over the rim of a schooner.

In fact, she'd be having a good time if it wasn't for Joe's brooding presence. He sat sideways in a booth, long legs stretched out, watching her dance with one of his friends, who had winked at her as he drew her away from Joe.

Could he be jealous? But she couldn't imagine him so petty. And, damn it, he'd brought her here!

When the dance was done, she thanked his friend and went over and tugged on Joe's hand. "How about a game?"

He shrugged and stood up, but the tightness pulling his dark brows together didn't ease. He played in silence, clearing the table before she had a chance to show him her stuff.

"That any way to treat the little lady?" another man asked, his voice slurred. "Let's rack 'em, young lady, and I'll be gentle."

She batted her eyes just for fun and simpered, "Why, thank you," but Joe didn't even crack a smile.

Also just for fun, *she* broke and cleared the table so her opponent never even straightened from his slouch against the wall.

A ballad came on, one she liked, though she didn't know who sang it. Teresa sweetly thanked her opponent and excused herself. Then she hauled Joe onto the small dance floor. The voice and harmonica cried out with sadness, and she almost felt tears in her own eyes. When she looked up into Joe's, she saw pain, and her instincts told her it had to do with her.

Before she could frame a question, he pulled her close again, the grip of his hands almost violent.

Though confused, Teresa accepted his need to shutter his emotions and to hold her close. She laid her head on his shoulder and let the music pour through her. This wasn't the time and place to talk, only feel. And, oh, she felt: his big hand, now flat against the small of her back, his thighs pressing hers, his heartbeat vibrating in her ear, the near groan that rumbled in his chest. He was warm and strong and solid, and she couldn't believe the inner part of him—the part he'd so carefully kept hidden—was any different.

The singer's voice became a whisper that eased into silence. For just a second nobody in the tavern moved; nobody shouted out a friendly insult, glasses didn't clink, a pool cue didn't strike a ball. Then normality resumed and Joe's hands fell away from her. Gruffly he asked, "You had enough?"

She nodded mutely.

He engulfed one of her hands in his and towed her through the labyrinth between tables in the long dark room. Teresa smiled and exchanged good-nights with his friends who'd welcomed her, but as far as she could tell, Joe didn't even see them. He wanted out of there, and bad.

Or else he wanted to be away from her. The thought came from nowhere and gave birth to a litter of others. Why had he been so quiet last weekend when they'd gone to Pioneer Square? He'd taken to stopping casually by her house a couple of times a week. So why not this week? She hadn't thought much of it—maybe he was working extra-long hours. Now his absence fit into a pattern she hadn't let herself see.

Had she said something? Done something? Good Lord, had one of her kids done something? But why wouldn't he say? Why take her out tonight, then sulk?

Beside her disquiet, annoyance began to grow. What the heck was wrong with him?

She waited until they were in the pickup, figuring it wasn't very classy to start an argument in the tavern parking lot. But the moment he climbed in and slammed his door, she asked straight out, "What's wrong? And don't say nothing."

Joe turned toward her, but she'd made a tactical mistake. It was too dark in here to read his expression. "Why can't I say nothing if it's the truth?"

"Come on, all evening you've been acting like Mark does after I've grounded him. Did I embarrass you in front of your friends?"

"They liked you," he said shortly, thrusting the key in the ignition and starting the truck.

"You were hoping they wouldn't?" she goaded.

They were out of the parking lot and a block away before he said, "I wasn't so sure you'd like them."

"Why not?"

This time he didn't answer at all.

"Talk to me!" Teresa snapped. He'd have her home in five minutes, especially the way he was driving. He burned rubber at every corner and failed to come to a complete stop—to put it politely—at a dark empty four-way intersection. And this was the man who usually drove as conservatively as Teresa's mother.

He swore, and as they passed under a streetlight Teresa saw how tightly he clenched the steering wheel. "I have nothing to say!"

Inner caution was telling her she should let up, but her temper had control. "Mark never does when I've grounded him, either. But he's ten years old. What's your excuse?"

They slammed to a stop. Only the seat belt kept her from shooting forward and bashing her head on the windshield. Vaguely she realized they were in her driveway.

"Goddamn it, what do you want from me?" Joe snarled. "A confession of some sin? Is that what you're prodding for? Well, save your prod for the cattle! If I had something I wanted to say, I'd say it. I don't."

She stared at him in shock. This wasn't the man she knew. And confession of sin? What in heaven's name was he talking about? All she'd wanted to know was why he was in such a foul mood and whether she had anything to do with it. Was that so unreasonable?

"Fine!" She fumbled for the door handle and almost fell out. "You've got a burr stuck in you somewhere, but if you don't want to talk, feel free to go pout in private!"

She heard him cursing behind her as she stalked across the yard. Then his pickup door slammed and she knew he was following her. She took the porch steps at a run and had her key in the lock before he laid his hand on her shoulder and swung her around.

"Don't I get a good-night kiss? Or was a date at the tavern not good enough to earn one?"

Fury surged through her. "You think kisses are a price I pay for dinner? Why, you son of a—"

She didn't get to finish. His mouth closed over hers, although considering his general nastiness, he wasn't as rough as she'd expected.

Maybe because her emotions were already roiled up, the surge of sexual hunger struck with unusual speed and power. Surge, hell, it was a tsunami. She grabbed on tight and kissed him back aggressively, anger and desire and hurt pride all coming out in the scrape of teeth on his lip and fingernails digging into his shoulders.

He mumbled something that sounded urgent, as needy as she felt, and then he yanked her so close their clothes hardly fit between them. And, oh, she wished those clothes weren't there.

He devoured her mouth; she fought back. His hands gripped her buttocks and lifted her against his erection; her hands found their way up inside his shirt and squeezed powerful back muscles. Both of them were gasping. Someone—it must have been her—whimpered.

His voice was hot and dark when he wrenched his mouth away and said, "Your kids? Are they here?"

She laid kisses across his rough cheek while she tried to think. Her kids. Where...

"No." Thank God. "No, Mark's spending the night with a friend, and Nicole got invited to an overnight birthday party with half-a-dozen other girls. I made her go."

"Then...?"

Did he even have to ask? "Step into my parlor," she whispered against his mouth.

Joe reached for her key, turned it in the lock and swung her front door open. Then he stunned her, not for the first time, by lifting her into his arms and carrying her across the threshold. He kicked the door shut behind them.

She'd have to think about the symbolism later. But symbols were powerful things; this one sent a primeval thrill through her that, stripped to the essence, meant "man claims woman."

He didn't set her down until he'd mounted the stairs and, after a rough "Which door?" shouldered it open.

A little bit of fear—well, nervousness, anyway—was chilling her by now. She hadn't done this in so many years. What if she'd forgotten how? She might not please Joe. She might hate sex at this point in her life, or with this man.

He saw the look on her face as he lowered her onto the bed, and his teeth gritted. "Second thoughts?"

"I...no. Just...nerves."

He murmured something strange then, one more thing she'd have to think about later. Unless she misheard him, it was, "I'm the one who has to measure up."

She knew he was more experienced than she was; witness the way he kissed her now, openmouthed and heated, coaxing and demanding and begging, all at the same time. Her thought processes went wavy, like a TV when the cable was out. If he said anything else, it was lost in static.

All she could do was lie there, sinking deep into the down comforter, and kiss him back. He didn't have to demand or beg; all he had to do was ask.

At some point he eased her sweater up and she let go of him long enough for it to be lifted over her head. He pushed himself up on his knees, a flush dark across his cheekbones, and gazed down at her as his big hand released the front catch of her bra.

Her sixteen-year-old self had regretted that she wasn't better endowed. Now she was grateful. At her age, big breasts would have started to sag, maybe gotten stretch marks. Hers were just enough to fill a man's palm, but not enough for gravity to have bothered with. They pleased him, Teresa could tell; he cupped them and stroked them and finally bent down to suckle them. She cried out and arched her back.

To equalize things, Teresa uncurled her fingers from the comforter and undid the buttons on his shirt. The sight of his bare chest gave her as much pleasure as hers did him. Muscles rippled under tanned skin as she spread her hands wide and rubbed his nipples under her palms.

He gave a half-laugh, half-groan, and reared back up to peel her leggings off. His eyes were so intense they were almost black, and the hand he reached out had a faint tremor. He laid his fingertips on her breastbone and let them travel downward, over her belly, finally to curl in the dark hair clustered below. She shivered, and his gaze shot back up to hers almost fiercely, as if he expected protest.

"That... feels good."

"I've hardly begun," he said hoarsely.

But it had never been her way to lie passively waiting to be pleasured. With the things his fingers were doing to her now, it was hard to concentrate enough to unbutton the fly of his jeans, but she managed. Of course, it helped to have a goal in sight.

Any illusion of lazy exploration vanished thereafter. She barely got to lay a hand on him before he was kissing her again with a desperation that inflamed her own. Legs tangled together, and his weight came down on her. Her legs parted then to receive him as though this was an everyday matter, but the shuddering pleasure of his slow barely contained thrust was new to her. Seeing the strain on his face, the molten glow in his blue eyes, she thought wildly, *It's never been like this. It can't be this good.*

But it only got better, more consuming, when he finally lost control. She wrapped her legs around his waist and her arms around his neck and met every pounding thrust with eagerly lifted hips. This wouldn't be for everyone, might even scare some women, but Teresa had never been afraid of the physical.

Her whole body seemed to convulse at the end, sending shock waves through her and wresting any final control from Joe. He made a guttural sound and drove deep into her one last time, his muscles rigid as his climax shuddered through both of them.

Eventually he rolled to one side, as heavily as though it was almost too much for him. Teresa moved enough to plaster herself against him for the sake of his warmth and the tangy scent of sweat and sex. His heartbeat under her ear was inexplicably soothing. They ought to talk; she was sure she had something to say, or ask, or...

But sleep was tugging her eyelids down, slowing her own heartbeat and the tempo of her breathing. She wasn't used to drinking much, so even the one overflowing mug of beer acted as a soporific, helped along by more exercise than she'd gotten since she didn't care to think. As if she *could* think.

Oh, well, was her last conscious speech to herself. *In the morning...*

The only trouble was, she was alone in her bed when the rain pounding on her roof awakened her to a gray depressing day she could see all too clearly through a window unshielded by blinds. It took her a minute to realize she hadn't expected to be alone; first she stretched, felt some aching muscles and a few lovely twinges deep inside that reminded her of the night before. Memories came flooding back, and she turned her head sharply. But the extra pillow didn't bear any indentation, and the covers on his side were smooth. He must have tucked her into bed and left.

Teresa tried to rationalize it: he might have had to go to work especially early today—on Saturday?—or maybe he was afraid one of her children would come home early and surprise them. But something else was already making her uneasy.

That fight—she still didn't know what it was about or how it had happened. He'd said something about her expecting him to confess to a sin. A sin? That sounded almost biblical. And the bit about how a date to the tavern hadn't earned him enough points for a kiss. Had she ever given him reason to think she despised taverns or small-town life or anything else?

And then there was his quietness last week in Seattle. And the way he'd disappeared for the intervening week. It must all mean something taken together, but she sure didn't know what.

She liked and admired Joe Hughes. In fact—a moan was torn from her—in fact, oh God, she was falling in love with him. Was in love. Loved. No matter what verb tense she used, the terror squeezing her chest didn't abate.

She was in love with a man who clearly had some problems with their relationship, who wouldn't talk about them, who'd made fierce urgent love to her, then fled the second she fell asleep.

And for the moment there wasn't a damn thing she could do about it but wait. And hope none of her fears came to pass.

JOE SWUNG THE AX and felt a satisfying *thunk* that vibrated up his arms as it struck, then fell free. The round of fir split into two. He upended both halves, swung again and again, splitting them into usable sizes. He tossed the pieces onto a growing pile, then rolled another round over. The work kept him warm despite the cold rain slanting by the open sides of his mother's woodshed. He'd hoped it would empty his mind, too, but nothing seemed to do that.

He didn't like knowing he was a coward, but however he tried to run away from the self-knowledge, he had to face it: he didn't have the guts to tell Teresa the truth. No, worse than that: he'd never let any relationship with a woman get so far he had to tell her his secret. Shying away himself was easier than being rejected. And wasn't that what a coward did? Took the easy way?

He grunted and lodged the ax in a chopping block, then began stacking the firewood along one side. It was pretty sad that the only reason he'd gotten around to finishing a job he'd promised his mother he'd do was because he knew Teresa would never look for him here. Yesterday, she would have been working, but today was Sunday and her day off. She'd wonder why he hadn't at least called.

Back when he was in high school, he'd been responsible for splitting and stacking all the firewood intended for the wood stove in the Hugheses' family room. Maybe the familiarity of the task was why today he felt close to his youthful self, who'd often been angry and bewildered.

He'd been a good-looking kid; he knew that. He could see his younger face in Alan's. Joe had been a jock, too. But there was one big difference between them: Joe had already been labeled a dummy. *Already.* Hell, who was he trying to fool? In a town this size, he'd been labeled by the end of second grade, when his parents kept him back a year. Worse, he'd labeled himself by the second day of first grade.

Still stacking wood, pausing only to wipe sweat from his forehead, Joe plunged into painful memories. He'd been pulled from class for special help since his earliest recollection, stigma enough. He'd been kept in the regular class rather than special ed, but he never belonged. Some years he'd been angry and in constant trouble. Other years, when he'd had a nicer teacher, he'd settled for slumping in the back and praying he wouldn't be called on. But even when he wasn't, the other kids knew. He was the class dummy. No girl would be caught dead flirting with him.

Now most of his classmates were long gone from White Horse. There wasn't much to hold them here.

But Joe Hughes, who had more reason to want to escape than any of them, was held here by bonds of steel. In White Horse, people owed the Hughes family or were bound by ties of friendship. They cut him slack when no one else would. But it also meant living without ever being able to make a fresh start where people didn't know him. Sometimes he felt as if he had a scarlet *D* tattooed on his forehead. Whenever he ran into someone he'd known all his life, he wondered whether they saw it, too.

His life's work was to earn respect. He was a good employer and he'd made money. Although he hadn't showed it, he'd reveled in the talk when he'd built his house, way too big for him, a showplace, with its wall of glass overlooking the valley. He regretted that he hadn't brought Teresa there. If she'd seen his house, would she despise him once she discovered the truth?

He hated himself for such thoughts. Why had he ever asked her out? Damn it, he'd been content with his life. He'd been a goddamn fool to tempt himself.

"Gracious, Joe, I didn't know you were here!"

He swung around to find his mother just inside the woodshed. She was protecting linen slacks and a silk blouse with an enormous umbrella sprigged with somebody or other's coat-of-arms.

"Didn't want to disturb you."

"I've scarcely seen you in weeks!" She leveled a mother's penetrating gaze on him. "You're not avoiding me, are you?"

No, only Teresa Burkett.

Lying through his teeth, he said, "I've been feeling guilty because I hadn't finished splitting this wood."

The look sharpened. It was like having a zoom lens trained on his face. "Which I won't burn until next winter. It could have waited."

"I like to keep promises."

She blinked, her still attractive expertly made-up face deceptively mild. "Lee was just commenting that he hasn't seen much of you lately, either."

"I stopped by his shop..."

"Two weeks ago."

"He notes me on his calendar?"

Her brow crinkled as though she'd just remembered something. "And Jess was complaining that you hadn't returned her phone call."

Did he tell his mother that he hadn't returned his sister's phone call because he was still irritated at her for the way she'd boxed him in three Sundays ago?

He stayed silent.

"Oh, well." She smiled brightly. "I won't badger you. I just wanted to remind you that next week we're congregating at your house. Let us know what the main course will be."

"I'll cook a turkey," Joe said recklessly.

His mother looked surprised. "But we'll be having turkey for Thanksgiving. Not that it matters," she hastened to add. "You can get such good prices on them right now."

He'd forgotten Thanksgiving. What would he give thanks for? His magnificent empty house? "You're right." He said the first thing that came out of his mouth. "Let's make it spaghetti."

"Fine." The penetrating gaze had returned; his mother was studying him as though she'd just noticed some peculiar physical symptom. "Of course, we did have spaghetti last time. You insisted on bringing the sauce so Rebecca wouldn't have to do so much cooking."

"Damn it!" he snapped, then sucked in a deep breath. "What do you suggest?"

"Maybe a nice ham?" It was an order, and he knew it. But she wasn't done. "Are you asking that new vet again? We all liked her very much. And her children were so well behaved."

"She was Jess's guest, not mine."

She pretended not to notice the set of his jaw. "Really? What a pity. Why, then, perhaps I'll suggest Jess bring her."

His teeth ground together. "Don't you dare."

She sniffed. "Well, I was just trying to help out. Since you seem to be a little slow."

They both froze. Stiffly Joe said, "I always have been, haven't I?" He turned away, rolled another round to a clear space and grabbed the ax.

Obviously distressed, his mother said, "I didn't mean—"

"No. Forget it." But it was God's own truth, as they both knew in their hearts. He wrapped his fingers around the smooth familiar wood handle and hefted the ax. "You'd better back up."

"I was on my way out. I'm meeting a friend for lunch, but I wouldn't mind canceling if you'd like to come in..."

"No. I have an appointment this afternoon."

He didn't look at his mother, but he could feel her hovering indecisively. At last she gave a soft sigh. "We'll see you next Sunday, then. If you decide not to cook ham—"

"Ham's fine." *Leave.*

She did, after only two more goodbyes, accompanied by patent hesitation. She really wanted to probe his soul and was disappointed by his refusal to allow it. He always had been the most frustrating of her four children. He knew he'd closed off whole parts of himself as a form of protection. They weren't the kind of doors you could open for some people and shut the rest of the time. Those wouldn't have been sturdy enough. No, the ones he had were six inches thick. He'd closed and locked them by the time he was ten years old. If he'd kept any keys, he didn't know where they were.

The moment he heard her feet crunching on the gravel as she returned to the house, he swung the ax. This, he was good at. His woodsman's eye chose the fault line in each piece, his muscles and nerves knew how to apply the ax with precision.

They knew too well. His mind was free to return to the original problem.

What in hell was he going to do about Teresa Burkett? How had he screwed up so royally that he had to hurt her to save himself?

And how was he going to live without her?

CHAPTER EIGHT

THE OVERNIGHT at Ariana's house had actually turned out to be kind of fun, even though Nicole hadn't known the other girls. They were all so friendly she felt ashamed of the way she'd been thinking of them.

Her birthday present for Ariana was a *Batman* video she'd said she didn't have. Wearing pajamas and nightgowns, the girls had all sprawled on the family-room floor, pillows scrunched under them, and watched it. The whole while they argued about whether Val Kilmer or Chris O'Donnell was cuter. Then they did makeovers using a really cool makeup kit that Ariana's parents had given her. Finally they stuffed themselves on leftover reheated pizza. The lights went off after that. Nicole fell asleep about the time the whispers were getting further apart and softer.

She'd gotten home just in time for Alan to pick up her and Mark for the second guided tour. He'd been busy last week, he said. Probably with another girl. But he hadn't tried to get out of this Saturday's plans. They bowled at the tiniest bowling alley she'd ever seen; it had only four lanes. She slaughtered Alan on the video games, then lost to Mark. This time she insisted on paying for lunch at a burger joint. When she said her mom had given her the money, Alan didn't argue. In the afternoon they went to a matinee showing of a movie she'd seen two months before, but she liked it better this time. Maybe that was because she sat next to Alan, who shared his popcorn and giant drink. He made a production out of drilling another hole in the plastic top so they could each have a straw. In a weird way, it was romantic. Mark just got his own drink.

While they were still sitting in the theater after the credits, waiting for the aisle to clear, Alan asked whether they were going to his uncle's for the next family Sunday dinner.

"Mom didn't say anything. I don't think so."

"Hasn't Uncle Joe ask your mother?"

"I guess not." Nicole looked to her brother for confirmation. He shrugged. She went on, "I think maybe they had a fight or something. He hasn't been around much this week."

"But Mom said they were going out last night," Mark put in.

"Yeah? Oh, well, maybe I'm wrong."

"Hey, do *you* want to come if he doesn't ask her?" Alan was looking at her, not Mark. "You can be my guest."

She hadn't actually dated that much. Mom wouldn't let her until she'd turned fifteen in May. Maybe that was why her heart beat way faster even as she tried to sound nonchalant, "I don't think I'd better. I mean, it might make your uncle feel like he should have invited us or something. I just don't think I should."

"I'm sure it'd be all right," he said persuasively.

Nicole shook her head. "I'd feel uncomfortable, like I shouldn't be there."

Alan seemed disappointed, but not sulky like some boys would have been. "Oh, well," he said, shrugging, "maybe he'll ask her."

"Maybe." But she didn't think so.

When she'd asked her mother later, Mom just said, "Not this time." She sounded almost normal, but she had shadows under her eyes, as if she hadn't gotten enough sleep. And she was rubbing her forehead, where she sometimes had tension headaches.

Mom hadn't had a headache in a long time. Not since their move. Even though she never took it out on Mark or Nicole, she used to act really stressed sometimes, and she was always taking pills for a headache. Maybe that meant she was happy here. At least until today.

Joe didn't drop by the following week, either, and Mom didn't say a word about him. On Wednesday Nicole came into her English class and bumped into Bill Nelson. She'd been avoiding his eyes ever since he'd called that time and wanted to take her out. Seeing him made her feel so guilty she tried to pretend he wasn't there. But now she couldn't avoid him.

"Umm . . . sorry." She bent to pick up a pencil the collision had knocked out of her hand. When she straightened, she saw that he'd sat down right behind her desk and wasn't looking at her.

Nicole took a deep breath. "Bill." She waited until he did look at her. "I'm sorry. I mean, not just about this. About the time you called. I was rude. Something had just happened that upset me, and . . ." She bit her lip. "I shouldn't have taken it out on you. I really am sorry."

He shrugged, squirming like a big puppy. "That's okay. Don't worry about it."

She felt better, freer, immediately. And the very next period, a note fluttered from Alan's hand right onto Nicole's desk as he sauntered into French class. She unfolded it.

"Want to go horseback riding Saturday?" was followed by a scrawled "A."

With the note tucked in her binder, it was hard to concentrate on conjugating French verbs. After class, she waited for him.

"Where would we go?"

"We can borrow Aunt Jess's Arabians. The thing is, we can't take Mark. She only has two horses. Do you think this time he could go to a friend's or your mom would get a sitter for him?"

"I'll ask." And if the answer was no, she'd pay somebody to kidnap her brother.

When her mother got home from work, Nicole waited a little while before asking. She'd put it off until tomorrow night if Mom wasn't in a good mood. But today she acted more cheerful, chattering as she put away some groceries. According to her, the dairy farmers were loosening up some.

"Today one of the worst old farts let me stitch up a wound on one of his prized producers. He showed me some ribbons she's won at the state fair. Mind you—" she made a face "—he didn't decide to trust me because my brilliant reputation is getting around. No, Joe's mother apparently suggested strongly to him that he give me a chance." She lowered her voice in mimicry. "Margaret Hughes is a fine woman." Another grimace. "I agreed that she is indeed, and he let me go to work. Of course, he was breathing down my neck the whole time, but since all he did was grunt when I finished, I figure I did okay."

"Speaking of the Hugheses—" Nicole tried for an it-just-occurred-to-me voice "—Alan asked if I'd like to go horseback riding Saturday. He can borrow his aunt Jess's horses. You treated one of them, didn't you?"

"Yes, and they're beauties." Her mother closed the last cupboard and turned to lean on the counter. A faint smile played around her mouth. "Funny thing is, she only owns two. Let me think. Could that possibly mean you want me to take Mark off your hands?"

Nicole abandoned pride. "Please, please, *please!*"

As her mother thought, Nicole prayed for a "yes," not a "maybe" or "I'll see what I can do," her mother's stock answers.

But this time Mom gave her a broad smile. "Sure. I'll figure something out. If worse comes to worst, he can go to work with me."

Nicole leapt up and twirled twice, finally hugging her mother. "Thank you, thank you, thank you! He is *so* cute!"

"He is pretty cute," her mother admitted. "Of course, he's also two years older than you..."

Nicole rolled her eyes. "I'm not dumb, you know. Besides, he told me he doesn't drink much, never does drugs, and he hated wasting his money the one time he got a traffic ticket, so now he drives like you do."

"A saint in the form of a teenage boy," her mother said dryly. "Oh, well, I don't suppose you can get into too much trouble horseback riding. As long as you wear your helmet."

"Mom!"

"That's my condition."

She'd look like a dork. "He'll think I'm a baby," she muttered, but her mother just gave her a look. "Okay, okay," she conceded.

Mom opened the refrigerator door. "I guess I'd better do something about dinner."

"Can we have tacos?"

"Oh, I suppose." Mom didn't sound enthusiastic. "They're quick at least."

"I'll grate the cheese," Nicole offered.

"Bless you, child." Her mother took out the frying pan and a pound of hamburger.

"You know," Nicole said casually as she stood on tiptoe to reach the grater on a top shelf in the cupboard, "Alan kind of looks like Joe. Mr. Hughes. Don't you think?"

Mom shot her a razor-sharp glance, which she met innocently. "I suppose there's a resemblance," her mother admitted. Acid crept into her tone. "Does that mean Alan is a hick, too?"

"*He's* going away to college next year. On a football scholarship."

"Yes, so Joe said." Mom's voice gave nothing away.

"Alan invited me to their Sunday dinner next weekend."

Her mother was breaking up the hamburger in the pan. Either she was concentrating really hard on that, or she didn't want to meet Nicole's eyes. "You can go if you'd like."

"I thought... well, if Joe had asked, and you said no..."

"He didn't."

"Oh."

Her mother turned and looked at her directly. "Are you trying to ask me something?"

Would Mom say it wasn't any of her business? She took a breath. "Are you still seeing him?"

Mom gave this strange smile that looked more sad than happy. "I don't know. And that's all I'll say for now."

Nicole, feeling awkward, mumbled, "I'm sorry."

Her mother gave herself a little shake. "I didn't uproot us to find myself a man. You know what I always say..."

She ought to. She'd heard it often enough. By rote, Nicole said, "Women are strong, capable and independent."

"Very good." Mom's smile was a little less twisted this time. She nodded toward the door. "Go ask Mark to set the table."

"Sure." Nicole plopped the bowl of grated cheese in the center of the oak table and kept going. The Nintendo was beeping in the living room.

But she stopped right outside the kitchen, thinking her mother was calling after her. Nicole poked her head around the door frame. "Were you talking to..."

Then she distinctly heard, "...capable and independent. Women are strong, capable and independent." More sharply, and still to herself, Mom said, "Remember that!"

Nicole retreated silently. Weird.

SHE WAS ONLY CRYING because she was chopping onions. Teresa wiped her streaming eyes on her sleeve and, lifting the cutting board, used her knife to scrape the diced onions into the minced beef she was browning.

Women are strong, capable and independent.

Teresa's every instinct demanded that she track down Joe and demand an explanation for his hurtful behavior. She wasn't a woman to wait timidly at home for the phone to ring.

But vying with that instinct were both common sense, which pointed out that she hadn't done such a great job of getting him to explain the last time, and pride, which didn't want him thinking she couldn't do without him.

She could of course. Hadn't she managed just fine all these years since Tom's death?

On automatic pilot, Teresa opened a can of tomato sauce and rummaged in the cupboard for chili powder. She could do without Joe; she just didn't want to. Damn it, they had fun together! She knew it wasn't one-sided. She couldn't be wrong about that. She wasn't wrong in thinking he wanted her as much as she wanted him, either. Their kisses had told her that much, never mind the other night.

She couldn't let herself think about the other night, at least not what had happened after he'd carried her up the stairs. It hurt too much to remember the intense way they'd come together, considering she hadn't heard a word from him since.

Had that been all he wanted from her? Was he the type who got a woman into bed, then dumped her? She didn't believe it.

Where had things gone wrong? She just couldn't figure it out. The first time she recalled Joe not being his usual self was the night they went into Seattle. But maybe he'd been quieter than usual when he stopped by the week before that? She couldn't remember.

Okay, then, focus on the evening at Pioneer Square. What could have happened to make him pull back into himself? She went over their conversation, what she could summon of it from her memory, but it hadn't been all that different from others they'd had. Maybe she'd talked more—just because he wasn't contributing much—but she didn't think she'd said anything offensive. Did he not like reminders of her marriage? Tom had been part of some of the stories she told. But Joe had *asked* her about her husband other times. He'd never acted as though he'd just as soon her past love life didn't exist.

Oh, hell, she wasn't getting anywhere.

Teresa tasted the taco filling and wrinkled her nose; she'd been a little heavy with the chili powder while her mind was elsewhere. She gave a mental shrug. At least she hadn't totally ruined dinner. That had happened often enough before. She liked cooking—she just had a tendency to let her mind wander. Tonight, for example, she was going to finish wallpapering the upstairs bathroom and she dreaded having to do behind the toilet. It was easy to get so distracted that she forgot the rice cooking on the stove or the meat loaf in the oven. The kids were used to it.

"Dinner's ready!" she called, and grabbed a trivet.

Mark made as much noise as a horse would galloping through the house. It must be those size-ten feet. Nicole came almost as fast, although she never did anything in a way that wasn't dainty and graceful.

"Tacos! Cool!" her son proclaimed, throwing himself into his chair. "Where's the shells?"

"You could have gotten them," Teresa suggested.

"But I'm washing the dishes tonight. I don't have to help cook."

"Carrying something from counter to table doesn't fall into the category of cooking."

Nicole gave her mother an "I am so much more mature" look, then said with exaggerated patience, "I'll get them."

"Thank you," Teresa said moderately.

Over dinner, she sounded them out about their respective days in school, which earlier had been declared "fine." When her probes didn't get anywhere, probably because nothing especially interesting had happened, she switched her line of attack. It was time to find out more about Alan Harstead. Thus far she'd accepted him as a gift from God—the teenage boy had to be the reason Nicole finally seemed to be resigning herself to the move. But it was also obvious that Nicole was beginning to get serious about Joe's nephew. Which meant Teresa's protective-mother instincts were issuing a warning.

She opened the subject by letting Mark know about the plans for Saturday. Initially his feelings were hurt, but he cheered up when she agreed to let him come to work with her. Nicole loved animals but hated blood, disease and death. Mark, in the way of boys his age, enjoyed his own pets but wasn't passionately drawn to any species in particular; on the other hand, he found blood and death morbidly fascinating.

Right now he fixed an eager gaze on her. "Are you going to cut anything open Saturday?"

Nicole scrunched up her face. "You want to *see* some poor dog's guts spilling out on the table?"

"Yes, I probably will do surgery," Teresa informed him, then added, "and thank you, but I do not allow guts to 'spill out.'"

"But I can see 'em, can't I?" her son asked.

"If you scrub first."

"Neat." He shoved an obscene amount of his taco into his mouth, which at least had the effect of shutting him up.

To her daughter, Teresa remarked, "It's been nice of Alan to include Mark in your outings."

"He's a saint, remember?" Nicole said pertly.

"Maybe he is. Not every seventeen-year-old boy would like having his date's little brother tagging along."

She'd been wrong. Mark didn't let a full mouth stop him from an indignant "Tag along? Like I wanted to go *shopping?*"

"I didn't mean that quite the way it sounded—"

"They weren't dates, anyway," Nicole said gloomily.

"Yeah," her brother gloated. "They didn't kiss or hug or hold hands or anything."

Nicole lifted her taco preparatory to launching it. "Shut up!"

Family dinnertime was so peaceful. Teresa raised her voice slightly. "We don't say 'shut up' to each other nor do we play with our food. As for you, young man—" she held Mark's gaze "—the fact that Alan was gentleman enough not to make you feel uncomfortable doesn't mean he isn't interested in your sister."

"Why would he be interested in *her?*"

Instead of losing her temper again, Nicole mumbled, "He isn't. He only took me out because *you* set it up, Mom."

"Because I..." Teresa set down her fork. "What?"

"Didn't you have Joe ask him to be nice to me?" Nicole probably had no idea that her resentful gaze also pleaded for a negative answer.

"I most certainly didn't." Was there any chance Joe *had* asked just that? Teresa didn't show her thoughts. "I'll have you know, the first time I met Rebecca, she'd already heard all about the new girl at school from Alan. He just hadn't figured out how to meet you."

"He could have walked up and said hi."

"Would you have been friendly?"

Resentment kindled anew, but Nicole was too honest to deny the accusation. "I don't know. Maybe. If he didn't sound like a farmer."

Teresa didn't have to ask what her daughter had against farmers; she knew. They didn't live in Bellevue, the mecca of sophisticated urban living according to the chronicle of Nicole.

"What did you do besides go to the movie last week?" she asked, instead.

They told her about bowling and video games and hanging out in a little store that would have qualified as a five-and-ten in Teresa's day.

"It was fun," Nicole concluded.

Mark shoved more taco in his mouth and mumbled, "Yeah," around it. Teresa tried not to look at him.

But the moment he'd swallowed enough to speak freely, he said enthusiastically, "I forgot to tell you about the dirt-bike course. It was really cool! These guys were shooting off hills and sliding around curves and they weren't afraid at all. Some of the guys were my age."

"Oh, boy." Teresa knew what was coming next.

"Can I have my own dirt bike? You told Nicole she could have a horse. Motorcycles don't eat all that hay or need new shoes."

"No, they guzzle gas and need new tires." Teresa looked at Nicole. "Alan didn't let either of you ride a dirt bike, did he?"

"You think he's dumb or something?" Nicole was scornful. "Of course not!"

"I'd wear a helmet." Mark's wide-eyed look said, *I'm a good kid. I'd never do anything stupid. You can trust me.*

His father had had a tendency to fall for it. Teresa said, "No. Maybe when you're older." To forestall him, she added, "*Way* older."

His expression told her he hadn't expected to win but hadn't given up, either. He had a way of wearing her down that she was certain was shortening her life expectancy by years.

Interestingly, Teresa caught a fleeting expression of satisfaction on Nicole's face. Mark wasn't in trouble, so that couldn't explain it. Teresa would have asked if she'd thought she would get an answer. But Nicole would just open her eyes wide and say, "I don't know what you're talking about."

Teresa got the kids headed for bed and decided she was not in the mood for wallpapering. Instead, she settled down on an easy chair in the living room, lamplight pooling on her lap where she'd piled veterinary journals she really ought to catch up on.

Who was she kidding? Her eyes glazed over and her mind circled back to the beginning: Joe, stiff and quiet that evening in Pioneer Square. She remembered him digging in his pocket and thrusting a ten at the wino. He had looked sympathetic, compassionate. It was the only emotion his face had showed all evening.

In her alarm, Teresa sat up straighter, heedless of the journals slipping to the floor. Good Lord, was Joe an alcoholic? Maybe a recovering one? No, he'd had wine that evening in Seattle, and a schooner of beer at the tavern. Okay, maybe he'd slipped, was running away from her to protect her from his worst self.

Even she rolled her eyes at this bit of melodrama. It didn't wash. Other than that flash of sympathy, she didn't have a reason in the world to think Joe had a drinking problem.

Okay, some other kind of problem. Rebecca had hinted at something in his past, something she felt he should tell her himself.

He'd been married once and murdered his wife. He'd been tried for sexual abuse. He'd bumped off his father. Each idea, as lurid as her son's imagination, sounded more ridiculous than the last.

Well, what then? Teresa wondered in exasperation.

Maybe he'd just discovered he didn't like her as much as he'd thought he did. Maybe she bored him. Maybe he didn't feel able to take on her kids. Maybe his family had hated her; although he hadn't begun his disappearing act for a couple of weeks after that Sunday dinner. Still, maybe he'd decided she was pushy, starting with weaseling her way in. Well, she hadn't, but she *had* jumped at the invitation, even though she'd wished it had come from him. But she'd accepted because she liked Jess and Rebecca. She wouldn't mind becoming friends with both his sisters. And, damn it, she wouldn't let him stop her!

She carried her indignation to bed, where it settled back into depression. She kept turning the same thoughts round and round: he'd lost interest in her, decided she was pushy (well, she was, and so what?), had met someone else.

But she wasn't satisfied with any of these explanations. Now, alone and in the same bed where they had made passionate love, she let herself remember. The way he'd touched her, the sounds he'd made, the near violent desperation. A man didn't make love like that with a woman who had begun to bore or irritate him.

One more thing hovered, something she'd intended to think about later.... She kicked her covers off and stared blindly at the window. There was the symbolism of his carrying her over the threshold. Maybe he'd just been in a hurry, but even then she'd been affected by the significance of the act. Surely it couldn't have been lost on him. It was more likely he was trying to say something without words, something stronger and more lasting than "Let's get it on, baby."

But still she was tantalized by a memory that frustrated her, sliding out from under her finger every time she closed in on it. Something he'd done, said—

That was it. She stuffed her pillows behind her and sat up in bed, thinking hard. He'd asked her if she was having second thoughts, and she'd said no, just nerves. Then he'd said hoarsely, "I'm the one who has to measure up." What had he meant? Why would he feel in any way inadequate?

It just didn't make sense.

Maybe not, but she thought that one remark was at the heart of whatever was bothering him.

Surely he wasn't idiotic enough to think she shared Nicole's prejudice against small-town rural America? Was he intimidated by her education? She did seem to remember rambling on and on that evening in Pioneer Square about art shows and operas and similar stuff she didn't miss at all. Could he have thought she was oh, so subtly putting him down?

But he'd done stuff she hadn't. She wouldn't feel put down if he talked about rodeos and county fairs and playing high-school football.

But those were all "hick" activities. Could he possibly think she secretly despised them, despite moving here?

Oh, she was getting so tangled up she'd trip over herself any minute. She'd never get an answer unless he gave her one.

He owed her that much, Teresa thought. And she wouldn't be shy about demanding it. Forget pride and common sense. She had an ugly feeling she'd never hear from Joe Hughes again if she didn't go after him right now.

OF COURSE, that was easier said than done, given life's little complications. It was already Thursday. Eric was doing farm calls, which meant the jam-packed schedule was all hers, never mind that she wanted to lay her head down on the desk and take a nap to make up for last night's sleeplessness. She was just getting into her car after work at five o'clock when a pickup truck came squealing into the handicapped spot. In the back was a black Lab that had been hit out on the highway. She ended up doing emergency surgery. By the time she had the dog stabilized, it was seven o'clock and she could only pray Nicole had put dinner on. That still left paying bills and nagging her kids into doing their homework. She did try to call Joe, but only got a brusque message on his answering machine. She didn't leave a message.

On Friday she had to go straight home from work because Nicole had a dance class at five and Mark would otherwise have been by himself. If the days had still been long and light, she would have been tempted to drive over to Joe's house after dinner and batter down his door. But late October had crept upon them, it was dark by five o'clock, and she couldn't face trying to find his property in the dark and rain, considering all she had was an address from the phone book. She did call again, listened again to his taped voice: "You've reached Joe Hughes. Leave a message."

She was tempted. Maybe he was standing there beside the phone waiting to hear *her* voice. Maybe he'd pick it up if she said, "Joe, are you there? It's Teresa. I really want to talk to you."

But caution held her back. If he was so eager to talk to her, he'd have called her himself. What she needed to do was take him by surprise, catch him off guard. She wouldn't do that by warning him she was coming.

Saturday was out; Nicole was going horseback riding with Alan, and Teresa was taking Mark to work with her. Sunday Joe would be occupied with his family. Although impatience was eating away at her, she would have to wait. Monday, she told herself. One way or another, she'd find him.

WEDNESDAY, WHEN NICOLE had called her best friend, Jayne hadn't even said hello. Instead, she'd announced dramatically, "Russ Harlan asked me out. Can you believe it?"

Like it was someone else, Nicole had heard herself squealing and saying, "Where's he taking you? Tell me all about it!"

This should hurt, she'd thought. Nervously she'd poked at the spot where heartache made itself felt. Nothing. She hadn't cared that Russ Harlan was taking out her friend, instead of her. She'd rather be going horseback riding with Alan Harstead. It was the first thing she'd really, truly looked forward to since the move.

For some reason, she'd been reluctant to tell Jayne about her date. Maybe she'd been afraid she'd jinx it. So even though part of her had wanted to brag, all she'd done was listen and make breathy sounds of envy. She hadn't said a word about Alan or horses or this coming Saturday.

She was sitting in geometry class on Thursday afternoon when she heard rain pelting glass. Oh, no! Nicole almost groaned when she turned her head to see, not a drizzle that might disappear overnight, but serious windblown rain. She *had* jinxed Saturday! She wanted it too much. It wouldn't quit raining until next spring.

The evening was dreary. Her mother came home late, shaking off drops of moisture and looking tired.

Blood stains splattered her pant legs. Queasy, Nicole looked away. She didn't even want to know what kind of animal had bled that much. Whatever had happened, Mom was as quiet as Nicole during dinner. Afterward, Mom disappeared upstairs to wallpaper, but then she must have changed her mind. That bathroom had been torn apart for weeks, and Mom just kept putting off finishing it. Nicole had the feeling she wasn't really enjoying remodeling the house. It had sounded fun, but the result was having at least one room a mess for weeks at a time. Tonight she called good-night and went back downstairs.

Alan didn't make any effort to talk to Nicole the next day, even though it was still pouring. She went home feeling really down. All evening she thought about tonight's football game, the last of the season. The White Horse Grizzlies were playing Cascade High School in Everett. If it had been a home game, Nicole would have gone. She imagined Alan, rain dripping from his helmet, his uniform muddy and soaked, his hands cold. Was he fumbling a lot?

She should have gone. Especially, she decided unhappily, since they wouldn't be going out tomorrow. He'd call and cancel, and then never get around to asking her again. Or the weather would stay bad; it was November. She could see it now: he'd smile vaguely at her when they passed in the hall at school, like he wasn't sure who she was. If her mother quit dating Joe, Nicole was sure Alan would drop her. She just knew he was only doing his uncle a favor, even if Mom denied it.

She fell asleep listening to the rain on the roof and awakened Saturday morning to silence. When she leapt out of bed and went to the window, she saw blue sky and scudding clouds.

"Yes!" She shoved open the closet and began digging in the jumble for her riding boots.

"Nicole!" Mom's voice carried up the stairs. "Is that you?"

"I'm awake," she yelled back. Her fingers closed on the smooth leather of one of her boots.

"Alan called. He wants you to call him as soon as you can."

The boot dropped from her fingers. Her chest became so heavy it hurt. He was going to cancel. It was just like she'd feared.

Her mother had promised to get Nicole her own telephone line, but so far they didn't have any phones upstairs. The house wasn't wired for them. In the green thermal knit shorts and oversize shirt she'd slept in, Nicole went downstairs. The phone was in the kitchen. Mom was sipping coffee and reading the newspaper at the table. She said, "Good morning," but Nicole was too depressed to agree.

Turning her back on her mother, who always pretended not to listen but probably heard every word, Nicole dialed. Alan answered.

"Hi," she said softly. "This is Nicole. Mom said you called."

"Yeah, listen. The trail by the river is going to be really muddy. I don't think we should go riding today."

"Sure." Her voice was flat. "That's okay."

"I'm kind of bummed out, anyway. I wouldn't have been very good company."

Bummed out? A light bulb went on.

"Is it the game?" she asked.

"Yeah, we got whipped. And I sucked." He was silent for a moment. "It's my fault we lost."

"It was raining really hard. I don't see how you could throw when the ball was that wet."

"Yeah, well, that was my job. Thanks to me, we're out of the playoffs." Again he paused. Nicole waited for that vagueness to enter his voice. "Maybe we can go some other time," he'd say. Or, "I'll see you later, okay?"

She opened her mouth to say it herself. She didn't want him to know how disappointed she was.

But he surprised her. "If the ground freezes, we could go tomorrow. Unless you're already doing something. Or your mom won't let you."

She couldn't quite keep the happiness out of her voice. "No, Sunday would be great."

"Like, eleven? Or will you be home?"

"When we go to church, we usually make it an early service. Eleven is great."

"See you then," he said, and disconnected.

She hung up, too, and turned to her mother with a big smile. "We're going riding Sunday, instead of today."

"I heard." For once, Mom didn't deny eavesdropping. She was too busy thinking something over with more than usual concentration. "I'd intended to do something then."

Nicole's excitement stumbled. "You mean, I can't go?"

"No, that's okay." Her mother's face cleared, and she rose to her feet. "I get off, God willing, at four today. I'll just do it then. If I'm late, call and order a pizza. I'll leave money here on the table.''

"What do you have to do?''

Rummaging in her purse, Mom appeared not to hear her. "I've got to run. Mark's still in bed. Tell him I'm sorry I didn't take him to work today, but he can come next weekend.'' She brushed a kiss on Nicole's cheek in passing. "Be good.''

She was gone, leaving two twenty-dollar bills on the table. Nicole stared after her. Her mother hadn't said, but Nicole had a feeling that wherever she was going today, it had something to do with Joe.

CHAPTER NINE

TERESA SLOWED her car and peered at the large black mailbox: 2963. Bingo.

A gravel driveway curved into a thick stand of cedar and fir. In the late-afternoon light the woods were dark, but an understory of ferns, salal and huckleberry crept out to edge the drive.

With startling suddenness, her car emerged into a clearing. Ahead was a magnificent modern home with a high peaked roof, river-rock chimney and gleaming windows reaching from floor level to beams. To one side of the driveway, Joe's chestnut quarter horse grazed in a fenced pasture; he lifted his head to gaze disinterestedly at her passing car. She reached a Y. One direction led on to the house, the other to a huge metal building set inconspicuously at the edge of the woods.

Teresa parked in front of the house and sat gaping. Joe lived here? The extent of her surprise made her think about her perception of him. It was easy to stereotype anyone; maybe, on one level, she *had* dismissed him as a local yokel.

But she didn't think so. It was more that this house was so big for a man who'd never been married. What did he do with so much square footage? Had he maybe intended to get married when he built it? He hadn't mentioned a near miss, but then she hadn't asked.

And she was beginning to realize how uncommunicative he really was.

She shook her head. Was she going to sit here until bedtime? Then she grimaced at the double meaning. There wouldn't be any bedtime with Joe Hughes until he did some explaining. And maybe not afterward.

Especially, a small voice whispered in her ear, if he's not interested anymore.

His pickup was here, but if he was home, it seemed funny he hadn't come out to see who'd driven in. Maybe, in a house this size, he hadn't heard her arrive.

She left her keys and purse in the car. All the better for a quick getaway. Going up to the front door and ringing the bell, Teresa wished she'd been here before, so she didn't feel quite so much like a trespasser. She couldn't help thinking that if he'd wanted her here, he would have invited her. She squeezed her eyes shut, summoning up a snapshot of his face, tender and exultant, as he made love to her. He had no business looking at a woman that way if she wasn't welcome in his house.

She'd heard the doorbell ring, but no one answered it. She turned and surveyed his domain. If he was in the barn, he'd have heard her. She supposed she ought to try the big metal building, since she'd come this far.

The sound of the door opening brought her around sharply.

"Yes?" Joe said curtly. Then he saw who was there, and a muscle jerked in his cheek. "Teresa."

The way he'd said her name told her nothing, not even whether she'd really surprised him.

Her heart was suddenly pounding so hard it sounded like a war drum to her. The two weeks since she'd seen him felt like two months. Two years. He was a stranger. She said uncertainly, "I was hoping we could talk."

For a long moment he didn't say anything, just stood there, intimidatingly handsome even in faded navy blue sweats. His eyes closed for a brief instant and he stood back. "Come in."

She did, before he could change his mind. He gestured her into an expansive living room furnished with leather sofas and beautiful wood tables, all low, with clean lines. From the slate-floored entry, her feet sank into rust brown carpet as thick and elegant as any she'd ever seen.

Even in her preoccupation with the man behind her, she couldn't stop a quick in-rush of breath when she saw the view through floor-to-ceiling glass on the back side of the house: the ground dropped precipitately into a river valley, beyond which rose snow-capped mountain peaks.

"Like it?" he asked quietly.

"How could I not?" She crossed the living room to the glass, part of her still taking it in, still awed; the other part of her was scrambling for the right thing to say. She was on the edge of a precipice in more ways than one.

"I have a big-screened TV downstairs, but nothing on it looks as good as my view. Sometimes I have trouble tearing myself away."

"I can see why."

Silence reigned after this inspiring exchange. Now what? Teresa took a deep breath and turned to face him.

Joe had shoved his hands in the pockets of his sweatpants. He stood with shoulders back, as though he were braced for some blow.

"Joe..."

"Teresa..."

They both spoke at the same moment. Both stopped. When she waited, he said with obvious difficulty, "I don't know why you've bothered to come talk to me after the way I've acted."

She willed herself not to fidget or slip into any of those ways women have of deprecating themselves: hunching shoulders, twining fingers, smiling meaninglessly. "I guess I'm just curious," she said, holding his gaze. "I thought we had something pretty decent going."

Again he squeezed his eyes shut, and his chest rose and fell on a long breath. But he was looking at her when he said, "This isn't your fault. It doesn't have anything to do with you."

"You just lost interest?"

"No! Damn it—" She saw his teeth as he bit off whatever was about to burst out. He breathed hard through his mouth. "I just realized that things were getting too serious. I couldn't see a future for two people as different as we are."

She felt cold. "How are we so different?"

He rotated his shoulders as though to relieve tension. The muscle in his cheek jumped again. "That night in Seattle reminded me. You're symphony, I'm country-western. You've got fifteen years of college—"

"Eight."

"—and I barely finished high school. I drive a pickup, you drive a Volvo. You're a reader, I'm—"

She lost her temper. "And you're not. So what? You think I can't face life unless I've got a man in the easy chair beside mine reading a good book? You think that's what counts?"

"Yeah, it counts." He said it quietly, simply, with stark pain she didn't understand.

Pleading for something, if only understanding, she chose her words with care. "What matters is how we feel about each other. Whether we have a spark, whether we enjoy each other's company, whether we like each other, respect each other." She shrugged helplessly. "I was falling in love with you, Joe. I'm probably some kind of brazen hussy to tell you that, but all I want to know is one thing—how you feel about me. Was I the only one who was getting serious?"

He bent his head, but too late to hide the grief twisting his features. It was a long moment before he ran a hand roughly over his face and met her eyes again, his own dark with whatever torment drove him. "You know better than that," he said in a voice that didn't sound like his own.

"Do I?"

His laugh could have been ripped from him. "You're going to make me say it, aren't you?"

How could she feel joy leavening the heaviness in her chest like tiny air bubbles expanding, and feel close to tears at the same time? "What's 'it'?" she asked, trying to sound flirtatious but failing.

"I was falling in love with you, too," Joe said roughly.

She wasn't sure who moved first, she or Joe; all she knew was that they ended up in each other's arms, both squeezing as if they were afraid to let go. She closed her eyes and listened to his heart pound as hard as her own. Mouth against her hair, he was murmuring things she couldn't quite make out that probably weren't meant for her to hear. His shirt was damp under her cheek, and she realized she'd wet it with her tears.

At last she understood one thing he said. "I'm an idiot."

She lifted her head enough to look up at him. "Yes, you are."

"I was an idiot before and I'm an idiot now. Can't you see?" Now he was the one pleading. "We're too far apart."

"We don't feel far apart right now."

He gave another of those laughs that told her how close he was to despair. "Oh, God, this doesn't settle anything."

But she didn't care, because he was kissing her with all the desperation and naked hunger she'd felt from him when he'd carried her over the threshold. He used his teeth and lips and tongue; his hips ground against hers and his hands were almost rough. Shaking with the force of his emotions pounding at her own, like a stormy sea that had met a bulkhead and was forced back to slam into the next wave, Teresa held on and gave him what he seemed to need: her.

With no finesse at all, Joe stripped off her turtleneck and began to suckle her breasts through her satin bra. The pull of his mouth awakened her body on the most primitive level. All she could do was twine her fingers in his thick dark hair and moan. He fumbled with the snap of her jeans and jerked the zipper down. He rubbed a bristly cheek against her belly above her skimpy satin panties. Now she was trembling from physical needs as much as emotional.

And then he froze. Embarrassment brought some of the heat that had been pooled between her legs to her face. Had she yanked his hair? Or stiffened, so that he was afraid he'd shocked her? But he stayed still, silent, head bowed against her. She looked down at the back of his head and didn't know what to do.

Finally he made a muffled sound, not speech, she thought, but anguish. Oh, God, what was wrong?

Teresa's fingers uncramped and she brushed his hair with her hand the way she did her kids' when they were upset. Soothing, calming, reminding him that she was here. Fear lanced into her chest, chilling her skin so that her flush faded and she almost shivered.

"Joe?" she whispered.

A shudder passed through him.

"Is...is something wrong?"

He muttered an obscenity, unusual enough coming from him to scare her even more. Then he sank back onto his heels and looked up, eyes red and face ravaged.

"I'm a coward," he said hoarsely.

"I...I don't understand."

"How can you, when you don't know me?"

That fear was turning into a vise around her heart. "Joe..."

He rose to his feet as stiffly as an old man. He zipped up her jeans and fastened the snap. She felt like a mannequin, made unmoving by dread.

His gaze rested on the damp circles on her bra, and he flinched. Now he didn't seem to want to look at her at all as he bent to pick up her shirt and handed it to her.

With him averting his face that way, Teresa felt naked, exposed. She couldn't get into her shirt fast enough.

That shame she didn't deserve made her voice brusque. "Tell me."

He looked at her, shied away. His Adam's apple bobbed. "I, uh, wasn't too good in school."

This was so far from anything she'd expected she gaped. "High school was twenty years ago. What difference—"

Now he looked angry, at last able to meet her eyes. "Maybe it was, but it taught me who I am. I can't forget, no matter how hard I try."

Her mind groped and came up empty. Helplessly she said, "I... I just don't get it. What are you trying to tell me?"

He glared at her with something akin to hate. He'd wanted her to guess, Teresa realized, to put it into words herself so that he wouldn't have to.

Joe swallowed again, took a deep breath. What he said was just audible. "I can't read."

Stunned, she whispered, "What?"

"I can't read!" he shouted. "How many times do I have to say it? I can't read. Did you get it this time?"

Her mind was working sluggishly. Joe couldn't read? But he ran a business! He had a driver's license. She'd always presumed he voted; he was well aware of news events and discussed them intelligently. Of course there were plenty of illiterates; she knew the facts. She'd just never met one.

Joe?

She realized suddenly that while she'd gaped at him, he had stood silent, stiff, hands curled into fists at his sides. A dark flush suffused his cheeks: shame.

Could she think of a single compassionate, thoughtful, sensitive thing to say? Of course not. She opened her mouth and out came, "I don't understand."

"Which part don't you understand?" Joe asked, voice cutting. "How I've hidden my disability? Or how you could ever have been attracted to someone who can't do something so basic?"

"Neither." She looked around almost blindly. "Can we sit down?"

"If you'd prefer." He sounded formal now; a distance had opened between them that might never be bridged.

She stumbled toward the sofa, as much in shock as if she'd just witnessed a traffic accident. She was making this worse for him, she knew, but she felt... She didn't know what she felt.

She sank down on the soft leather. Joe sat, too, at the far end. The distance between them was real, then, not in her imagination. He had made it real, with his anger and shame.

"Why do you hide it?" she blurted.

"I don't altogether." He spoke stiffly, the normal fluidity transformed into something robotic: emotionless, jerky. "Half the people in White Horse know, although probably some of them have forgotten."

"But you didn't tell me."

He looked away. "It's not exactly something I'm proud of. It... seemed irrelevant to our dating."

"Until you could tell I was getting serious." She saw now the pattern that had eluded her, why he had begun retreating when he did. Why he had made love to her but hadn't called the next day.

"Until I realized *I* was getting serious," he corrected her.

Now she studied him with real perplexity. "But if it wasn't such a secret, why didn't you tell me? Why just end our relationship without giving me a chance?"

"A chance to feel sorry for me?" He rose to his feet as though he couldn't bear to hold still. "To hide your disdain?"

If the turmoil in his eyes hadn't been so evident, she might have gotten mad. He'd said he was falling in love with her, but love involved a certain amount of trust and liking, neither of which he was exhibiting now. But she suspected he wasn't judging her. It was himself he disliked, himself he considered too inadequate to be worthy of her.

She stood, too, and said quietly, "You're wrong to think I won't love you because you have a learning disability. You haven't undergone some horrible change in my eyes just because you've told me something about yourself that I didn't know. It must be difficult for you—"

"Difficult?" He gave a harsh laugh. "Lady, you have no idea."

Still softly she said, "Will you tell me?"

She saw the instant the fight left him. His shoulders slumped and he sank back down onto the sofa. Elbows resting on his knees, he bowed his head.

Teresa's heart cramped. She knelt before him and cradled his face in her hands, lifting it so that he had to meet her eyes. "You don't have to tell me anything if you don't want. I love you, Joe. To quote you, I don't scare off that easily."

He searched her face without hope, only desperation on his. "To quote...? Oh. Your kids. That's hardly the same thing."

"You're right. It isn't. The existence of my kids affects every moment we spend together. The fact that you can't read doesn't. Look how long we've known each other, and I never guessed."

His expression and voice remained bleak. "Now that you know, you'll never see me the same way again. You knew kids like me when you were in elementary school. They just weren't your friends. Why should they be? You were college-bound. They were the dummies, the dropouts. I'll bet you don't have a single friend or even close acquaintance who's illiterate. If you'd known I couldn't read, I doubt you'd have invited me into your house for lunch that first day."

Her temper sparked. "You don't think much of me, do you? You were there doing a job for me. I was being pleasant."

"Is that all?"

No, it wasn't all of course; she had been attracted to him even then, hoping if she made the first move, he'd follow up on it. She couldn't swear she would have felt the same if she had known, if Jess had said, "My brother is illiterate, but he's a good logger." Perhaps she *would* have seen him with different eyes. But that was then and this was now. Now she did know him, whatever he said to the contrary; now she was in love with him.

Which meant she owed him honesty. "Maybe not all," she admitted. "I can't say what I would have felt then. All I know is what I feel now. The way I still see you."

"And how's that?" He tried to sound sardonic, uncaring, but with her hands resting on his thighs, she felt his sudden tension, the way he braced himself.

Very deliberately Teresa said, "I see a successful businessman, a rare employer who thinks of his men ahead of profit. How many other logging outfits keep the men employed even during the slow season? I see a man who until today I didn't realize was rich. More important, I see a man who is unfailingly kind, gentle and patient. Who puts up with the rotten behavior of my teenage daughter, who has time for my son. Whose sense of humor matches mine. I see a man who makes my heart beat faster than is good for my health."

"And who has lied to you."

She gave a twisted smile. "But you never did lie, and I'll bet you wouldn't have. You'd have told me if I'd stumbled over your secret, wouldn't you?"

His jaws clenched. He released one small word. "Maybe."

She was thinking aloud now. "That's why you hated our evening in Seattle, isn't it? I suppose you thought I'd figure it out in the bookstore."

Voice raw, he said, "I couldn't even read the god-damn menu."

"And I never guessed," she said wonderingly. "How do you do it?"

"Does it matter?"

"Yes, it matters!" She looked reprovingly at him. "I'll bet you compensate by being better at other things than most of us are. You couldn't have become as successful as you are, especially given a handicap, if you weren't way above normal in intelligence. Don't you sometimes feel proud of what you've accomplished? How can you still think of yourself as a 'dummy'?"

"Easily." He sounded weary. "I went to school for thirteen years straight, and every day I was told, one way or another, that I was dumb. The only thing I was ever good at was math, and not always that. Teachers like story problems. I could have done 'em in my head if I hadn't had to figure out what the words meant first. From the time everyone else learned their letters, I knew I was a failure. I was always slower. I'd take a test, and by the time I reached the third problem, the time was up and everyone else had finished fifteen. Teachers thought I was lazy, or defiant, or..." His throat worked. "Who knows? It's done. I survived. But you wonder why I see myself the way my teachers saw me?"

"They didn't diagnose you as dyslexic?" Teresa asked, shocked. "You mean, you went all the way through school..."

He grunted. "Eventually they figured it out. I was pulled out of classes for special help, which didn't do a damn bit of good. Usually the aide was as impatient as the teachers. The reading they put in front of me looked so simple to them. They just couldn't understand why I couldn't see it the same way."

"And your parents?" She was almost afraid to hear the answer.

"They were different." He made a sound in his throat. "If it weren't for them, I'd have turned into a juvenile delinquent. But they really tried, even though they didn't understand what was wrong, either."

"I'm sorry." Teresa grasped his hands and squeezed. "I wish I'd known you then. I wish—"

"You wish what?" His eyes let her see his bitterness. "That you could have stuck up for me? Been my best friend? Don't romanticize this. I wasn't kidding when I said you went to school with dozens of kids just like me. You weren't *their* friend, were you?"

Embarrassment closed her throat. He was right. She hadn't been. She'd hardly noticed those kids who were struggling. About the only time she had was when the teacher made students take turns reading aloud, and she'd become bored and impatient when someone stumbled over the easiest words. She never would have made fun of them or been cruel, but she hadn't done anything positive, either.

"Don't worry about it." Joe turned his hands over and returned her clasp. He tried to smile. "That's life. Kids are self-centered. Growing up changes that, when everything else goes right."

Tears stung her eyes. "It must have gone right for you, despite school."

"Yeah, I was lucky. My parents helped me as much as they could. My big brother beat up anybody who gave me too hard a time. My sisters tried to get me dates. None of them was ever ashamed of me."

"No wonder your family is so close."

"Yeah, I suppose that's part of it." He lifted Teresa's chin and kissed her, his lips lingering for only a handful of seconds, only long enough for her pulse to quicken, for her to reach up and grip his shoulder. Then he pulled back.

"I want you to go now." He grasped her elbows and lifted her to her feet. "If you stay, it'd be too easy for you to say things you don't mean."

"Like, 'I love you'?"

A shutter had dropped, leaving his expression remote. "Yeah. Let all this sink in for a while. Pity is the last thing I want. I'd rather say goodbye right now than know that's what you feel. So think it over. Be honest, Teresa. Imagine how you'll feel when your friends and family find out I can't read. If you're ashamed, it'll eat away at our relationship."

"Joe—"

"No." His voice was inflexible. "I mean it. Go."

He wouldn't let her say another word. He hustled her out the front door and closed it in her face.

She wanted to hammer on it with her fists and yell, "I don't have to think! Damn you, Joe Hughes, I love you!" But in her heart, she knew he was right. How *would* she feel when she had to explain his disability to uncomprehending friends? She should think long and hard.

Even if she already knew the outcome.

SHE TRIED IT OUT on the kids that evening.

Teresa waged an internal war first: would Joe hate them knowing? But if her relationship with him continued, Nicole and Mark would have to find out eventually. She couldn't let his dyslexia continue to be some kind of terrible secret. It was heartbreaking enough that he'd been ashamed of himself. If she was ashamed, too, then he was right. Now was the time to break off their relationship.

She waited until dinnertime, when she, Nicole and Mark had some of their best discussions. Mark had already wolfed down his stroganoff and Nicole was daintily finishing hers when Teresa said, "I want to talk to you guys about something."

"Are we in trouble?" Mark asked.

Teresa smiled at him. "No, it doesn't have anything to do with you two. I went to see Joe today. You know he's been acting a little strange lately. He finally told me why. It turns out that he's illiterate."

Watching their faces, waiting for a reaction, she held her breath. This was worse than telling a friend. Now she was anxious not only for Joe's sake, but because she wanted them to demonstrate the kind of behavior she had tried to instill in them. She wanted them to prove that she was really a good parent.

Talk about ego! she thought ruefully.

What she got was an anticlimax. "What's that?" Mark asked.

Nicole dropped her fork. "He can't *read?* But...but he's a grown-up!"

"There are plenty of grown-ups who can't read. As many as twenty-five million adults in America can't." She'd looked up the subject in the encyclopedia as soon as she got home. "Most of them aren't as successful as Joe is. The prisons are full of them. Probably the welfare rolls are. Imagine what would happen to you if you couldn't even read the classified ads in the newspaper or fill out a job application. And most of these people can't help it."

"But I could read when I was five." Mark's face was scrunched up. "It's not that hard."

Looking appalled, Nicole just stared at her mother. *"Joe?"*

Teresa answered Mark. "It was easy for *you.* You must have noticed some kids in your class who struggle with it."

"Well, sure, there are always some dumb kids..."

Teresa had to repress a surge of fierce protectiveness that would have made her voice sharp. "Not necessarily dumb," she corrected. "Some of them at least will probably be diagnosed as learning disabled. Have you ever heard of dyslexia?"

Nicole nodded, but Mark shook his head.

Teresa leaned forward, elbows on the table. "Well, basically, somebody who is dyslexic can't process what he sees on the page the way you or I can. There's nothing wrong with his eyes. Glasses won't fix his problem. And dyslexics don't all see words in the same wrong way, or it might be easier to figure out how to help them. Some dyslexics see words turned around. What you or I would read as 'was' looks like 'saw' to them. Or they might just reverse some letters within a word. Or the text might seem to jam together so there aren't any blank spaces to separate words. Most dyslexics can learn to read with lots of help, but never very fast. They have to concentrate too hard to unscramble what they're seeing."

"But isn't that dumb?" Mark asked tentatively.

Teresa shook her head. "Someone can be dyslexic and a genius. Thomas Edison was dyslexic. So was Albert Einstein and George Patton, the World War II general. There are actors and writers and businessmen who are dyslexic. It doesn't have anything to do with intelligence. There's just one small thing wrong in their brains. It makes it hard for them to read, and sometimes to do math. It doesn't mean they can't think well. In frontier days, it wouldn't have mattered very much. Most people couldn't read, anyway, and those who could didn't much because books weren't available. But in the modern world, it matters a lot. If you can't read quickly, you'll fail in school. People get impatient with you. They *will* think you're dumb. Sometimes, dyslexics start believing they are. They try to hide the fact that they can't read. Joe is one of those."

Face still screwed up, Mark said in puzzlement, "But what's it got to do with us? Why did he quit coming over here?"

"I think he finally realized that we'd find out one of these days. He was ashamed."

"Oh, no!" Eyes wide, Nicole clapped her hand to her mouth. "That night when I asked him for help with my homework! He got this weird look on his face and said he barely graduated from high school."

A lump in her throat, Teresa nodded. "And what did I do but insist we go to a French restaurant, where he couldn't figure out what the menu said, and then I dragged him into Elliott Bay Bookstore and kept shoving books in his face and telling him he'd love them. He must have felt awful."

"Oh, Mom!" Nicole wailed. "I was thinking such mean things!"

"Only because you didn't know." Teresa laid her hand over her daughter's and gently squeezed. Her confidence in her kids had been rewarded. Resentful as Nicole could be these days, she was reacting exactly as Teresa had hoped she would. She continued, "He was so good at covering up his problem, we had no idea he had it. I have faith that neither of you would knowingly be insensitive."

Nicole's eyes had filled with tears. "But why didn't Alan ever say?"

"I suspect that Joe swore everybody in the family to silence. At the very least, they thought he should be the one to decide who he wanted to tell. Rebecca hinted one day, but I didn't get it. How could I? Joe's too...too competent. He's good at his job, he's up on current events, he's articulate. I never for a second dreamed—" Her voice caught.

"Is he mad that you found out?" Nicole asked.

"No, he's the one who told me." Teresa tried to smile. "The thing is, he figures it means he isn't good enough for me."

Mark stared at her in shock. "But he's a really cool guy! You don't care if he can read, do you?"

His sister shot him an angry look. "Of course Mom doesn't! Don't be dum—" She clamped down on the word.

For a moment all three sat in silence broken by Teresa's sigh. "You don't have to worry about what you say. Joe's *not* dumb. We all know that."

Shyly Mark asked, "Is he going to start coming over again?"

"I hope so." She ruffled his hair to hide her own emotion. "He's afraid I'll be ashamed of him. I have to convince him I won't."

"You can do that, can't you?"

Seeing his eagerness, Teresa felt a wrench in her chest. Mark cared too much. Joe was just what he'd needed, a worthy object of his hero worship. Trouble was, this hero might, in the end, not be able to swallow the fact that she'd gone to college for eight years, while he couldn't read the newspaper.

He'd told her to think, to be honest with herself. She had a feeling he was doing the same. She knew her own conclusion. But what would his be?

CHAPTER TEN

SHE HADN'T EXPECTED to feel so nervous, just because this was the first time she'd been alone with Alan. Nicole stole a shy glance at his profile. He was frowning at a slow driver in front of them.

"Jeez. Thirty-five miles an hour. Come on, lady." Then he groaned. "Oh, no!"

Nicole looked ahead to see what he was complaining about. A tractor was pulling onto the highway. It wouldn't be going very far, experience told her—probably just from one field to another—but it was moving slower than a baby crawled. Alan slapped the steering wheel in frustration.

"Hey," Nicole said tentatively. "We're not in any hurry."

The rigidity in his shoulders eased. His smile was wry. "Yeah. You're right. Mom says I'm the most impatient driver she knows. She hates riding with me."

"My dad was awful." Funny, she'd forgotten that. "He'd swear and fume and yell. Mom would get so mad at him."

"Does it make you sad to think about him?"

She looked inward and was surprised to find that, this time, talking about her father hadn't hurt. "It's been so long," she said slowly. "I missed him a lot for the first couple of years. I mean, you just assume your parents will be there. Mom used to tease Dad by saying she'd teach me to drive, not him, because he'd be a bad influence. Next semester I'm taking driver's ed, and it will be Mom who teaches me, like she said. But I know she didn't mean it. We never thought..." Now it did hurt, but only a little, an ache like a fading bruise.

"Yeah, I always thought that, too," Alan said. "Maybe it's not the same, because my dad's not dead, but he's not here, either. He's always promising to show up and then not making it, or bragging about what a good football player I am, but he never comes to the games. It's worse since he got married again and they had a baby. He's like someone I hardly know, but I still have to visit once in a while."

"Maybe that would be worse," Nicole said. "At least my father can't help not being here."

Alan nodded. "I guess that's what I was trying to say."

She was silent for a moment as he accelerated past the tractor, bumping its way into a frozen field of brown stubble. Tentatively Nicole said, "But you have a stepfather now. Do you like him?"

Alan's voice warmed. "Yeah, Sam's cool. He lets me drive his Mercedes sometimes."

That wasn't exactly what Nicole had been probing for; she didn't want to drive Joe's pickup truck if he married her mother. But she could tell Alan was happy that his mother had remarried, which reassured her.

It also got her to thinking about what Mom had told her and Mark at dinner last night.

"Mom said your uncle Joe can't read."

"He told her?" Alan sounded surprised.

"Yeah. I think he and Mom really like each other." A month ago that knowledge had bothered her. She was still confused, but not as much. If he made Mom happy, was it so bad if she remarried?

Yeah, because it would mean staying here forever, she reminded herself.

Well, yes, she admitted silently, but—

"Do you mind?" Alan asked, echoing her thoughts.

They'd turned into a long gravel lane that passed a Christmas-tree farm. Carved gates already had multicolored lights strung overhead.

At his question, Nicole moved a little uneasily. "I'm not sure. I guess I haven't made up my mind. He's okay, but it's...I don't know, kind of scary. Does that sound dumb?"

Dumb. There was that word. She winced, but Alan didn't seem to notice.

"No, I was a real jerk when my mother started to see Sam. I really hated him for a while."

Nicole glanced at a sign beside the lane: Pilchuck Riding Stables. Ahead she could see a white farmhouse, then long barns and a huge covered arena.

"Wow," she breathed.

"You really like horses?"

"Mmm." She was craning her neck. "Mom said I can get one, but I haven't made up my mind."

"Why?"

She gave her standard answer. "I'm hoping Mom changes her mind and we move back to Bellevue."

"Still?" He parked and turned off the engine in front of one of the barns.

Had she hurt his feelings? Before she could have second thoughts, Nicole blurted, "Today I'm glad I'm here."

He smiled, and the look in his eyes made her blush. "Good."

Suddenly she wasn't at all sure she wanted to move back to Bellevue.

TERESA WAITED almost a week, just to convince Joe she'd thought seriously about their future. Then, on Friday night, she called him.

When she heard his real voice, not the canned one on his answering machine, she said hurriedly, "Hi, this is Teresa. The kids and I were wondering if you could go Christmas shopping with us in LaConner tomorrow."

His answer was a long silence. Pulse already racing, she started to see colored dots in front of her eyes. Oh, Lord, she was holding her breath. She gasped in some air just as he spoke.

"Is this invitation supposed to have deeper meaning?"

"Yes," she admitted baldly.

Another pause. "I didn't think I'd hear from you."

"That's because you have no idea what a prime catch you are."

If his laugh sounded a little rusty, as it had when she'd first met him, Teresa was still glad to hear it.

"You can itemize my superior qualities tomorrow," he said. "I think I can stand to hear them."

"Just so I don't give you a swelled head," she teased.

"Oh, I don't think there's any danger of that."

His wryness brought a lump to her throat. She had to clear it before she could say, "Nine-thirty too early for you?"

"Nope. I thought you worked on Saturdays."

"We switched this weekend. Eric had plans for Sunday."

"With Eric, they're usually beautiful ones."

"This one's named Louise."

Another laugh, better than the first. "I do believe the new loan officer at SeaFirst is a Louise."

"How do you learn everything so fast?"

"Well, in this case, Rebecca went into the bank and ended up being introduced to Louise whatever-her-last-name-is. She happened to mention it to Jess, who called Mom right away. Mom told Lee, who made sure I heard the news."

Teresa shook her head, laughing. "And you couldn't control yourself for the excitement."

"Right." His amused voice sounded like the Joe she knew.

"I'd better go." A high-pitched battle was erupting from the living room. Unfortunately it was live action, not a particularly violent television episode. "My kids are trying to kill each other."

"Think of the problems that would solve." He laughed again. "I'll come by your place in the morning."

She hung up, smiling. The fizzle of excitement in her chest was even able to withstand the settling of an argument that began with, "Mom, I was watching that movie you said I could watch, and *he* keeps changing the channel to Nickelodeon!"

"'Rugrats' is on, and you said..."

By the time they'd simmered down, they'd missed half of both programs. With unwonted sternness, Teresa sent them to bed with permission to read a good book for half an hour.

She wondered what Mrs. Hughes had said when she sent *her* brood to bed. "You can all read a good book, except for Joe who can't?" Life must have been full of land mines for Joe and his parents.

And now it would be full of land mines for her, Teresa suspected.

The first one appeared the next day when the only parking spot on the narrow shopping street in the small town of LaConner was smack in front of a tempting bookstore. Getting out of the car—she'd driven so the kids didn't have to ride in the cold back of Joe's pickup truck—Teresa sneaked a glance. But when Nicole wandered toward the door, Teresa said sharply, "We can look at books another day. Unless you plan to buy one for a present."

"I don't mind," Joe said, but his mouth had a grim set.

Teresa smiled determinedly at him. "Christmas presents first today. We all have our lists, right, troops? Okay, march!"

"This how you get the dairy cows in the barn?" Joe asked her, humor relaxing the tension in the line of his mouth.

"That's me, an irresistible force."

"I know just how those cows feel," he murmured, but his smiling glance took any sting out of the words.

They had fun that day. Even Nicole cooperated, at her cheerful best. LaConner was a charming town strung along the edge of a sluice lined with sailing and fishing boats, some already sporting Christmas lights on their gunwales and masts. More lights festooned shop windows and wrapped the fragrant branches of beautifully decorated trees just inside.

For the first time, Teresa was made aware of how near Christmas was. Other years, she would have had her shopping almost done by now. This year, she'd been so busy painting and wallpapering and deciding on carpet colors, she hadn't even *thought* about Christmas.

Making decisions would be the hard part here, she could tell, once she'd seen the work of local craftsmen and the unusual imports sold in the shops. The shopping wasn't the entire charm of the town; tables in restaurants looked right over the water and the occasional boat, slowly gliding past and leaving a long silver wake. Joe mentioned that there was a museum up on the hill, as well as a handsome Victorian mansion that had been a showplace at the turn of the century and was now open to the public.

"We'll come back another day," Teresa promised the kids.

Joe became the packhorse for their parcels. Every time he got too loaded down, he'd ferry bags back to the car. Even he bought a few Christmas presents: for Jess, a fat humorous rendition of a horse in chocolate brown ceramic, its eyes bulging comically and its ears flopping; for Rebecca, a hideously expensive but elegant terra-cotta pot for her brick courtyard.

Teresa watched to see if Joe fell in love with anything in particular, but she never did see him exhibit the kind of wistful longing she felt for ten or twenty different things, starting with a carved swing that would be bliss on summer evenings on her front porch. Eyes closed, she rocked back and forth for a moment, imagining it. Ah, well, later. When the major remodeling was done and Christmas past.

She kept watching Joe, but, thinking back, she remembered how stark the decor in his house was. If he liked simple and uncluttered, he probably wouldn't want any of the wall hangings or gewgaws she saw.

Teresa was exhausted by the time they called it a day. She wished she could revive when Joe pointed out the antique stores on the way out of town, but her feet refused to consider any more shopping.

"You a gardener?" Joe asked.

"I intend to become one. When we bought our house in Bellevue, the yard had already been laid out and planted by a landscape designer. Takes all the fun out of it. Why?"

He nodded toward the fields that stretched ahead of them. "Those are planted with tulips and daffodils. You ever been up here in the spring?"

"Years ago. I'd forgotten."

This land was a floodplain, flat and rich. Here and there were farmhouses built high off the ground to withstand the floods that still washed over the banks of the Skagit River every few years. The day was crisp and clear; she could see for miles across the low land to the Cascade Mountains, and especially Mt. Baker, which had a plume of steam rising from its caldera.

"This is the time to plant bulbs, you know," Joe went on. "Roozengarten sells the best bulbs you've ever seen. We're not far from it."

"All right, all right," Teresa agreed. "Just so I don't have to dig 'em up out of the field."

The lines in his cheeks deepened with a smile. "I think we can assume they do that for us."

The earth in Roozengarten's display gardens was black and crumbly. They dug up all their bulbs every year and replanted them in the fall, a clerk told Teresa.

"But some will come back and even multiply if you leave them in the ground, especially if you fertilize faithfully," he added. "Look for the ones that say they naturalize well."

To Teresa's surprise, Nicole eagerly helped her choose tulip and daffodil bulbs from the rows of bins. Teresa kept waiting for a snippy remark about how they might not be in White Horse next spring to see them bloom, since it was still possible that they'd return to Bellevue. But Nicole didn't say a word about moving again.

Teresa glanced at her daughter, whose face was animated as she answered some question Joe had asked. Maybe she was finally adjusting, wonder of wonders.

Or—a horrible thought struck Teresa—maybe Nicole was in love. That might be even worse than having her sulky.

Well, no. Almost anything was better than that.

The day had gone so well Teresa hated to let go of it. Back at her house, just after they'd climbed out of the car, she asked Joe if he'd like to stay for dinner. "It's nothing fancy, I knew I'd be tired, but if I don't get distracted and burn it, I make a half-decent meat loaf."

"Do you often get distracted?" he inquired.

She batted her eyelashes. "You could distract me any old day."

A smile showed in his eyes. "I prefer my meat loaf unblackened."

"Oh, phooey, and we could have had such fun," she said with mock disappointment. "So, are you afraid to stay?"

"Seems to me I've told you before—I don't scare off easily."

The kids had disappeared into the house. Teresa stood on tiptoe and kissed Joe on the mouth. He reacted the way she'd hoped: his hands closed around her waist and he kissed her right back, but with serious intent. She swayed toward him and just for a moment lost herself in the feel of his lips and his thumbs, drawing circles through her shirt right beneath her breasts.

When his mouth lifted from hers, she whispered, "I'm glad."

He looked down at her for a long moment, lines carved between his dark brows, giving his face a grim aspect. "I only hope you won't regret this."

"I won't," she told him huskily, "if you don't."

She felt the long breath he expelled. "We may both be sorry," he muttered.

Teresa touched his cheek. "I'll turn you into an optimist yet."

"I already am." A swift wicked grin transformed his face. "I'm staying for dinner, aren't I?"

"Rat!" She pretended to punch him, then tucked her hand companionably in the crook of his arm and steered him toward the house.

In the kitchen she said, "Stay and talk to me."

"Why don't I bring in everything you bought first?" he suggested. "That way you can concentrate."

She put her hands on her hips and scowled. "I never should have admitted to my little flaw."

Again she saw the grimness. "I have you beat in that department."

Before she could think of anything to say, he turned and went back out, grabbing her keys off the kitchen table on his way. Damn it! she thought, slapping the hamburger into a bowl. Was this going to be hovering there between them from now on? She couldn't watch every word so she didn't graze his thin skin. It'd be better if they talked about it openly, if she showed she wasn't rendered uncomfortable by his admission.

The only trouble was, she had no idea whether he wanted to talk about it, too, or whether her probing would be unwelcome.

But they couldn't just pretend his dyslexia didn't exist! If they were to have any hope of a future, she had to know if he wanted and would accept help, whether she ought to tell other people, whether her reading in front of him would seem likc a slap to his self-esteem.

In fact, they had a ton to work out. Why not start tonight?

The meat loaf came out perfectly, and everyone's good moods lasted through dinner. Then Nicole disappeared upstairs to call one of her Bellevue friends, and Mark went back to the television.

"I'm weak." Teresa sighed. "His brain's getting warped."

Joe leaned one hip against the kitchen counter. "From what you've told me, there's nothing wrong with his brain."

She shot him a nervous glance, but she couldn't detect any tightness to his mouth or undertones in his voice.

"No, but I wish he'd read more by choice." She gave another sigh. "And then there's Nicole. Do you have any idea what my phone bill is every month?"

He accepted the dish towel she handed him. "You mean, she calls her friends in Bellevue?"

"Constantly! Last month, my bill was more than two hundred dollars." She attacked the dirty pan in the sink with unnecessary force. "I'm weak where she's concerned, too. She's been so unhappy I didn't want to crack down."

"She didn't sound unhappy today," he observed.

"No, she didn't," Teresa agreed thoughtfully. "Did you know she's seeing your nephew, Alan?"

"He mentioned taking her and Mark shopping for his mother's birthday present."

Teresa's hands stilled. "You didn't, um, ask him to spend some time with Nicole, did you?"

"Why would I do something like that?" Joe looked at her incredulously.

"Maybe for the same reason your family has been marshaled to ease my way with the dairy farmers?"

"Ah..."

Teresa raised her eyebrows.

"Okay, I plead guilty on that one." Joe set down the dry meat-loaf pan and reached for a wineglass. "Is it working?"

"It hasn't hurt," she admitted. "Your mother seems to be a popular lady."

"In more ways than one." He shook his head, smiling. "I suspect she's turned down several marriage proposals since my father died."

"Would you mind if she remarried?"

"Nah. Of course not. None of us would. But I'd be surprised. She likes her peace and quiet when she isn't lording it over the family. I can't see her getting used to some other man's bad habits."

Teresa turned off the water and reached for the hand towel. "She may surprise you one of these days."

"Maybe." His blue eyes were suddenly intent. "You're a generation younger, but you're in the same boat. Don't you worry just a little that you'll take some man in only to find out that he drives you crazy?

Snores and leaves his dirty socks on the floor and shaves into the sink without rinsing?"

"Tell me this isn't you we're talking about."

The way a slow smile grew on his face was enough to convince her she didn't give a damn if he dropped his dirty socks anywhere he wanted.

"I don't know if I snore," Joe said, "but I'm tidy enough."

"And here you scared me." She went to the stove. "Like a cup of coffee? Tea?"

"Tea if you have herbal or decaf. Coffee keeps me awake."

She put on the kettle and got out two mugs. "Joe?" Her back was to him.

"Mmm?"

"Do you mind if we talk about your dyslexia?"

She sneaked a look and saw that he was slowly shaking out the wet dish towel and hanging it up. It seemed like forever before he said impassively, "No. What do you want to know?"

"Well..." Was this incxcusably nosy? But it was too late for second thoughts. "Can you read at all? I heard you tell Nicole you'd graduated from high school."

He faced her at last, arms crossed as he leaned back against the counter. "Yes, I can read some. Given enough time and no pressure. It's... a struggle. And yeah, I did graduate, but not on my own merits. They kept passing me along. My parents had me held back one year, but it didn't make any difference. After that, I think the teachers just wanted to get rid of me."

"Surely not!" She was probably naive to feel shock, but she couldn't help it.

"Sorry." His expression was remote. "That's the way it works. In fairness to them, keeping someone back doesn't do much good. I couldn't learn to read. Another year wouldn't have done it. As it was, I knew I stuck out. They took pity on me."

"But—" The kettle began to whistle, and she gave a start. Lifting it off the burner, she poured. "Did you always get bad grades? You must have dreaded report-card time."

"After a while, I didn't care." He shrugged, but something in the tilt of his mouth told her he wasn't telling the truth. "My grades in math weren't bad. Shop, PE, art, even Spanish I did okay in. Most of it was memorization. I learn things I'm told pretty easily."

She nodded. "How do you handle the office side of your business? I mean, you must do billing and advertising and taxes and—"

"I have a secretary. The numbers I can deal with. She writes the letters."

He didn't look angry, so Teresa asked one more question. "How did you get a driver's license?"

"A friend who works in the Motor Vehicles office. He read the questions to me. I proved I could read the road signs, so he gave me my license."

Teresa nodded again, thoughtfully. "I can see why you're stuck here in White Horse."

"You sound like your daughter." There was an edge to his voice.

"My daugh— Oh." She flushed. "I didn't mean it that way. I love it here. But I chose it." She lifted the tea bags from the cups and carried them to the table.

Joe pulled out a chair and turned it around, then straddled it and rested one arm on its back as he reached for the mug.

"I shouldn't have jumped on you. You're right. I *am* stuck. People here are always ready to help out. After all, I'm a Hughes. But you know—" he was gazing down into the mug "—that's half blessing and half curse. I can't leave."

Here she felt as if she'd found home, and to him the same place was a prison.

"Do you want to?" she asked, voice low.

He set down the mug and rubbed the back of his neck. "Oh, hell, I don't know. You have no idea how many times I've asked myself the same thing. My sisters and brother all chose to stick around. Maybe I would've, too. I'm happy enough with my life, I guess."

"But you've never married."

"I've never been quite sure what I wanted. Nobody I've known all my life." Joe grimaced. "And anybody else would've had to find out. I know for damn sure I don't want pity. And I don't like feeling—" he hesitated, shifting uneasily "—inadequate."

"Is that how you feel with me?" She quit breathing, waiting for his answer.

His eyes, vividly blue, met hers. Roughly he said, "I'm afraid I might."

"But you're..." She struggled for the right word.

"A prime catch," he filled in dryly. "I know."

"You don't believe it, do you?"

"Would you like me if I did?" Was that a smile that played with the corners of his mouth?

She made a face. "Probably not. I worked with a guy once who was sure he was God's gift to women. I never could convince him he was sadly mistaken."

"There you go." Definitely a smile. "At least I'm modest."

Teresa stood up and came around the table. She wrapped her arms around his neck and murmured right into his ear, "Cute, too."

"It's nice to know I have two fine qualities." He turned suddenly, so that his mouth was a hairbreadth from hers. "Any more you'd like to mention?"

He might sound teasing, but something told her he really wanted to know why she'd come after him that day at his house. If he'd listened at all then, he hadn't believed her. And no wonder.

"Um—" Teresa pretended to think "—you can lift one eyebrow."

"Me and Errol Flynn."

"You're sweet."

"Every boy's ambition."

"Patient."

"Maddening, is how Jess puts it."

"But then, she's probably *not* patient."

He kissed her, his chuckle tickling her lips.

When Teresa came up for air, she continued, "Years ago, I went rafting down the Colorado River. It was...oh, exhilarating and scary and..." She couldn't find the right words. "It was an unforgettable rush." Brushing her mouth across his, she murmured, "That's what kissing you feels like."

"God almighty, lady." His voice was gravelly. "You have to say things like that when your kids could walk into the room any minute?"

"You asked," she said simply.

"Yeah, I like being frustrated as hell." His fingers tangled in her hair and he kissed her again, hard. When he let her go, Joe rubbed his hands across his jean-clad thighs. "Any more of that, and I may have to sneak back in your bedroom window later."

"Conveniently enough, there's a walnut tree right outside my bedroom."

His eyes darkened. "That an invitation?"

Teresa hesitated, more tempted than she would have liked to admit. But, "No, I'm afraid not. That's not exactly the example I'd like to set for my teenage daughter. Especially if your nephew is anywhere near as persuasive as you are."

Joe shook his head. "Struck out again. Listen, I'd better get home. How about dinner tomorrow night? Just you and me?"

"So long as I'm not late."

"Good." This smile hadn't been intended to be sexy, which made it even more so. "Six?"

"You're on. Come on, I'll walk you to the door."

They kissed again on the front porch and yet again after he opened the driver-side door of his pickup truck. Teresa didn't want him to drive away any more now than she had after their first date. She seemed doomed to feel insecure where he was concerned. He'd spent the day with her, but that didn't mean he wouldn't still have second thoughts. What would it take to make him feel inadequate? Any reminder of his disability? Unconscious condescension on her part? Would he give her enough time for them to understand each other?

Locking the front door once she'd come in, Teresa didn't go any farther. She just stood there in the entry hall, waiting for a half-formed idea to present itself.

If Joe could read some, was there any reason he couldn't improve? Her eyes widened. Teaching reading had come a long way since he'd been in school. Plenty of adult illiterates were making progress with tutors. There were all kinds of new techniques. Just imagine how good he'd feel about himself once he could read with confidence.

She'd have to think about how to suggest it, but the basic idea excited her. If he wanted, she'd tutor him herself, but she wouldn't be hurt if he preferred to go to someone else. That way, it couldn't come between them. He could surprise her with his progress and not feel as if he was disappointing her if he didn't make any.

Maybe Monday she'd call around, Teresa decided, just to find out what was available to someone like him. That way she wouldn't promise him something that didn't exist. After all, she was no expert. But for his sake, she could become one.

"Time to turn off the TV!" she called to Mark.

Tomorrow afternoon she'd go to the library and find some books on dyslexia. That would be a good start. She'd wait a little bit before she sprang this on Joe, so he wouldn't think it was a requirement to qualify for a relationship with her. Of course it wasn't; she didn't care whether he could read or not.

He was the one who cared, the one who would be freed from his cage. She could understand why he'd been afraid to try again. But now that he'd had the courage to admit his disability to her, maybe he'd be willing to face it head on. For his own sake.

CHAPTER ELEVEN

NICOLE STUFFED her jeans and sweater into her backpack and then straightened to look at her reflection in the small mirror above the sink. She tugged her leotard so it covered her bra strap, then poked a few wandering strands of hair back into her French braid. There. She was ready.

She took jazz dance right after school on Tuesdays. She'd walked over from the high school along with a couple of the other girls. So far, Ariana was the only real friend she'd made, but in a casual way some of the other girls were starting to include her.

Joe's niece Steph, who'd come from the middle school, whisked past Nicole into the bathroom the moment she came out. Nicole hung her pack on a hook in the waiting room and went on into the big high-ceilinged room where dance classes were held. A mirror covered one whole wall; bars were affixed to the two side walls.

Nicole immediately began to warm up, touching her toes, stretching, eyes fixed on the mirror to be sure she didn't slump or make graceless movements.

The instructor, Joan, was a tiny woman in her early twenties whose mass of dark red hair always seemed to be slipping out of its confines. She was a study in perpetual motion, bouncing with enthusiasm. The high energy of jazz dancing was a perfect match for her; Nicole couldn't imagine Joan accomplishing the slow studied elegance of ballet.

The moment the girls had all arrived, still tugging at their leotards and sitting on the polished wooden floor to pull on ballet shoes, Joan clapped her hands for attention.

"Girls, I have news today. We've been asked to participate in a Christmas program in the high-school auditorium on December twenty-second. Several choirs are performing, as well as the high-school jazz band. If you're interested, what we thought we might do is choreograph a dance to accompany a reading of *The Night before Christmas.* We'll have to hustle to learn it in time, and we'll undoubtedly need several extra rehearsals the last week. So first let me ask you—do you want to do this? Will anybody be out of town?"

Excited chatter broke out. Joan asked for a show of hands. Nobody was planning to be away. Everybody wanted to do it.

"Great." She flipped pages on her clipboard. "I've assigned parts rather than holding auditions, given the shortness of lead time. If anybody hates what I ask you to do, talk to me after class. Oh, and we'll need costumes, of course, at least one change for some of you."

Nicole hung back as the others waited eagerly. It sounded like fun to her. She loved to perform. But she doubted she'd be given any major part; after all, she was the newcomer.

"Steph," Joan said, "I'd like you to be the father, the one who is telling the story, although you won't actually be narrating it. Nicole, we'll have to pad you, but you have a gift for the comic, and I think you'll make a charming Santa Claus. Liz, Sarah, Jessica, you'll start as children, and you, Jessica, as a mouse, then you'll become reindeer." She named five others to be reindeer, as well. Some girls would be snowflakes and then toys that Santa would pull from his bag. "Okay, let's start thinking about choreography. Children, you'll be curled in some blankets. Mouse, you need to be asleep, too, as the opening stanza is read. ''Twas the night before Christmas, when all through the house,/ Not a creature was stirring, not even a mouse.'"

They would paint a backdrop to serve as a wall with the fireplace in the middle, they decided. Stockings would be hung.

"Can we get a small Christmas tree and decorate it, do you think?" Joan asked. "If there won't already be one on stage. Let me make a note to ask."

One of the girls said, "My parents own a Christmas-tree farm. I'll ask if they'll give us the tree."

"We could all bring a few ornaments," Jessica suggested. "Or maybe make some stuff ourselves, like a popcorn garland."

They were all excited by the time class ended. Outside the girls separated, some to the waiting cars, the rest to walk home. As Nicole waved goodbye, a chorus of voices recited, "'But I heard him exclaim, ere he drove out of sight—'"

Walking backward and laughing, she yelled back, "'Happy Christmas to all. And to all a good-night!'"

At home she rushed in the front door. "Mom! Where are you?"

"In the kitchen."

Her mother turned, smiling, from the stove as Nicole dropped her backpack and did a pirouette.

"Guess what?" She didn't wait. "My jazz class is going to perform in a Christmas program. We're choreographing a dance to go with a reading of *The Night before Christmas.* And guess what?"

"You already said that. Let's see." Mom pretended to think. "You get to be the mouse and I have to make the costume."

"Better!" Nicole rose en pointe and twirled, arms lifted above her head. "Joan picked *me* to be Santa Claus. It's the best part in the dance. She said I have a gift for the comic. Cool, huh?"

"Very cool." Her mother hugged her. "*Do* I have to make the costume?"

"Uh, maybe. Probably. Unless we can borrow one."

"You're a little smaller than most Santas. And I presume you don't want to dance in big black boots."

"Maybe I could wear black leggings and, like, red knickers? And then a pillow to be my stomach?"

"Sounds good to me. The hat ought to be easy. It won't kill me to get my sewing machine out. And I'm pretty sure I have a wide black belt. Listen, why don't we go look at fabric on Sunday? We can go to Mt. Vernon. I've heard there's a good bookstore there—for some more Christmas shopping."

"Sure, why not?" Nicole grabbed her backpack and started to leave the room.

"Don't you want a snack? Dinner'll still be a while."

"I'm not hungry," she called back, and bounded up the stairs.

She called Ariana first. Ariana was almost as excited as Nicole. "My church choir is going to be in that program, too."

"I wish you were in my dance class," Nicole said.

"You haven't seen me dance." Ariana sounded cheerful. "I'm the world's worst klutz."

"But dance makes you more graceful."

"*Nothing* is going to make me more graceful. At least not until I get tall enough to match my feet. And that may not happen. Mom's always saying, 'You've *got* to have another couple of inches of growing in you. Otherwise, why are your feet so big?' "

"They're not that big," Nicole said loyally. It was weird, though, that Ariana wore size-eight shoes and was barely five feet tall.

They talked for a while longer before Ariana had to go so she could start her homework. "You're lucky not to have Mr. Holland for English," she moaned. "He *always* gives homework. He'll probably give it over Christmas break."

Still hyper, Nicole phoned Jayne next. Her friend launched right in. "Do you think your mom would bring you down to Bellevue next weekend? I mean, not this one, the one after? *My* mom says if you want to spend the night, we could drive you home the next day. We could hang out at Bellevue Square all day and then do something in the evening. Maybe Mom would let us throw a party, so you could see everybody."

"Um...sure." Instead of feeling a burst of elation, Nicole thought, Would Alan ask her out that weekend? He hadn't said anything after their ride. Well, she still had *this* weekend. And she didn't want him to think all she did was wait for him to call. "I'll ask. The only thing is, my mom works on Saturdays. Do you think I could spend Friday night, instead, and then you could bring me home Saturday after we go shopping?"

"Or you could spend both nights!"

Nicole wasn't sure she wanted to. Later she'd figure out why.

"I'll ask," she said again. "You weren't planning to do anything that Friday, were you? Like with Kelly or Russ?"

"I'm not speaking to Kelly right now. She's gotten *so* conceited. I mean, she has the lead in the school play, and the only people she has time for are the other drama students."

Kelly always had been conceited. She took classes at the Seattle Children's Theatre Drama School, and every day you had to figure out what role she was playing now. Nicole had never understood why Jayne liked her.

"What about Russ?" Nicole asked.

There was an odd little pause before Jayne said, too quickly, "I don't know if I'll see him again."

"You mean, he hasn't called?"

"Yeah, but I made an excuse." For a moment, only the sound of breathing came over the wire. "You won't tell anyone, will you? I mean, not even your mom?"

Nicole had been lying on her stomach across the bed, but now she scrambled upright. "Of course not."

"He...well, he came on really strong. Like I was supposed to spread my legs just because he paid my way into the movie theater. When I wouldn't, he got mad."

"He didn't hit you, did he?" Nicole held her breath.

"Not...not really." Another strained silence. "But he started the car and took off so fast, I didn't have my seat belt on, and then he had to stop practically right away, and my head hit the dashboard. I've got this big bruise on my forehead. I didn't tell my parents where I got it."

"But it wasn't your fault!"

"No, but you know my dad. He'd want to call the police or something. He probably wouldn't let me go on another date for a year."

"Russ Harlan." Nicole shook her head. "He's not even the jock type you figure is half-crazy on steroids."

"You don't believe me?" Jayne asked belligerently.

"Of course I do! It's just so bizarre. I mean, we've both liked him for so long."

"I haven't liked him as long as you have." Jayne let out a sound that might have been a sob. "I felt so guilty when he asked me out! I was afraid you'd hate me!"

"I didn't mind." There was a time for lies, Nicole figured. "It's not like I had some claim on him. I'll never see him again."

"Do you care?"

"Are you nuts? After he treated you like that?"

Definitely another sob. "I miss you."

Jayne hadn't missed her back when Russ Harlan first asked her out and when she was suddenly best friends with Kelly. Nicole tried to summon some resentment, but it wouldn't come. Staying best friends with someone you hardly ever saw was hard. Maybe impossible. Jayne hadn't dropped her; Nicole had moved. And for the first time she admitted to herself that she wouldn't be going back. Her mother wasn't going to change her mind. And just because Nicole had been miserable didn't mean Jayne had to be.

"I miss you, too," Nicole said softly, blinking against a rush of tears. Spending the weekend with Jayne would be fun in a way, but it wouldn't be the same as when they did everything together. Nicole couldn't step back into her old life as if nothing had changed.

And when she thought about her role in the Christmas play and about Alan and Ariana, Nicole wasn't even sure she wanted to.

IT HARDLY SEEMED possible that Thanksgiving had arrived. They'd been in White Horse—in this house—for three months. Make that three years, and she'd still be an outsider as far as some of the community was concerned, Teresa thought ruefully. Three years from now, some of the farmers would still be watching her suspiciously.

Bending over the hot oven, she gingerly tested the wing of the turkey. It came loose in her hand. She grabbed a couple of hot pads and lifted the heavy pan onto the stovetop.

Two cats sat watching her hopefully. "Later, guys," she told them. "If I gave you some now, you'd burn the sandpaper right off your tongues."

Once she'd popped the sweet potatoes into the oven and opened a can of food for the cats, Teresa returned to her reflections. Despite some frustrations and Nicole's resistance to the move, Teresa was glad she'd made it. She had never been happier in her work. Mark was thriving at school and with his new friends. The cats and dogs loved their new home. And, unless she was mistaken, even Nicole had finally accepted the inevitable and let herself notice that some things here in White Horse weren't so bad.

It was a little unnerving to realize how much of their adjustment was due to the Hughes family, however. Her own romance with Joe, the grudging willingness of some of the dairy farmers to give her a chance, Nicole's turnaround... All were thanks to Joe and Alan and the family support they'd mobilized.

Even the changes in her house were thanks to a Hughes—Rebecca. She'd helped Teresa pick out the new vinyl floor in here and the lacy valance and blinds. Unfortunately no Hughes had volunteered to strip or reface the kitchen cabinets, a job Teresa dreaded. It was fun to choose the materials, but she was getting just a little tired of spending evenings painting and papering, and not being able to use one of the two bathrooms because the plumber had it torn up. He'd have worked faster if *he* had a teenage daughter who lived in front of the mirror.

The doorbell rang and Teresa hurried to answer it, still wearing her apron. She flung open the door to greet two friends she hadn't seen since they'd helped her on moving day.

"George, Beverly, how wonderful to have you here!" She hugged them both. "I'm so glad you could come."

George Dobson had been Tom's fraternity roommate in college. They'd married women who liked each other on sight. Beverly was a prosecuting attorney in Seattle, and George was a software designer with a young firm that hoped to be the next Microsoft. His hair was receding now, but he was a handsome assured man. Beverly hung up her purple wool cape—typically flamboyant, and why not, if you were tall, voluptuous and raven-haired?

"What can I do?" she asked, handing Teresa the pumpkin pie she'd brought.

"Keep me company." Teresa smiled at them. "Both of you. Tell me what's going on in your lives."

"We won't have anything left for the Christmas letter," George complained before leaning over to kiss her cheek. "You look great."

"I feel great. Oh, here's Nicole."

Beverly enveloped Teresa's daughter in a bone-crunching hug.

The teenager looked almost misty-eyed. "It's cool that you came."

"Ah, the language takes me back." George kissed her cheek, too. "We said 'cool' at your age. Tell me 'groovy' has come back in style."

"Not in my lifetime." Nicole made a face. "It's really lame."

"That's a new one," he conceded.

In the kitchen Beverly insisted on donning an apron and carving the turkey while Teresa peeled potatoes and put them on to boil, then cut up broccoli. Nicole set the table in the dining room—wallpapered in long sessions the last two nights—and George straddled a kitchen chair in a way that reminded Teresa of Joe.

"Okay," he said. "Tell all."

Teresa told them about Eric and the practice, chattered about the house and what she intended to do to it, and bragged about the kids.

Nicole rolled her eyes on one of her trips into the kitchen to collect silverware and dishes. "Did you tell them about your boyfriend, Mom?"

"Boyfriend?" they repeated in chorus.

Teresa sent a meaningful look after her daughter, who didn't appear chastened. Then she said, "That word is so...so..."

"Adolescent," Beverly supplied. She gave an evil smile. "Is 'lover' a better choice?"

"I have to have some secrets." Teresa backed up, laughing, when Beverly brandished the butcher knife at her. "Okay, okay. You'll meet him later, I hope. His name is Joe Hughes, and he invited us to his family's Thanksgiving dinner, but I declined. I've been wanting to have you guys up, and...oh, I just wanted to have this Thanksgiving in our own home. It seemed appropriate. But he promised to try to come by in time to say hello."

"What's he do?" George asked predictably.

"He's a logger."

"A *logger?*" Belatedly, George must have realized that incredulity was not a polite response, because he cleared his throat and forced a humorous tone, "You'll be drummed out of the Sierra Club."

Teresa tried not to sound irritated. "I don't belong. And he's not the kind of logger they battle. He has a good-sized crew that works locally. They took some trees out for me. They do tree-topping, clearing so a house can be built, that kind of thing."

"So he's the boss."

"That's right." Teresa hated feeling defensive. Why was she? So what if Joe didn't have two college degrees? He could hold his own in any conversation, and he wasn't just a logger, he was a businessman.

"How do the kids like him?" Beverly asked more tactfully.

"Mark adores Joe." Teresa glanced to both sides to be sure Nicole wasn't in the room. Even then, she lowered her voice. "Nicole has been determined not to like anybody or anything in White Horse, including Joe, but she's coming around. Partly because of a romance with his nephew, who is a senior in high school. But do me a favor—"

"Mum's the word." Beverly turned to her husband. "Right?"

"Why's everybody looking at me?" He stood up. "I can tell I'm not wanted. Where's Mark?"

"I have a suspicion he's in the living room playing Nintendo. With the sound turned down so I don't notice."

"Aha! He's met his match. I'll go take him for every cent he has."

Beverly looked after him, her expression fond but exasperated. "He's a sweetheart, but he has the tact of a two-year-old. We were at a dinner party, and I overheard him telling two other couples how much I weighed! I could have killed him! He *knows* how sensitive I am about it, but, to quote him, the words just floweth forth."

Teresa had forgotten. She hoped to God he wouldn't say anything grossly tactless to Joe. Or grill him about his educational background. Oh, Lord, maybe this hadn't been such a good idea. If only she *knew* what would upset Joe.

How true, but she reminded herself that she'd never find out if she was afraid to mix him with her other friends. She had to take risks.

She relaxed over dinner. George was witty, Beverly insightful. They both treated the kids like equals—it was a pity, she thought, that they'd never had their own. Strangely she had no idea why they hadn't. Had they tried and failed? Or just chosen to put careers first?

Beverly helped her clear the table for pie and coffee. As though she'd read Teresa's mind, Beverly said suddenly, when they were briefly alone in the kitchen, "I don't want to make a general announcement, but I think I'm pregnant."

"That's wonderful!" Teresa set down the dirty plates and gave her a hug. "George knows, I presume?"

"Nope, not even George. I'm not positive, and I don't want to raise his hopes until I am. We've been trying for years, you know."

"No, I didn't know. You've never said, and I hated to ask. I figured if you wanted to talk about it, you would."

"If only my mother had half the sensitivity." She grimaced. "Actually, George and I waited until I was thirty—I wanted to get to a certain point in my career before I took time off. Once we decided the moment had come, I just assumed I'd get pregnant. When it didn't happen right away, it didn't seem like a big deal. I mean, we were both busy. But after two years, we went for testing. The doctors tell us there's absolutely nothing wrong. But we've been trying now for five years. Can you believe it? I'm just praying this isn't a false alarm."

"I'll add my prayers." Teresa glanced over her shoulder when she heard voices nearing. "You'll let me know?" she asked quickly.

"Are you kidding? I'll trumpet it to the world."

Teresa was just cutting the pumpkin pie when the doorbell rang. Nicole and Mark raced to get it.

"It's Joe!" Mark yelled. "And somebody's with him."

"Shush!" Nicole snapped. "They'll hear you." She apparently opened the door decorously. "Hello, Mr. Hughes. Hi, Alan."

"Is this the nephew?" Beverly whispered.

Teresa nodded and hurried to meet them. Joe appeared in the doorway before she reached it. Instead of kissing her, he nodded. "I hope you don't mind my bringing Alan."

"Don't be silly," she said warmly. "Joe, I'd like you to meet some old friends of mine."

"I object to the 'old,'" George said, grinning as he stood to extend a hand to Joe.

"If you weren't balding..." his wife contributed.

"'Old' was just a figure of speech," Teresa said.

"Probably a balding one," he muttered.

Everyone was laughing by the time Teresa managed introductions.

Teresa cut two more pieces of pie. She'd left room at the long table for Joe, and Nicole produced another chair for Alan. Cream and sugar made the rounds. Teresa complimented Beverly on the pumpkin pie and tried to think of some innocuous topic for conversation.

George forestalled her. "Teresa tells us you're a logger."

"That's right."

Joe *sounded* no more than polite; was he feeling defensive? Teresa couldn't tell.

"I gather timber prices just shot up with the latest environmental legislation. Is that affecting you?"

"Only in that I can pay more for timber and make more. The mills are hungry right now, and they'll take anything they can get. I expect to see some go out of business."

"Where do you stand on these issues?" Beverly asked, looking interested. "Are you with the rest of the timber industry?"

"No, actually I'm not, assuming there's any common ground at all." Joe set down his fork and leaned forward. "Partly it's because my self-interest isn't necessarily the same as the big outfits that are logging national forest land. In fact, I tend to profit when they're suffering. But I'd be opposed to stripping old-growth forests, anyway. Common sense says if we had a free hand, we'd cut it all down within a very few years. Then we'd be right where we are now, and the old-growth forests would be gone forever."

George arched his brows. "That's an unusual stance for someone in your profession."

Joe met his gaze calmly. "I know others who would agree with me. We aren't all taking potshots at spotted owls."

Conversation moved on. Joe asked what they did for a living. Then George edified everyone at the table with a description of a video game he was dreaming up on his own time.

"It sounds cool!" Mark said enthusiastically.

"He's just complimenting me because I whipped him at Ghost Rider."

Beverly stuck an elbow in his ribs. "At your age, I wouldn't brag about your skill at some silly game."

"Silly game!" he and Mark exclaimed as one. With help from Teresa's son, George began a learned discourse on why video games were fine training grounds for young scholars and athletes. They sharpened reflexes and encouraged creative thinking, if he was to be believed. "And," he added smugly, "if a kid is good enough, he can grow up and design software like I do and make piles of money."

"Yeah!" Mark declared, then shoveled in a last bite of pie and mumbled around it, "That's what I want to do."

"I thought you wanted to be a paleontologist," his mother said.

"I could design software about dinosaurs. Or maybe stuff that would help paleontologists find the bones. You know, like in *Jurassic Park.*"

Teresa laughed. "Why not?"

Of course, then they had to discuss the sequel to Jurassic Park, and whether the book had been too obviously written as a movie script with a little description thrown in.

When Beverly looked at Joe, he shook his head. "I haven't read it."

"Not a Crichton fan, eh?" George asked.

"No."

"What do you read?"

Teresa tensed, but Joe's expression didn't change. "I'm not much of a reader."

She smiled brightly. "He's taken up cow penning. It looks exciting."

His gaze flicked to her, enigmatic. After an odd little pause, he drawled, "It'd be a little less exciting if I could stay on the horse. Sometimes I think I'm crazy to take up something like that at my age."

"But that's how you stay young." Beverly gestured grandly. "You age when you're plodding along in the same old rut."

George ran a hand over his high forehead. "You mean, the hair would *all* be gone if I hadn't tried bungee jumping?"

"You didn't!" Teresa exclaimed.

"Damn right I did. Bev wouldn't join me. That's why she has to dye her hair to cover up the gray."

This time, his wife punched him in the ribs in earnest. While they were still wrestling, Joe decided it was time to go. Teresa couldn't help wondering if he wasn't making his escape before he was put on the spot again.

Alan went reluctantly. Teresa walked them out after the general goodbyes, but Joe did no more than drop a brief kiss on her lips before he got in his pickup, slammed the door and backed out.

Although the late afternoon was chilly, Teresa stood in the yard for a moment, watching him go. She thought the hour had gone pretty well. Beverly and George had liked him, she could tell. She'd worried about nothing.

Yes, but weren't they close enough friends that she'd end up telling them eventually? Why hadn't she, just as under other circumstances she'd have mentioned that Joe was diabetic and couldn't eat the pie?

Maybe because she wasn't sure Joe would want her to. He might consider it his private business. Look how long he'd taken to tell her. On the other hand, Teresa thought, he might assume she was ashamed of him if she was too careful not to mention his dyslexia.

In fact, had he already decided she was ashamed just because she'd changed the subject so quickly the second someone asked him about his reading?

She was starting to trip over her own thoughts. Would he, wouldn't he? Should she, shouldn't she?

What if she invited George and Beverly up again soon? Or wanted Joe to go with her when she met them for dinner in Seattle? There were plenty of things they might talk about that he wouldn't be able to contribute to. Would he hate that? If he sat there silent, would she be self-conscious?

Would—

Forget it! she told herself. It would all work out. She'd ask Joe what he preferred. She'd ask so matter-of-factly he couldn't accuse her of being embarrassed about his problem.

Next time she saw him, Teresa vowed. It had been hard to raise the subject last time, but if they couldn't talk comfortably about Joe's dyslexia and what it meant to both of them, it would become this yawning hole they both tiptoed around.

And Teresa preferred to set her feet firmly on the ground.

CHAPTER TWELVE

AT THE VERY TOP of the aluminum extension ladder, Joe leaned carefully to his right. The string of lights was still an inch from the hook. He stretched just a little farther and settled the string over the rusting hook at the peak of the roof.

Thank God it was already there; otherwise, he'd have to be pounding nails in, too. He didn't mind climbing trees, never had, even though topping them could be considered a dangerous occupation. But he hated ladders. They were too damn flimsy. Teresa's firm grip on the bottom of this one didn't reassure him. Holding on might make her feel better, but if the ladder started to slide sideways with his two hundred pounds at the top, she could no more stop it than he could win a spelling bee.

Still, she'd been determined to put up Christmas lights on her old house, and better him up here than her. He winced just thinking of her thirty feet above the ground, gaily singing carols as she hung out over space.

The next couple of hooks were within easier reach. One more stretch, and it was time to move the ladder. Again.

He climbed down, claimed a kiss to fortify himself and shifted the ladder five feet toward the corner of the house. As he climbed it again, Teresa was talking, more to herself than him, he deduced.

"Maybe I'll buy another string or two. They'd be pretty in the small cedar." A pause, then musingly, "Maybe those twinkling white ones. No. Red!"

The "small" cedar was almost as tall as her house, but not big enough for him to scale. It'd be the ladder again. Joe groaned to himself. Who'd have guessed she'd be almost as Christmas mad as his sister Rebecca? He'd bet his last dollar that Sam was climbing ladders today, too. Just like Teresa, Rebecca believed in getting those lights up the second Thanksgiving was decently laid to rest. Joe didn't know why they bothered to wait. Why not put 'em up in September? The stores were already sucking in susceptible Christmas shoppers almost before the kids were back in school. And if this was September, his fingers wouldn't be threatened with frostbite.

He enjoyed Christmas Day itself. He wasn't any Scrooge. The family closeness was always reassuring, and exchanging presents was fine, although it had been more fun when his nieces and nephews were still of an age to want toys. Now he had to guess what teenagers wore/read/listened to, and who the hell understood them?

But Teresa was prepared to revel in every moment of Christmas tradition. The lights went up this morning; this afternoon, they were going to the Santa Claus parade. He was pretty sure Mark didn't still believe in Santa, which meant they were going to freeze their butts off just to wave at Ed Hardecker, the pharmacist, dressed up in red flannel. But Joe didn't mind, if it made her happy. Her happiness drew him, as though she were a small flame over which he was warming his hands.

When he finally put the extension ladder away, Teresa plugged in the multiple strings of lights, and Mark and Nicole came out to join them in gazing at the house, made festive. Winter hadn't officially arrived, it being only the second of December, but you couldn't tell by the weather. The thermometer read twenty-nine degrees, and frost clung to branches and the grass where the weak sunlight hadn't touched. Teresa was bundled in sweater, hat and gloves, but her nose was as red as those lights she wanted to put in the cedar. Unlike some women, she looked cute with rosy cheeks and nose.

Or maybe he was prejudiced.

They'd had dinner last night and gone to his place afterward. She couldn't stay long, she'd warned him, but the countdown to a climax hadn't taken either of them even as much time as she'd allowed. She pushed all his buttons, and apparently he did the same to hers. All he had to do was look at her, and he wanted to be between her legs.

He shifted a little uncomfortably and turned his attention back to the house, still painted white, although Teresa swore that, come spring, it would be russet rose or lemon yellow or pine-forest green or some other fancy color. She changed her mind every day. Mark liked pine forest, Nicole winter blue-gray. Joe seemed to remember voting for sandstone tan with teal trim.

A couple of times he'd let himself think that this house would never be painted, that by spring Teresa would be wearing a wedding ring and living in his house. Probably painting his house, currently stained cedar. But he didn't let the picture form often; he still didn't quite believe she really meant it when she assured him that his dyslexia wasn't any different than her tendency to get lost. Everyone had strengths and weaknesses, she said. Her feelings for him hadn't changed just because she now knew he wasn't perfect.

Perfect. It was almost laughable.

The kids were racing around the yard now, the dogs barking after them. Laughing, Teresa snagged Mark, whirled him away from Nicole, then took off, both kids after her. The laughter had a clear ring in the cold air. Joe stood watching with his hands in his pockets, a sense of unreality gripping him. The scene was too much like a painting on a Christmas card: lights sparkling on a white farmhouse with a deep front porch, dark evergreens, the bright splash of sweaters and parkas as Teresa and her kids played. Family. Home. And he was part of the picture.

Funny that Teresa never mentioned getting lost, while she wanted to talk incessantly about his disability. Why could he read numbers and not letters? What had they tried in school? Would he be embarrassed if she told people? And on and on.

Joe understood that she'd have questions. He tried to hide his discomfort with the whole thing. Damn it, he didn't want to talk about it! The fact that he wasn't like other people, couldn't do something so basic to their lives, he pushed out of his mind as much as possible.

Teresa's probing was starting to make him dwell on his failure, and he didn't like it.

He drew in a long breath of cold air and let it out with a sigh.

"Deep thoughts?"

Startled, he blinked to find that Teresa, red-cheeked and bright-eyed, was standing right in front of him, head cocked to one side like an inquisitive cat.

"Oh, yeah," he said. "My thoughts are always deep."

Her laughing eyes told him she knew a joke when she heard one. But at the same time, she tucked her hand in the crook of his arm and raised her voice, "We're going to be late if we don't get a move on."

Mark dodged behind her, avoiding his sister's feints. "Yeah, I want to be in front, in case anybody throws candy. The guys at school said you can get tons at parades."

"Mostly the Fourth of July one," Joe said. "This is smaller." Actually, he wasn't positive. He hadn't been to the Santa Claus parade. It was one of those things parents and kids did. He felt a little funny about going, as though he was a fraud. The hero worship in Mark's eyes when he looked at Joe sometimes made him feel the same way. What happened when the boy found out he couldn't read? Talk about feet of clay.

The sidewalks lining the main street weren't as packed as they were for the Fourth of July, but a surprising number had turned out, considering how bitingly cold the day was. The atmosphere was cheerful; the older folks sat on folding chairs while the kids perched on the curb at their feet. Most every store had Christmas lights on. The lampposts were wrapped like candy canes. A policeman rode up and down the street on his ten-speed. Peters' Furniture was giving away red, green and white helium balloons, which children held clumsily in mittened hands. In the clear winter day, the mountains seemed to rear right over the town.

A steady stream of people stopped to say hello to Joe or Teresa. Half-a-dozen people smiled and said something to her like, "You were right, that medicine did the trick. You should have seen Leo tear up a tree yesterday as if he'd never been hurt." Even those who'd known Joe his whole life were polite enough not to show what an odd pairing they thought he and the vet made, but Joe was conscious of being on display. Some of them must have been marveling.

The parade started right on time. It wasn't all that different from the one on the Fourth of July. Just shorter. A couple of logging trucks led it, horns blasting. Fire districts sent their red and yellow engines and tanker trucks, the firemen making everybody jump by sounding the siren every block or so. Two floats were designed by local Christmas-tree farms. Horses pranced and puffed out clouds of steam, more rising from their flanks. The high school marching band played carols that sounded more ragged than usual, thanks to frozen fingers. At the very end, Santa drove a sleigh mounted on old car axles and pulled by Clydesdales, with their huge hooves and feathered white legs. Everybody clapped and cheered and whistled.

And the candy flew. Mark's buddies were right. Loggers and firemen tossed it out the truck windows. Santa flung handfuls from his bag. Even Nicole let herself be childish, dodging out to snare her share.

Walking the half mile home afterward, Teresa teased her kids and snatched a few pieces of wrapped candy from their bulging pockets. In those seconds, Joe walked alone, feeling oddly isolated. The feeling went away the moment Teresa reached for his gloved hand again.

He was disconcerted—or maybe scared was a more accurate word—by how much he had come to depend on her warmth and smiles and kisses. Life hadn't seemed all that empty before he met her. Okay, there were moments here and there: seeing a family go by, the toddler riding on Daddy's shoulders; watching a romantic movie—alone; Rebecca's wedding to Sam.

This last had hit him hard, because he could see how much in love they were, and because Sam reminded Joe of himself in some ways. Sam had been pushing forty, too, and had never been married. Joe remembered the first time Rebecca dragged Sam to a family dinner, how reserved he was, how lonely even when surrounded by all the Hugheses. At Rebecca's wedding, Joe had suddenly, fiercely, wanted what Sam had found: a woman who loved him enough to claw her way over the walls that set him apart.

When Teresa rose on tiptoe just then for no particular reason and kissed him on the cheek, Joe thought maybe he had gotten that lucky.

So why couldn't he just accept it? Why was he waiting for the other shoe to drop?

Today he had an obvious reason. He and Teresa, at her insistence, were having dinner with an attorney and his wife. They were newcomers to town, like Teresa. It was natural she'd become friends with them. It was equally natural that he hadn't. Normally the only way Joe would have rubbed up against an attorney was if he dropped a tree on someone's house and was being sued.

But thanks to the woman who had just kissed him, he was having dinner with someone else who had enough college degrees to make him feel about two feet tall. And there wasn't any way in the world he could get out of it. Teresa mixed happily and willingly with his friends. He owed her as much in return, even if he had to fake it.

He went home to change clothes and came back to pick up Teresa. They were eating here in town, at the Mexican restaurant where he'd taken her on their first date. She spent the short drive assuring him he'd like the new couple.

"I think Jordan said something about having horses. Maybe he's interested in cow penning."

Maybe, Joe thought, but more likely he did dressage or show jumping or something else that fit his place in society. He carefully didn't mention his skepticism. Teresa would have—rightly—chewed him out for stereotyping someone he'd never even met.

The couple were already at the restaurant. Joe's mental picture of Jordan was immediately demolished when the man, dressed in baggy cords and a rumpled sports shirt, rose to his full six-five and extended a big meaty hand.

"Teresa tells me you're the brains and money behind Hughes Logging," he said heartily.

"Makes me sound grander than I am," Joe said, "but that's essentially true. I'm some of the muscle, too."

"Let me introduce my wife," Jordan said. "Megan, meet Joe Hughes."

His wife must have been nearly six feet herself and was model thin. But unlike Teresa's Thanksgiving friend, who'd worn enough jewelry and makeup to buckle a strong man's knees, this one didn't appear to give a damn about clothing or any other feminine art. She wore something shapeless and tan, belted at the waist, and her hair was carelessly bundled up on the back of her head. No makeup; freckles sprinkled her nose and her lips were pale. But her gray eyes were friendly, her smile warm, and Joe relaxed infinitesimally.

She was an artist, Jordan explained. A potter. "I'm pretty sure," he added fondly, "that Megan always wears clay-colored clothes so she can foot a pot on her way out for the evening without worrying if she gets some slip on her sleeves."

"My secret's out," she agreed amiably.

They ordered and in the lull afterward used corn chips to scoop up the salsa while they chatted.

Jordan, it turned out, had two quarter horses; so much for stereotypes. One was for Megan, who was willing to go on trail rides so long as her husband promised not to move faster than a lazy rocking canter. When Jordan found out that Joe cow penned, he sat up straighter. "I've always wanted to give that a try. Any chance I could join you sometime?"

"No problem. I'll call you."

"Will I be the only beginner?"

Joe had to grin at that. "I'm a real amateur myself. So are half-a-dozen others. If you don't mind a laugh at your expense, you'll be right at home."

Inevitably the conversation worked its way around to education—Jordan and his wife had two kids in the school system. They were unhappy with the physical state of the high school.

"Why the hell hasn't a bond issue to build a new one passed?"

"Recession," Joe said. "This is a logging town, and the industry is depressed. People don't want to increase their taxes."

"All the more reason to make sure the kids get a good education. Logging will never revive to the point where kids can count on growing up and working side by side with their fathers."

"I agree," Joe said mildly. "I have a niece and two nephews at the high school right now. They're all college-bound."

"Where did you go, Joe?" Jordan asked.

Just like that, Joe tensed. Beside him, he felt Teresa stir.

"I didn't go to college. I started logging summers when I was in high school and made such good money I never thought of doing anything else."

He immediately despised himself. He hadn't flat out lied, but he'd sure implied that he could have gone to college if logging hadn't beckoned. He should have admitted he was dyslexic. He was a gutless wonder.

Megan was nodding seriously. "I didn't, either. I was lucky to have a wonderful art teacher in high school, and once I'd earned enough with summer jobs to buy my own wheel and kiln, I started selling my work. I think potting is all instinct. You've got the touch or you don't."

"Whereas any idiot can become a lawyer. Just has to go to school long enough," her husband said cheerfully.

Any idiot who can read a book. Joe gritted his teeth.

"Becoming a veterinarian takes memory more than anything," Teresa said. "They shove so much at you—chemistry, anatomy, pharmacology, symptoms, diseases. It's overwhelming the first year."

Joe let himself relax again, though he had a sour taste in his mouth left by his cowardice.

But his relaxation was premature, he discovered, because the next thing the other three were talking about was books. What they'd read, hadn't read. Reviews, journals, newspaper articles. Maybe he was imagining it, but Joe thought Teresa was being unnaturally vivacious, filling every gap in the conversation before it could be used to question him.

He sat silent, the kernel of anger in his chest swelling. He didn't even know who he was angry at. Her? Himself? Fate? Or maybe it wasn't anger at all, but shame, an emotion that cut just as deep.

A pause came; Teresa opened her mouth to speak. Joe overrode her, his voice too loud. "I'm dyslexic. I have to wait for the book to come out as a movie."

They all stared at him. Was the anxiety in Teresa's eyes for him, or for the hideous social situation he'd created? Neither the attorney nor his wife seemed to know what to say. Hell, what could they say?

Megan was the first to speak. Softly she said, "That must be difficult. I don't read that much myself. I'd rather be working at the wheel. But day-to-day life seems to require a huge amount of reading."

He felt the dark flush on his cheeks. "I get around it."

"You've done damn well despite dyslexia," Jordan said. Joe couldn't decide whether his tone was patronizing or not.

"I do all right," he said curtly.

"You must."

End of conversation. Nobody asked whether Joe could read the newspaper headlines, or how he'd gotten his driver's license or ran his business. The other couple were either lacking in curiosity or were sensitive to his misery.

Books weren't mentioned again. Jordan admitted his practice was still in the red; he'd mostly done wills so far. They talked about how Megan made the rounds of crafts fairs in the summer, the exorbitant cut galleries took, her impatience with the necessity of repeating the same pieces.

"I hate to turn down special orders," she said, shaking her head, "but usually customers want something identical to other work I've done, just in a different color. I get bored easily."

Her husband gave her a lopsided grin. "Megan hates the necessity of making a living. It threatens her artistic integrity."

"But I can understand her feelings," Teresa said immediately. "Even in my line of work, I like variety. Low-cost neutering clinics are important, but I'd go nuts performing the same surgery over and over. Never being faced with a challenge."

Megan poked an elbow at her husband. "Even Jordan likes a challenge. We moved here to open a practice because he was so bored with the work he got stuck with when he was but a lowly member of a giant firm."

"The secretaries did more interesting work than I did," he grumbled, but not very seriously.

Joe didn't say anything. He had never been more cripplingly aware of how circumscribed his life was. Had he become bored with his work? He'd never let himself consider the possibility. He couldn't do anything else. Yeah, it provided minor challenges, but not the kind these people would understand. His were physical or financial, theirs artistic and intellectual. Another brick in the wall between them.

Nobody seemed to expect him to contribute to the conversation. He had the uncomfortable feeling that now all three were conspiring to keep silences from stretching out. They spoke too quickly, too brightly, never looking expectantly at him.

His relief was almost painful when the waiter cleared the table and presented the bill. He and Jordan argued briefly and agreed to split the total. They made their way toward the door, the two women with their heads together. Just outside, Jordan held out a hand.

"Good to meet you, Joe. Don't forget to call sometime about the cow penning."

"I won't." He shook the other man's hand, surprised to feel a few calluses on it.

Teresa hugged both, then let herself be helped into Joe's pickup. Once he circled it and got in, too, she said with forced vivacity, "Well, did you like them?"

"They were all right." He knew he sounded sullen, ungracious. Damn it, they *were* nice people; they just weren't his kind.

"You didn't like them." Her disappointment came through loud and clear.

"That's not what I said."

"But it's what you meant."

Oh, hell, they were having a fight. The street was well enough lit for him to see that Teresa's chin was up, her eyes glittering.

Tension gripped his neck and shoulders. "No, that's not what I meant."

She didn't listen. "You don't like Jordan because he's a lawyer. You wouldn't have liked him no matter what."

"I have nothing to say to someone like him."

"You've always had plenty to say to me."

"Have I?" he asked quietly.

"All right," she snapped, "now what are you implying?"

"Maybe sexual attraction has put blinders on both of us." He felt like a bastard the minute the words were out. It wasn't what he really feared: what if attraction had put blinders on *her?* What if one day she rolled over in bed and realized she'd just had sex with a big dumb logger? He squeezed the steering wheel so hard his fingers ached.

Now she'd blast him. Tell him where he could go and meantime where she never wanted to see him again: her house and her bed.

The silence stretched on. He shifted gears unnecessarily. He had to look at her. A traffic light ahead turned yellow and then red, giving him the chance. They were leaving the street lamps behind, so her eyes were shadowed but her mouth was soft.

"You're wrong." Her voice came out as gently as an autumn leaf falling. "I see the man I'm lucky enough to be with. Even if he is dense about a few things."

"Dumb is the word I would have used." His jaw muscles ached.

"Okay, dumb."

Shock stabbed at his chest to hear her agree in that soft sweet voice.

"There's nothing wrong with your brain," she continued, "except a little malfunction where reading is concerned. And so what? You get by just fine as you are. No, the thing you're dumb about is yourself. You're so sure you're worthless, nobody can convince you otherwise, can they? I sure can't seem to."

He heard her from a distance, the words only slowly penetrating. She wasn't saying what he'd feared; of course she wasn't. Even if she thought it, she wouldn't say it.

"I know my worth," he said hoarsely.

"Do you?"

"I'm good at what I do. I'm not bad-looking."

She laughed, took off her seat belt and scooted across the bench seat to his side. Her lips brushed his jaw, and one of her hands was— Good God, what was she doing? Suddenly more than his neck was tightening up.

"Go on," she murmured.

He cleared his throat. "People seem to like me well enough."

"You have a good sense of direction," she suggested.

"I know where your house is," he croaked. She had his jeans unzipped and her hand right inside. He now had a pretty good idea what she was doing. He wasn't *that* dumb. He just hoped like hell she wasn't going to zip him back up—assuming that was humanly possible—kiss him good-night in front of her house and leave him to suffer.

He didn't have to worry. She nibbled at his ear and whispered, "I bet you know a good place to park. A private place."

"Anybody ever tell you you're brazen?"

She pulled her hand back. "Am I shocking you?" Genuine anxiety underlaid her light tone.

He turned the pickup onto a dead-end road he knew. His crew had done some work here just a month or so ago.

"Oh, yeah," Joe said. "Can't you tell how much you've shocked me?"

Her small hand tested him experimentally. "I see what you mean." Her voice was a little huskier than usual and sexier than hell.

They passed one house, its porch light shining out of the darkness. The road dwindled to gravel and finally to rutted mud. He slammed on the brakes, backed into a turnaround overhung with vine maples that were surrounded by smaller fir and hemlock and shut off the engine.

In the new silence, he asked, "Private enough for you?"

"I think this'll do." Her mouth was exploring his jaw and ear again.

This time he turned his head to meet her. She'd worked him to a fever pitch, and if she wanted sweet and slow, she was out of luck. He took her mouth, his tongue plunging hard and fast. She sighed and melted against him, wax softened by the heat. He wanted her that way, soft and pliable. He tore her shirt open; she moaned and reached for her own bra clasp. Her breasts spilled into his hands, and he squeezed.

His mind fogged. A frightening urgency gripped him. Somehow he'd fallen to his knees on the floor of the passenger side. He lifted her skirt, one of those gauzy calf-length jobs. Her thighs were smooth. No panty hose, thank God. His mouth hadn't even left hers, and he was yanking her panties off, yanking his own jeans down. She whimpered and arched, breasts pale in what little moonlight fell through the windshield.

Joe lifted his head long enough to part her legs and drive into her in one powerful thrust that lifted her hips. Her fingernails bit into his shoulders as she held on while he rode her with brutal passion. Her breath was sobbing out, his as harsh as if he was outrunning a widow maker. In. Out. She felt so damned good. Her ankles locked behind his back, she clenched, gripping him so hard he had to fight her to withdraw. He was swearing, things coming out of his mouth he'd barely thought before. When her ripples started, they wrenched him into spasms that had him gutturally crying out. He'd never felt anything like this. Never been ripped open until his heart was exposed, and it felt better than anything ever had.

She was crying out his name at the same time, as though in it was her salvation. He heard wonder and desperation and love. She'd wanted and needed this as much as he had.

The night air cooled him quickly. He went from the peak of Mt. Olympus to his knees on the floor of his pickup cab. Her legs had relaxed and she lay on the seat like a rag doll, her breasts showing white and her skirt bunched around her waist.

There was nothing much more foolish than a man with his pants around his ankles—or his knees. It was hard to cuddle a woman the way you would in bed, and rest her head on your shoulder and tell her how beautiful she was, when your shirttails were framing a part of you that suddenly wasn't so impressive.

He didn't move for a second, unsure what to do. Pull his pants up? Tell her she'd made him happier than he'd ever expected to be?

What came out was a rough, "Did I hurt you?"

Her voice was breathy. "If you did, I didn't care. Don't care."

He swore under his breath. "I had about as much self-control as a fifteen-year-old boy his first time."

Her eyes opened at last, he could see that much, though he wasn't sure what expression they held. Her mouth had a wistful curve. "You know what a woman dreams about where her man is concerned?"

"No. I guess I don't."

"She dreams about being the one woman who can shred his control. She wants to see him so desperate for her he loses it completely."

His heart cramped, just a sharp moment of pain/ecstasy to remind him that he still wasn't sure of her.

"I guess I gave you that," he said.

"Yes, you did. And it was sweet."

Sweet. Oh, yeah, it was that all right.

"You getting a little chilly?" he asked awkwardly.

"I may never get chilly again," Teresa murmured in a voice that sounded on the edge of sleep.

"Well, unless you want to do it again..."

"I don't think I could," she said, but on a rising note, as though she was giving it some thought.

He gave it a little, too, but he never had believed in anticlimaxes.

A pun. It amused him, maybe because he was slap-happy. Or just happy. He realized that he had never felt this way before—actively happy, versus contented.

He also felt somewhat less foolish once he got his jeans up. In the dark he couldn't find her panties, which made her giggle, but he fastened her bra and gently eased her skirt down. He even buckled her seat belt, since she made no move to do so.

Then he drove her home, steered her to her own door and unlocked it for her, kissed her good-night and headed on to his own place. He didn't suffer at all.

CHAPTER THIRTEEN

"HOW COME YOU CAN'T read?"

Mark's question was followed by an appalled silence. Nicole could hardly believe her ears. Hadn't Mom taught Mark *anything?* Talk about rude!

They were all in the car—Mom and Joe in front, Nicole and her stupid little brother in back—on their way to pick out a Christmas tree. Mark had been pelting Joe with questions about logging. *He* wanted to cut down the tree today all by himself. Joe had been explaining about leaving a few inches of trunk so the tree could grow again, and demonstrating how to use a crosscut saw. He seemed surprised that they'd never actually cut down their own tree before. Everyone Nicole knew in Bellevue either had an artificial tree or went to a lot where the noble and grand firs were already nailed to wooden stands and you simply bought the prettiest one.

Nicole had just been thinking this might be fun, especially since it had snowed yesterday and enough had stuck to make the ground a frosty white.

Then, all of a sudden, Mark just blurted it out: *How come you can't read?*

Joe had his head turned, so Nicole could see his face in profile when he flinched. Her stomach flipped over. He hadn't known their mother had told them. From the way he was looking at Mom, it was obvious he wasn't happy.

The silence was charged enough for Mark to get the message. He shrank back in his corner and shut up.

Mom said in a fake-calm voice, "Mark, it's rude to ask personal questions."

No kidding.

"That's all right." Joe sounded as lifelike as a chunk of wood. His face was expressionless. It must have been hard for him to say matter-of-factly, "I just don't see the words the same way most people do. Letters crowd together or they change places, so I'm seeing them backward."

Of course, her brother figured that because Joe had answered at all, it must mean asking in the first place was okay. "Can't you just get glasses?"

Didn't he *listen?* Mom had told him!

"Afraid not." Joe still sounded stiff. "My problem isn't really my eyes. It's the part of my brain that processes what my eyes are telling it. That can't be fixed so easily."

"Do you see everything else backward?" Naturally Mark wouldn't let it go. "Like, Nicole's sitting on this side of the car and I'm on the other side?"

"No. Most things I'm okay with. Some people who are dyslexic get left and right confused and have trouble with fine motor coordination—they might fumble buttoning their shirts. Or they might not follow directions very well—they can't seem to remember them in the right order. Problems vary."

"Oh." Mark lapsed into silence just long enough for Nicole to start to relax. Then he said confidently, "But it doesn't matter to you, does it? I mean, not being able to read."

"Doesn't matter?" Joe's voice had frozen now. "Why wouldn't it matter?"

Mark squirmed. "Well, because... I mean, loggers don't have to read, do they?"

"Of course they have to read!" Nicole turned on her brother, her tone blistering. "Everybody has to! Gol, you can't go to the grocery store or pay taxes, or...or *anything* if you can't read! It must be really hard, so don't be so dumb!"

Her cheeks were flushed with anger. Or maybe embarrassment. Had she made things worse? Defiantly she met her mother's gaze in the rearview mirror. She couldn't tell if Mom approved or not.

"'Dumb' isn't my favorite word in the whole world," Joe said, sounding odd. "But you're right. It is hard. It used to be worse, before I...adjusted. And I'm lucky I have a way of making a living that doesn't require a college degree or writing letters or doing research. If I'd been bad at math, too, I'd still be working for someone else, instead of having my own business. Estimating timber value and costs can be pretty complex."

He said the last part the way Nicole said something she knew her mother wouldn't believe. Like he had to defend himself, but he was already sure they'd think he was dumb. A couple of months ago, she would have. She'd been shocked enough that her mother was dating some logger. If she'd known he couldn't read, she would have used it as ammunition to convince her mother they didn't belong here.

Why was it different now? She frowned, staring out the car window into a forest so tall and dark hardly any snow had filtered to the ferns beneath. Partly it was different now because she had started to kind of like Joe. He'd helped them put up the Christmas lights and explained the algebra she didn't get and had a snowball fight with Mark yesterday. He was okay. Having him around was . . . well, cool. It felt right.

She'd gotten used to White Horse, too. She didn't know how she'd feel if Mom suddenly announced they were going back to Bellevue. She'd had fun last weekend with Jayne, but it hadn't been the same as it used to be. She'd felt like a visitor. She *was* a visitor. And there were things she liked about it here. Her dance classes were not as strict as at her last dance school but more fun. And Ariana was nice, and so were some of the other kids. And then there was Alan—

"Are we almost there?" Mark was bouncing up and down in excitement, as though no one's Christmas spirits had been squashed. He had the sensitivity of . . . of one of those black-and-white cows the school bus went by every day.

The forest ended as abruptly as if someone had drawn a line with a ruler, and now the car was passing a snowy field of wispy trees only a couple of feet tall. Douglas Fir, a sign said. On the other side of the gravel road, the trees were larger and their branches stiffer. They passed field after field, all labeled. In each, the trees were planted in rows, all exactly the same height. Finally Mom turned the car into a slushy muddy parking lot that was probably grassy in the summer. There must have been close to a hundred cars already here.

Even though she'd worn boots, Nicole said, "Yuck," as she got out and sank ankle-deep through a thin crust of ice. They all put on their gloves and coats and hats, and Joe carried the saw. When Nicole looked around, she could see flashes of color between trees in every direction: bright-colored parkas and hats and snowsuits. People were wandering through the fields of Christmas trees trying to find the perfect one.

"Do you know what kind you want?" Joe asked.

"A tall one." Mom's nose and cheeks were already pink from the cold air. "Not a Douglas fir. I hate sheared trees. A noble or grand, I guess."

Mom *always* wanted a tree that turned out to be too tall for their ceiling. But Joe, who didn't know that, only nodded. "Let's pick up a map that shows what's growing where."

Across from the parking lot, Christmas lights were strung along the eave of a long shed where you were supposed to take your tree once you'd cut it down. Watching, Nicole saw the people who worked here measuring the trees, then bundling them in burlap so they could be tied on the cars. You paid by the foot; Mom was going to be really sorry when she got her tree home, found out it was too tall and had to cut off five or ten dollars' worth.

They sold other stuff here, too: wreaths and holly swags and ornaments. Following the good smells, Nicole discovered you could buy coffee and cocoa and some kind of hot spiced cider, too.

While Mom and Joe studied the crude sketch of the fields, Mark was looking at the ornaments. With tiny price tags stuck to them, they hung along a clothesline.

"Hey, Mom!" He grabbed her sleeve and tugged. "Can I have this one? Look, it's really cool. See? It's a logger, like Joe."

Carved out of wood, it *was* pretty cute. You could even see the seams in his blue jeans and the laces on his big chunky boots and the head of the ax he carried slung over his shoulder.

"It does look like Joe." Mom was laughing. "He even has blue eyes. Sure. Let's have them hold it for us while we go pick out our tree."

Nicole was waiting for them when she heard someone call her name. "Hey, Nicole!"

She turned and her heart stuttered. Alan was loping toward her, looking even bigger than usual in a blue parka.

"Hey," he said again, stopping in front of her. He was breathing hard, like he'd really hurried.

"Hi," she said. "What are you doing here?"

"Mom and I came to pick out a tree."

"Not your dad? I mean, your stepdad?"

"Nah, he had to work. Hi, Uncle Joe. Mrs. Burkett." He exchanged high fives with Mark.

Joe's face was solemn, but his eyes were smiling. "So, you sold your mother on it."

Alan gave Nicole a sidelong nervous look. "Yeah," he said like it was no big deal, "she wanted to get a tree today, too. She said Sam would have to live with it."

Joe shook his head. "Bad move."

Alan grinned. "He told me I could control her. We figured she's not going to get down on the ground and saw the tree herself, right? So I just refuse unless I approve."

Nicole was finally getting it. "You mean, your mother likes big ones, too?"

"I wish." Alan made a face. "She always picks out some really ugly stunted tree she feels sorry for. You wouldn't believe some of the trees we've had."

Rebecca came puffing up. Her stomach had gotten a lot bigger since October. Probably none of her coats fit, which explained why she was wearing a sweater that had to be Sam's, with the sleeves rolled up about ten times.

"Hi, everyone." She had this twinkle in her eyes. "I wish I could say this is a surprise, but the truth is, my son dragged me out of the house and said we absolutely had to get a tree today. I sort of had a suspicion why."

Everyone smiled except Mark, who looked puzzled and Alan, who was glaring at his mother. Nicole really did get it now.

He'd wanted to come today because she was here! He liked her! *Yes!* she thought, even as she blushed.

Yeah, but if he liked her, why hadn't he asked her out since the second time they'd gone horseback riding? It had been *weeks!*

Joe took pity on them. "Shall we get on with it?" he suggested.

Somehow they ended up in pairs, Joe and Mark in the lead, Alan and Nicole next, and Mom and Rebecca straggling in the rear. Nicole kept her gaze fixed ahead. Her brother was swaggering along in imitation of Joe's loose-hipped walk. Mark was talking nonstop, too, like he always did when he wasn't watching TV or playing Nintendo.

"I want to be a logger like you," he announced. "You can be outside and climb humungous trees and fly helicopters and even drive a logging truck."

Nicole couldn't hear what Joe said, but she could see he was being patient. He probably didn't mind too much. Everyone liked to be admired.

Nicole sneaked a glance sideways. When she met Alan's eyes, she looked shyly away.

"Did you have fun at your friend's house in Bellevue?"

"You knew about that?" she asked in surprise.

"Yeah, somebody mentioned it." He paused. "I had to go to my dad's last weekend. I'd have rather done something with you."

All her unhappiness whooshed away, as if he'd unclogged a drain. She smiled at him.

"Hey, look at those trees!" He veered off, grabbing her hand and pulling her after him. They were quickly out of sight of the others, although another family was up ahead, the man down on his knees sawing awkwardly while his wife and kids watched. Alan zigzagged to the next row of trees. The second they were all alone, surrounded by greenery, he stopped so suddenly Nicole bumped into him.

At first she thought Alan had grabbed her shoulders because he was afraid she was going to fall. But the next thing she knew, he'd bent his head and was kissing her. His lips were cold—probably hers were, too. But warmth surged through her, as if she'd swallowed some of that hot spiced cider. Except this was better.

It was over in a second—she was *really* blushing now, and Alan was smiling at her. Just in time. Mark pushed through the branches. Behind him came the others, Rebecca with her hands over her belly as though she had to hold it up.

Nicole was afraid of what her face might show. She didn't dare look at Alan again.

Fortunately her mother crowed with delight. "You've found the perfect tree!"

Nicole turned to see, her gaze crossing Joe's. He lowered his left eyelid in a wink meant just for her. She ought to have been embarrassed. Instead, she grinned like some kind of idiot.

It was the best day of her life.

"I SHOULD HAVE listened to you." Teresa sounded more disgruntled than apologetic. "I never learn."

Joe shoved away Golda, who was determined to see what was going on. He sawed off another of the lower branches and tossed it aside. He breathed in the familiar pungent scent of crushed fir needles and sawdust. "You've done this before?"

She sighed. "Every year. Why don't trees look as big as they turn out to be?"

He couldn't answer that one. He'd told her. But he knew better than to remind her. Instead, he rolled the tree a quarter turn on the frozen lawn and began sawing another branch off. He'd have to take eighteen inches off the trunk, he estimated. Even then, the tip would brush her ceiling.

She crouched beside him, looking absurdly young sitting on her haunches, arms crossed over her chest for warmth, nose and cheeks bright red. "I should be doing that. It's my fault."

"I don't mind." He didn't. Everybody had their eccentricities. Rebecca had gone home with another ugly tree. She always did.

There was something else he did mind, though, something that had been rubbing up against him like wet jeans chafing. Before he could have second thoughts, he said, "Mark caught me by surprise today. I didn't realize you'd told the kids about my dyslexia."

She looked startled. "I thought they should know. Would you rather I hadn't?"

He frowned down at the saw, unmoving in his hand. "Nicole doesn't think much of me already."

"I'm not so sure." Teresa's expression was thoughtful. "Did you notice the way she leapt to your defense? Once she's decided to like someone, she's loyal."

"She also likes slapping her brother down."

Teresa grimaced. "True. But in that case, she would have been sarcastic and superior, not mad."

He grunted and began sawing again. A branch dropped off; he adjusted the angle and went after the next one.

"Mark worships the ground you walk on." She dangled it before him like a carrot before a donkey.

"He's at an age where boys all want to be test pilots or firemen or cops. Anything physical and dangerous. A couple of years, and he'll see me differently."

She laid a mittened hand on his thigh. "You know, we don't grow up loving our parents or respecting them because of their professions. It takes other qualities. More important things, like whether they listened to you, helped you when you needed it, let you make mistakes and then dusted you off afterward."

Joe's hand slowed again. Her words reminded him of a story Sam had told him once. Alan had despised Sam at first, but one night Sam got a phone call well after midnight. Alan had been drinking and had the sense not to drive home, but he didn't want to call his mother. Sam drove all the way here from Everett, picked up Alan at his friend's house, dropped him off at home, didn't say anything judgmental. Their relationship had changed after that.

So maybe she was right. After all, if he'd really been Mark and Nicole's father, they wouldn't think anything of his dyslexia, unless they were briefly embarrassed about it as teenagers. And teenagers were embarrassed about their parents' hairstyles, choice of clothes and just about everything else. So what was one more thing?

"Maybe," he said cautiously.

"Anyway, I've been thinking," she said. "Maybe you still could learn to read. I mean, educators know more about dyslexia than they used to. There must be new methods."

Like what? he thought. A cattle prod to shock slow learners every time they screwed up?

"I'll look into it if you want." She was careful to sound casual, but underneath was something edgier. Excitement. Determination. She wasn't used to failing at anything, so she figured if she tried to cure him, she'd succeed.

"I gave it thirteen years. That's enough."

His brusqueness didn't slow her down. She was already saying eagerly, "For you, school was a vicious circle. The worse you did, the harder it would have been to concentrate, to believe you *could* do it. But now there wouldn't be any of that kind of pressure on you. You could take your time, and when it doesn't go well, the only person you'd be disappointing would be yourself."

And you, he thought bleakly.

"There must be things you'd really like to read." Now she was coaxing. "You could work on a book of your own choice, not some textbook. I'd give you any help you want and leave you alone when you prefer.

Just think about it, Joe. It's never too late to change ourselves."

She had no idea what she was asking. He didn't look at her. "I get by fine the way I am."

"Of course you do!" She was convincingly indignant. "That's not why I'm suggesting it."

"Then why are you?" His anger was stirring, but Teresa never noticed.

"Because it bothers you that you can't do it. Because if you learned to read competently, you'd know you were living the life you've chosen, not the one you were boxed into."

It sounded good all right. But he didn't think she understood that she might as well be assuring a diabetic he could quit checking his blood sugar if he wanted to badly enough. Some people who were dyslexic could overcome it, even go to college. His was too severe. The only method that worked for him was patience, and he'd run out of that.

"Will you think about it?" she implored again.

"I can do that." He was lying, but maybe that would satisfy her. "Now, let's see if this tree'll fit in your living room."

TERESA KNEW darn well that Joe was only humoring her. Resistance had radiated from him in waves so palpable she'd been reminded of a dog she'd seen a few days ago for a routine appointment. The owner had hauled the poor thing into the examining room, even though the dog's legs were braced in an I-won't-go-and-you-can't-make-me stance. But on the smooth vinyl floor, his claws couldn't gain any purchase, and he found himself willy-nilly in that room without having taken a single step.

It was actually a pretty good analogy. The dog was there for his own good—he needed those vaccinations, though he didn't understand that. Joe didn't want to admit he needed anyone's help, either, but once he was partway, he'd see that she was right. She was going to push and prod for his own good, not because it mattered to her whether or not he could read.

That gave her an idea for a Christmas present for him, something she'd been stewing about. She hadn't yet thought of anything that satisfied her. New gloves or a handsome belt buckle were the kind of thing you could buy for anyone. An uncle you saw once a year. Your brother-in-law. For Joe, she wanted her gift to hold meaning, to be special.

It would be a kind of promise to him. And maybe a temptation, like a skimpy black minidress would be to a dieter ten pounds away from getting the zipper up.

She'd taken care of almost everyone else. Her out-of-town packages had gone. Her son was easily satisfied: a couple of new Nintendo games, a chemistry set, some high-top basketball shoes he'd coveted, and several books for him to read by flashlight in bed.

The real money went for Nicole's present, a lovely Arabian mare. She'd belonged to a girl who had left for college this fall and lost interest. Joe's sister Jess knew the horse and had recommended her. The girl's parents agreed to deliver the mare on the twenty-fourth in midafternoon. Teresa spent Monday, when the kids were in school, cleaning out a stall in the ramshackle barn and checking the fence. In the afternoon, she visited the feed store in town and bought the necessities: hay, grain, brushes, buckets, hoof pick. She felt safe in assuming that neither of the kids would go in the barn.

Saddle and bridle had been part of the package with the horse. Teresa had brought them home and wrapped them in a big box. She could hardly wait to see Nicole's face when she opened it.

She'd picked up some nails at the feed store, too. Now, pounding one in to secure a fence rail, Teresa decided she'd go shopping the following Monday for Joe's gift. She knew just what she wanted. In the meantime, she'd continue to research reading disabilities.

Snow started to fall that evening. Teresa awakened early to at least six inches of the stuff. She sipped coffee and listened to the radio, waiting for the school report. She wasn't surprised that White Horse was among those districts on the closure list. Bus routes covered miles of narrow country roads. If the buses couldn't run, there was no point in holding classes.

The telephone rang at eight. It was Eric, suggesting she stay home, too.

"Business will be slow, and we won't be making any farm calls."

"I won't argue," she said. She felt sort of like the way Nicole and Mark would when they woke up to find there was no school and enough snow on the ground to play in.

Later, she and the kids bundled up and went out to build a snowman. She was wrapping his neck with an old muffler when a snowball smacked her in the back.

"Hey!" She turned to see Joe by the corner of the house, grinning at her. Her heart did a little dance and she was suddenly breathless. It was like the first time she saw him, excitement and shock and shyness all mixed up. In jeans, boots, wool hat and navy parka, he was devastatingly handsome.

Which didn't stop her from grabbing a handful of snow and letting it fly. She got him right in the chest. Of course, that might have been a strategic error. His eyes narrowed and he advanced on her purposefully. Nicole and Mark retreated, laughing.

Teresa circled behind the snowman. "I was just paying you back!"

"And I'm going to pay you back." He feinted left, then dodged right and snatched her. But instead of shoving her down in the snow, he kissed her, lips cold and breath warm.

Then he looked at the kids. "Want to go sledding?"

"We don't have a sled," Mark said.

"But I do."

"Cool!"

"Where do we go?" Nicole asked eagerly.

It turned out he'd brought two, one the kind with wooden slats and steel runners, the other a plastic toboggan. "Borrowed 'em from Lee," Joe told them.

They all changed to dry gloves, shut the dogs in the house and walked to the best hill in town, or so Joe assured them.

A dozen or more kids, ranging in age from toddlers with their parents to teenagers, were already there. The hill ran two long blocks and enough sleds had already gone down to polish the packed surface of the snow.

Nicole and Mark went first, Nicole on the toboggan, Mark on the sled. They shot down the hill neck and neck, whooping with glee.

Next turn, Teresa took the toboggan, Joe the sled. Teresa sat with her legs stretched out in front of her, and Joe lay down on his stomach. Using their hands, they pushed off for all they were worth. The cold wind stung Teresa's eyes, and the houses to each side of the road blurred. She dodged some kids walking back up, almost sideswiped Joe, righted herself and kept going. The speed was unbelievable, exhilarating.

At the bottom her toboggan slowed and finally came to a stop right beside Joe, who'd rolled off his sled and lay on his back in the snow.

"I haven't done that in years," he said, grinning up at her.

"Kids make you young again," she told him. "Or old faster, I'm not sure which. It varies from day to day."

"And averages out, so you age at the normal speed."

She laughed and offered him a hand. Instead of coming up, he pulled her down in a sprawl across him. Whether he was going to kiss her or not, she never knew, because a couple of teenage boys pelted them with snowballs. Joe retaliated, then they started back up the hill.

They went down again and again. About the time Teresa was getting too cold to continue, a neighbor hauled out a burn barrel and started a fire in it. Everybody gathered around and warmed their hands, then started up the hill pulling a motley assortment of sleds, plastic saucers and toboggans, and even a few flattened cardboard boxes.

They kept on until midafternoon. Joe and Mark had a snowball fight all the way home. After promising to come back for dinner, Joe headed to his own place to shower and change.

Teresa luxuriated in the longest hottest bath she'd had in a while. She could have fallen asleep right in it and slipped underwater without a fight, but she kept remembering the feel of Joe's lips and the flash of white when he smiled at her.

Even knowing he was coming for dinner, it was all she could do to make herself get out of the tub. She pulled on some big wool socks, an old pair of sweat-pants and a sweatshirt that didn't match. She skipped drying her hair, just braided it down her back and wandered into the kitchen, where she started opening cupboards in search of something to make for dinner.

Fried potatoes and leftover ham, Teresa decided. And for balance, a fruit salad.

She was still peeling potatoes when the doorbell rang.

"I'll get it!" Mark yelled.

A minute later Joe came into the kitchen. "I expected to smell homemade bread baking."

"Hah! In your dreams. I had better things to do today."

"Much better." He came up behind her and kissed her neck while she sliced potatoes. "Anything I can help with?"

"Mmm." She tilted her head to one side. "Do that again."

He kissed her nape and worked his way around to her throat. The paring knife fell out of her nerveless hand. Somewhere in there, Joe butted right up against her, so she could feel his arousal. His hands slipped up under her sweatshirt and cupped her breasts.

"This what you had in mind?" he asked huskily.

"It's a start," she whispered.

"It'll have to hold you." He tugged her sweatshirt down and stepped back. "I'm hungry, woman."

She laughed even as she groaned. Damn it, he had no right to get her worked up like that when they couldn't follow through. Of course, she didn't mind knowing that he was worked up, too.

Teresa turned around, smiled sweetly, scraped her fingernails teasingly down the ridge distorting the fly of his jeans and said, "Well, in that case you can start the fruit salad."

He muttered something she pretended not to hear, found another knife and the bowl she'd set out, and began peeling an orange.

She finished slicing potatoes and dropped them into hot oil, turning them as she chopped the ham. Joc assembled a fruit salad with an easy competence most men couldn't match. Of course, he'd lived alone for fifteen years or so. He'd have starved to death if he hadn't learned to cook.

He was in an unusually lighthearted mood, as though a day spent playing had loosened him up. It made her realize how much unspoken tension had been sticking rough edges between them lately, poking at just the wrong moment. Was it all to do with his reading disability? she wondered. It didn't make sense.

Well, not to her, but she wasn't the one battling feelings of inadequacy, the one other kids had called "dummy" so often he'd come to believe it. Maybe the tension made a lot of sense from his point of view.

So, did she just ignore the problem and hope it went away? Or was it not the tension that was unspoken, but his problem? How often in conversation did they head in that direction and then veer away? He hated talking about it, that was obvious, but maybe they were worse off *not* bringing it out to air. If she was right, and he could learn to read better than he did now, then the whole issue would evaporate.

Still, she found herself reluctant to say anything that would mar the good mood that even her kids felt.

Until, over dinner, Joe asked if they needed to go Christmas shopping without their mother.

Mark's face lit right up. "You mean, you'd take us?"

"If you want." He slanted Teresa the kind of smile that raised her blood pressure. "I wasn't sure if you had anybody to take you."

"Alan offered." Nicole sounded, if not snippy, a quarter of an inch away. She'd been so pleasant lately—thank God—that this was a rude reminder of her behavior a couple of months ago.

Maybe she feared Joe was assuming the place of father in their family. He probably was. Unlike Mark, Nicole remembered her own father well and still grieved his loss; it wouldn't be unnatural for her to defend his place. Actually, on the whole she'd accepted Joe rather gracefully, considering her age and resentment of the move.

"That's fine," Joe said amiably. "Just didn't want you to be stuck for a chance to shop for your mother."

Mark thrust out his chin. "I'd rather go with you."

Joe smiled at her son. "How about Saturday, while your mom's working?"

Nicole scowled as Joe and her brother settled on a time. Clearly she didn't like being excluded, however much she'd sneered at the original offer. It wasn't easy being a teenager. The very word meant a mass of contradictions.

Teresa let out an unconscious sigh. Enough undercurrents were swirling around this table to make her wonder if the business of dating and remarrying was worth it. Was there ever a moment when everybody was happy at the same time?

Just then her eyes met Joe's across the dinner table. The look he gave her was unexpectedly intense, as though he'd sensed her doubt. His eyes were so blue she couldn't look away. Her heart thrummed in her ears and her fork stopped halfway to her mouth. Was he trying to tell her something? Reassure her?

It was over in a flash; neither of the kids seemed to have noticed, she decided after surreptitious glances. But her mood had altered again. Oh, yes, Joe was worth any amount of adjustment—on her part, as well as the kids'.

Joe and Teresa left Mark clearing the table and Nicole loading the dishwasher, taking their coffee into the living room.

Teresa had gotten as far as painting the walls the color of clotted cream and installing blinds made of wooden slats stained maple. New carpet was as rich in color and texture as the glass-fronted bookcases that flanked the fireplace. On the other hand, the blue sectional couch clashed abysmally, but she was too conscious of the cost of remodeling the rest of the house to go out and replace furniture wholesale.

The tree, of course, took pride of place. She plugged in the lights before she curled up on one end of the couch.

Joe had to move a cat to sit down. "Clyde or Sal?" he asked.

"Sal. Cowardly Clyde was named for a reason. He'd have been long gone when he saw you coming."

"Cowardly Clyde?"

"He and Sal were part of a feral litter of kittens. It took us ages to tame them enough to catch them. We called him Nervous Nellie until we discovered she was a he. Sweet Sally turned out to be male, too, but we were so used to calling him Sal, it stuck." Inspiration hit like a light bulb over the head of a cartoon character. She put down her coffee cup and went to one of the bookcases. Over her shoulder, she said casually, "'Cowardly Clyde' came from a children's picture book. Have you seen it?"

He hadn't become suspicious yet. "I don't think so."

"I couldn't make myself give away all our picture books just because the kids outgrew them. Especially the ones with animals in them. Like *Amos, the Story of an Old Dog and His Couch.*" She grabbed it and *Cowardly Clyde.*

Plunking herself next to Joe, she set the two books on his lap. "We used to have an old dog who wouldn't stay off the couch. I finally gave up and put the couch, which was in its death throes, in the garage for the dog. We didn't get rid of it until he died."

Joe was thumbing through *An Old Dog and His Couch* and smiling. Teresa rested her chin on his shoulder and read the story as he turned the pages.

"Can you read text like this when there's not so much on a page?"

He stiffened, just enough that she could feel it. But he answered, "With a struggle. If I use my finger to keep my place and think about whether every word fits the context."

"Mmm." She wasn't seeing the charming illustrations anymore. Instead, she was thinking. "Does it make any difference what the print is like?"

"You mean, how small or the style?" When she nodded, he shook his head. "I don't think so. Capital letters are easier than small ones. Maybe because as a kid you learn those first."

"Is it easier to read aloud or to yourself?"

"Aloud. Or at least whispering words to myself." Now his arm was rigid. "They forbade that in school. You weren't supposed to move your lips."

Teresa sat back so she could see his face better. "Seriously? Why on earth would they do that? Lots of people move their lips when they read. My dad always did."

"It slows you down," he said simply.

She was both incredulous and outraged on his behalf. "But they must have realized that someone overcoming a handicap like yours wasn't ever going to read a thousand words a minute!"

Joe grimaced. "Educators tend to believe everyone should learn by the same method and at the same speed."

"I don't think that's so much true anymore. Mark's teacher not only lets the kids work at their own reading level, he encourages them to choose spelling words that will challenge them. Even in math, he has several different groups."

"Then maybe they've learned something." Without even opening *Cowardly Clyde,* he set the two books aside with an air of finality. "I'd better be getting on home."

Glancing at his untouched cup of coffee, she rose, too. "Will I see you tomorrow?"

"I'll try to stop by."

She walked him to the door, where he kissed her briefly but thoroughly and said good-night. He didn't seem angry or upset, but his earlier playfulness was gone.

Well, she'd known that prodding him would sometimes be uncomfortable for both of them. But the more they talked about his problem, the less it would be so. Her goal was to reach a point where he'd read to her. She had to believe that wasn't far away.

Now, if he just liked her Christmas present . . .

CHAPTER FOURTEEN

PRESENTS UNDER HIS ARM, Joe walked in the front door of Teresa's house to the smell of mulled cider, fir needles and something cooking he couldn't immediately identify. Didn't everybody have turkey or ham on Christmas Eve? Sniffing, too, the dogs crowded in with him.

Mark, who'd answered the door, was bouncing up and down with excitement. "You know we open our presents tonight, don't you? But Mom says we have to wait until after dinner. I'd rather open them now."

Joe shrugged out of his coat and hung it on the rack by the door. "You asking me to be the voice of reason?"

"It wouldn't do any good," the boy said gloomily. "She says she likes to torture us."

"Well, anticipation *is* half the fun."

"But maybe, if you said it's all right, she'd let us open the ones from you." Mark gazed up hopefully.

"We'll see." He sounded like a parent, Joe realized. He wasn't sure how he felt about that.

Nicole appeared in the doorway to the living room. "Did you put it up?" she whispered.

Joe grinned. "Yep. Wanna see it?"

"We might give it away," she whispered. She raised her voice to a normal level, "Do *you* know what's in the big present for me?"

"How big?" He followed her. Tonight the tree was brilliant with lights and glass ornaments shimmering in every color imaginable. Among the handsome teardrops and balls were homemade ornaments of crumbling clay or popsicle sticks crookedly glued together and covered with glitter. The golden star atop the tree bumped the ceiling.

Heaps of presents barely fit beneath the lowest branches. A few in front must have been wrapped by Mark. Joe was touched to see one with his name on it. In the midst of the presents, Joe spotted the face of a black cat, blinking sleepily at him. He nodded at it. "Does he climb the tree?"

"Yeah, and it makes Mom really mad," Mark told him.

Joe looked for a place to put his contribution. "Appears there's more than enough presents," he teased. "I think I'll just take mine on home."

Mark's eyes got big. "You wouldn't do that! Would you?"

"Of course not." Joe knelt and added his two to the abundance. "You might not give *me* a present."

"I got you a good one, too," Mark said eagerly. "You want to see it?"

Joe didn't have a chance to answer.

Nicole was almost dancing with impatience. "Look! This huge one's for me. Do you suppose Mom put something little like a watch inside just to confuse me?"

"You tried picking it up?"

"It's *heavy*. But Mom might have put in rocks or something."

He smiled at her. "Actually, I have an idea what it might be. You'll like it."

"I'd like it better if I could open it now!"

He laughed and left them poking and prying and weighing all the packages with their names on them. He'd reached the kitchen when he identified the mysterious smell.

"Lasagna."

Teresa turned from the stove, her smile as radiant as the Christmas lights. "Joe! I didn't hear you arrive."

"I've been admiring the tree."

She wrinkled her nose at him. "You mean, the presents. Nicole and Mark are both dying to start ripping."

He kissed her. "Looks like enough gifts for ten people."

"Mmm." She rubbed her cheek against his. "Their grandparents seem to think they're deprived. And then there are the aunts and uncles. I could skip shopping and the kids wouldn't even notice."

He watched as she peeked in the oven. Lasagna on Christmas Eve?

As though he'd spoken aloud, she said, "It's a family tradition. My grandmother was famous for her lasagna. She passed the recipe down to my mom and then me. We have turkey tomorrow."

"I like lasagna better than turkey, anyway." And he, too, would be eating turkey tomorrow, at his mother's house. Christmas Day was the gathering of the clan. He'd invited Teresa, but she had gracefully declined. "The kids'll want to play with their new stuff. Besides, Christmas is for family."

She and her children were beginning to *feel* like family to him. He usually spent Christmas Eve with Lee or one of his sisters and their families, but it had felt perfectly natural to come here, instead.

Just as it had felt natural to attend the Christmas program at the high school to see both Nicole and his niece Stephanie in *The Night before Christmas.* He had sat between Jess and Teresa, watching Nicole's comical jaunty Santa Claus and Steph's bemused, nightcapped gentleman discovering a fantasy was true. He would have been there, anyway, for Stephanie and Jess's sake, but then he would have been a stand-in for the absent Roy. Whether he was there or not, Steph had to deal with her father's refusal to bother coming. This time Joe belonged; he knew Nicole had been pleased that he intended to come, even if she tried to hide it.

And now tonight. Despite the apron, Teresa was stunning. Her dark hair was coiled in two gleaming rolls that met in back and were held by a gold clasp with tiny bells that tinkled softly when she moved. She wore a simple red dress, high-waisted, that fell almost to her ankles. It was some plushy fabric: velvet or velour or velveteen, he couldn't keep them straight despite having grown up with sisters. It felt almost as nice to touch as her smooth skin did.

To his eye, the dress and the graceful line of Teresa's neck demanded a necklace to go with the gold hoops she wore in her ears. He was almost sorry he hadn't bought her something like that. Pretty and feminine. But he thought she'd like his present. He'd made it himself: a porch swing with a curved back, a garland of roses carved along the arch. He'd come by the other day when she was at work and installed the sturdy eyes in a porch beam. Tonight he had quietly hung the swing on his way in. He had in mind a place on his own back deck where it would hang just as well, in case she didn't stay in this house. But it was just an idle consideration; he didn't let himself think too far down that path.

They said grace at dinner and meant it, as one does on those rare occasions when one stops long enough to look around and appreciate the good in life rather than grumbling about the annoying or frustrating.

The kids wished that it had snowed now that they had two weeks vacation to enjoy it. Joe couldn't remember the last time he'd seen a white Christmas. At most, a couple of snowstorms hit a year that left enough on the ground to sled or cross-country ski.

"We didn't have a good hill at our last house," Mark explained. "That's why we didn't have a sled. But we should get one now, shouldn't we, Mom?"

She smiled vaguely. "Oh, I suppose. I don't even know where you'd buy one."

"Hah!" Nicole crowed. "That means we're getting one for Christmas! That's what's in the big box!"

"Now, what did I say to make you think that?"

"She wouldn't just give it to *you,*" Mark said. "And I don't have any package that big under the tree."

Teresa smiled at them. "Some of the presents might not be under the tree."

"That's true," Joe agreed, eyes resting on Teresa.

"Okay." She held out a table knife in mock threat. "Where is it?"

"Can we show her?" Mark begged. "Huh? Can we?"

"Not until we open presents," Joe said sternly. "Remember, half the fun is the anticipation."

"Yeah, remember, Mom?" Nicole taunted.

She scowled, first at Joe, then at the kids. "All right. We'll open presents *before* dessert."

"Cool!" Mark looked at his sister. "Let's eat fast."

They both shoveled in. Joe tried not to watch. Anyway, he was tempted to follow suit. The lasagna lived up to Teresa's billing.

He, Nicole and Mark finished before their mother. She took a leisurely bite, chewed slowly, swallowed, then sipped her wine. An eternity later, she lifted another tiny mouthful with the fork and started over.

She suddenly dropped her fork with a clatter onto the china plate. "All right already! Quit staring!"

Joe looked at the ceiling. Mark slouched down and stared at the floor. Nicole began sketching swirls into the sauce left on her plate.

Teresa took one more bite. She was still swallowing it when she jumped up. "You win! Let's do it."

"You mean, we don't have to clear the table first?"

"It'll keep." She almost tripped over the black Lab, who was hoping for tidbits. "Well, let me put the lasagna away. Just to make sure nobody jumps up on the table."

The casserole dish safely covered and in the refrigerator, she closed her eyes and allowed herself to be led out onto the front porch.

Joe stopped and let her go.

"You can look now, Mom!" Mark was back to quivering with excitement. "Look what Joe made you!"

The expression on her face was all Joe could have hoped for. "Oooh," she breathed. "It's beautiful! You made it?"

He nodded. It was worth every moment in his shop to watch her caress the arms, sanded to a satin finish, run her fingers over the carving and finally sit down.

She gave a little push with her feet and started rocking, gliding back and forth just as smooth as could be.

"We had a porch swing like this when I was a kid," she said dreamily. "It was in the Midwest, you know. Everybody sat out on their porches on summer evenings. You could hear the crickets and the kids playing out in the street and the neighbors fighting." She smiled in the way she might have if she'd forgotten she was talking to anyone but herself. "The Dobsons fought a lot."

Joe eased himself down on the swing beside her. "Did you get your first kiss sitting out there on a summer evening?"

Her face cleared and she laughed. "No, that was out behind the gym. Come on, guys, I'm freezing."

The kids surged back in the house. She gave Joe a quick soft kiss. "Thank you," she whispered.

"You're welcome," he whispered back, and deepened the kiss.

On the way into the house, he realized he didn't care what she'd gotten him. He couldn't think of anything that would be meaningful in and of itself. But he did hope he'd chosen reasonably well for Mark and Nicole. It was more important than he wanted it to be that their eyes should light up and they should grin at him.

"Big box last," Teresa told Nicole. "No, don't argue. I have a good reason."

Mark was already tearing into his packages. Cats gathered and pounced on ribbon and wallowed in wrapping paper.

"Cool!" Mark declared, and moved on to the next package.

Sitting cross-legged on the floor, Nicole was opening her gifts more daintily, if almost as fast. Joe held his breath when she reached for his and tore off the paper. Inside was a small box, and inside that—

"Oh!" she exclaimed. Inside were earrings, tiny horses carved out of onyx. "Like Black Beauty," she said tremulously. "That book always makes me cry." Fumbling in her haste, Nicole took off the gold posts she was wearing and put on his earrings. When she bent her head to put the posts in the box, the small black horses seemed to be galloping.

She looked up at him, eyes bright. "Thank you. They're beautiful."

"You're welcome." They exchanged a smile uncomplicated by resentment or wariness.

Mark, unnoticed, had torn open his present from Joe. It was a set of pewter knights, some mounted in full suits of armor, others on foot with swords or staffs. Each rested in his place in a case lined with velvet.

"Oh, wow," he breathed. He took two out, both mounted and with their lances held to the ready, as though they were charging each other in battle. Mark set them apart, facing each other, and was reaching for more when a black cat—Sal—stuck out a paw and batted one of the knights.

Everyone laughed, and Teresa reminded him he had other gifts to open. He carefully picked up the two knights and set them back in their places. Mark grinned at Joe. "These are really rad!" Not just cool, Joe noted. The boy's face was alight with adoration.

It was dumb—no, poor choice of words—ridiculous to feel such warmth at being the kid's hero.

Joe opened his gifts from the kids. Mark's was handmade: a crude clay figure of a logger, probably a school project. It had a certain folk-art charm, but it also carried a load of emotion. Other kids had probably been making something for their mothers and fathers. Mark had chosen him.

"I love it," he said simply.

Nicole had given him an organizer that clipped onto the window visor in his pickup. "I noticed you just set your sunglasses on the dashboard," she said.

"And they're always falling on the floor," he admitted. "I should have had one of these years ago. Thanks, Nicole."

Teresa gave him a sweater knit in chunky cotton yarn. "Blue for your eyes," she said, "and no, I didn't knit it. I used to knit, but I never seemed to finish anything. I have half a dozen sweaters for the kids upstairs in my cedar chest. Every one of them is missing a sleeve or the front or—"

"It's beautiful," he said.

After that, he sat back and watched the kids tear, admire and tear again. He remembered thinking once that Teresa was like a small blaze he warmed his hands over. He realized tonight that it wasn't just her. It was family, home, uncomplicated acceptance.

He'd had that from his family while growing up, although it was tainted by the rage and frustration he felt all the time. They still gave him that kind of love, but now his family had broken into three or four smaller units that came together every once in a while. Sometimes he almost felt lonelier at the monthly gatherings than he did when he was alone. And when one of his siblings invited him to join them for Christmas Eve, he felt like an outsider. This was the first time since he was a boy himself that he'd felt as if a family was his.

Maybe they were. Or could be. Maybe whether he could read or not truly didn't matter.

"Time for the big one," Teresa said gaily.

Nicole leapt up and dragged it from behind the tree.

"Now, guys," their mother said, "this one is mostly for Nicole, but I expect her to share it. With me *and* her brother."

"Maybe it *is* a sled," Mark suggested, scooting over next to his sister so he didn't miss a thing.

Nicole ripped, exposing a cardboard box. "A brass lamp?" she said doubtfully, reading the side.

"Keep going."

She pulled open the top and her eyes got wide. "A saddle? And bridle? Oh, Mom!" She shot to her feet. "Do you mean . . . ?"

"You might want to go out to the barn." Teresa's voice held a smile.

They all put on coats and gloves and traipsed out. Nicole ran ahead, and Teresa held her son back. "Let her meet her horse by herself."

"You said she had to share!"

"Which means you can ride it sometimes, but the horse is Nicole's. She's the one who always wanted a horse."

"Does that mean when I'm fifteen you'll get me a dirt bike?"

"I won't promise," his mother said dryly.

Joe hadn't seen the horse, although he'd played a part by coming to get the kids this afternoon and taking them to his place for a few rides around the pasture on his quarter horse. To avoid making them suspicious, Teresa had agreed only with ostensible reluctance, making them promise to be home by four so they had time to clean up before dinner.

They found Nicole in the stall, face buried against an arched chestnut neck. The mare was nuzzling Nicole's shoulder, mouthing the collar of her shirt. It looked to Joe as if the bonding was going just fine.

Eventually he and Teresa walked back to the house, leaving the kids in the barn.

"Nicole'll want to sleep there," Teresa said comfortably from inside the circle of his arm.

"She'll probably kick Mark out."

"Oh, I don't know. She's feeling benevolent right now. Christmas spirit."

He grunted an agreement. He was enjoying even this short stroll, though the night was nippy. He liked feeling Teresa's hip bumping his, her arm around his waist, her thumb hooked through his belt loop.

And he liked the way her cheeks turned pink. Inside, she kissed him, gave him an uncertain smile and said, "I have another present for you."

"Really?" he drawled, not sure he had as much faith as she seemed to that her children wouldn't reappear and interrupt them.

But that wasn't what she meant, for she turned away and, from a drawer, produced a package wrapped in white paper printed with green trees and festooned with a cascade of green curling ribbon.

His reactions were slowed down, amplified in a strange way, as though he stood outside himself watching. Pleased surprise shifted slowly, like gears grinding, to apprehension, then disbelief. She wouldn't have bought him a book, would she? But the damned package was sure shaped like one.

That didn't mean anything. It could be a box, or if it was a book, it could be the coffee-table kind with photographs or art.

But it didn't seem big enough for that. He took the package from her, weighed it in his hands. She watched him anxiously, ready to be delighted when he liked her present, but not sure he would.

He didn't know what his face showed. His hands were clumsily working at the ribbon, then neatly slicing the tape so he could fold back the paper.

Any hope that he'd been wrong died when he saw the cover. It looked vaguely familiar. Maybe it was one of those she'd shoved at him that night in the Elliott Bay Bookstore. A Post-it note was stuck to the jacket. He stared down at it, but the turmoil he felt didn't allow him to concentrate enough to read even that.

"All it says is that I'll help you read this book." Her attempt to sound gay and chatty didn't disguise her nervousness. "I know you'll love it. I thought you might get more excited about reading if you were working on a book as fascinating as this one. You can go at your own speed. I promise not to nag. I use up all my nagging on the kids!"

Anguish was eating its way through his numbness. "Do you?"

"What do you mean?"

"Use up all your nagging on them?"

Teresa stepped back and her chin came up. "What are you suggesting?"

"Haven't you been nagging me? Isn't that what all the prodding and poking has been about? Isn't *this*—" he held out the book "—nagging?"

She'd paled. "I didn't intend—"

He didn't give a damn what she'd intended. His head felt as if it might explode with the humiliation and anger swelling inside him. "Why the hell did you talk me into going on with this relationship when you knew I'd be an embarrassment to you?"

"You're not—"

He leaned toward her, speaking between gritted teeth. "Let me tell you something, for the last time. I did my best in school, and I failed. Every word I read is agony. If I have to perform with a printed page to be good enough for you, then it's hopeless."

Her eyes were huge, shocked. "I never meant—"

He felt sick. Every hideous moment in school spent frantically trying to decipher the words in front of him while the rest of the class sneered or laughed, culminated in *this* moment, when the woman he loved subjected him to the same kind of humiliation.

Joe threw down the book. "Next time," he said hoarsely, "let a man know what you expect of him."

He turned and walked out. Behind him was silence. She didn't move, didn't say a word. So much violence churned within him right now, he didn't know what he'd have done if she had tried to stop him.

He drove half a mile and pulled over. Letting his head rest against the cold steering wheel, he tried not to cry. He never cried, hadn't since about second grade. Crying ripped him open and exposed the terror within.

Muttering an obscenity, he wiped his eyes on his shirtsleeve. He'd defended himself all his life against what had happened to him tonight. How had he let things go so far with Teresa when he'd known all along what the end would be? He wasn't good enough for her. Why the hell hadn't she believed him when he'd tried to tell her?

He knew the answer to one question, why he'd let himself be persuaded that she was different, that he could have what he'd yearned for and briefly imagined was actually within his grasp. It was the dream of having a family, kids to look up to him, a woman who loved him despite his flaw.

That was what hurt the most: that his dream had been dangled so close in front of him he could see every detail as clearly as reality just before she yanked it away.

He didn't usually let himself acknowledge his loneliness. But tonight it was swamping him. He was adrift in a rowboat in the open sea, and waves were washing over the side.

Nor would it get any better. He loved Teresa Burkett, and he'd lost her because of his inadequacies. He might spend the rest of his life looking for her, reaching for her, and finding only emptiness.

"OH, MY GOD, what did I do?" Teresa whispered. She could hear his pickup driving away, and still she stood there stunned.

If I have to perform with a printed page to be good enough for you, then it's hopeless.

She turned and stumbled to the couch. She curled into a little ball on it, knees drawn to her chest and her face buried in her crossed arms.

He was gone. Over and over, she relived the contempt on his face for her, the loathing for himself. Why hadn't she seen what a terrible thing she was doing to him?

Teresa began to rock. She was sinking into a bottomless well of loss. He was gone. He hadn't listened to her. Why should he? He'd told her things she doubted he'd ever told anyone else. She knew how he had suffered, how inadequate he felt. She, all nobility, had assured him it didn't matter that he couldn't read; he'd made meaningless a problem that stopped some people.

And then what did she do? She tried to fix his problem. Under the guise of "helping," she'd managed to convince him that he had to learn to read to please her.

Tears were hot on the sleeve of her dress. Still she saw that terrible look on his face. "I'm sorry," wasn't going to be enough.

SHE WOULD HAVE to tell the kids of course, but she didn't want to spoil Christmas for them. She dried her tears before they came in, told them Joe had gone home and said to wish them merry Christmas, and listened, smiling, as Nicole talked—endlessly—about her horse.

"I'll call her Rosie, too, since she's used to that. Except when I'm showing her, of course." The mare was registered under an unpronounceable Arabic name which apparently translated to "rosebud." Thus Rosie. "It'll be really cool to show her. I wonder if she's ever been shown before."

"Her last owner had a wall of ribbons," Teresa said. "She and Rosie competed in everything from trail riding to costume and even some jumping, according to the girl's parents."

"Wow, jumping." Nicole got a rapt look on her face. She was probably picturing herself elegantly attired competing in the Olympic games. "I hope I ride well enough." She gazed at her mother with sudden doubt. "Do you think I do?"

"If you don't now, you will shortly if you ride every day."

Nicole hardly listened. "Did I tell you Ariana has a horse, too? Hers is half Arab. I can hardly wait to tell her I have one now, too. I can join 4-H with her." She bounced on the couch. "Of course, once I'm showing Rosie, we'll have to figure out how to get her there. I mean, maybe we should think about getting a trailer."

"And a pickup to pull it?" Teresa said it in a tone that implied, *Dream on, kid.*

"Well, you know, I will be able to drive pretty soon," her daughter said innocently. "Instead of getting a second car, maybe we could get a pickup."

What would her friends in Bellevue think if they could hear her now? The 4-H club and a pickup truck! She'd come a long way.

Teresa relented and smiled. "You're right. We might want to do that."

"Cool!" Nicole leapt up. "I'm gonna go call Ariana if that's all right."

"She might not be home."

"She said she would be. They don't do anything special Christmas Eve."

"Then go right ahead."

Nicole twirled, darted from the room, then popped her head back in. "Hey, Mom?"

Teresa pinned another smile on her face. "Yes?"

"Thank you. Rosie is the best present ever."

"You're welcome," she said gravely.

Nicole gone, Teresa glanced at Mark, who was using the coffee table to arrange his pewter knights in battle formation.

Without looking up, he said, "This is my best present. All the other guys have is G.I. Joe and Batman and stuff like that. They're going to be jealous."

"I'm glad you like it." Teresa prayed he wouldn't notice the catch in her voice.

"You liked Joe's present, too, didn't you?"

Oh, God. She'd forgotten her porch swing. Would the time ever come when she could sit in it and rock back and forth on a quiet warm evening, and not think about Joe? Not remember his big hands, as deft at touching her as they had been at working with the wood?

She was such a fool.

"Is something wrong?" Mark regarded her anxiously.

"No." She knew her smile wasn't entirely successful, but her son seemed satisfied. His head bent again, and he made a minute adjustment to the position of a foot soldier.

"Joe said he has a friend with a logging truck who'd give me a ride some day. He said maybe his friend would even let me ride in the cab in the Fourth of July parade. I could throw the candy. You don't think Joe will forget, do you?"

She ought to tell him. But she couldn't. Not now. Please, not now. She would cry for sure. "No," she said shakily. "I don't suppose Joe will forget."

"I knew he wouldn't." Mark nodded in satisfaction that she'd vindicated his judgment. "He never forgets anything."

"You really like him, don't you?"

Mark lifted his head again. Hair tousled, he looked so much like the five-year-old boy who had listened uncomprehendingly as she explained why he would never see his daddy again. This wouldn't be quite as bad, but close. Joe was the first man Mark had really cared about since his father's death. Losing Joe, too, would devastate her son. Her own heart wouldn't be the only one breaking.

"Yeah," Mark said carefully, "he's really cool. I was thinking—I mean, wondering . . . well, that is, do you think you might marry him?" The last came out in a rush.

She could almost feel the shards in her chest, splintering still further. She couldn't seem to speak, didn't know what to say.

The truth, she thought. Tell him as much of the truth as you can bear.

"If he ever asks me to marry him," she said, her voice tremulous, "I'd say yes."

Mark studied her for a long moment, his eyes serious, then gave another decisive nod. "Good."

Teresa watched for a moment as he went back to his play. Then she looked above his head at the wall clock. How long until she could send her children to bed? How long until she could let herself cry?

CHAPTER FIFTEEN

TERESA KNEW it wouldn't do any good, but on Christmas day she left a message for Joe on his answering machine. He'd be at Rebecca's of course; he hadn't even put up a tree at his house. She told herself she wasn't being a coward. She would have waited until she had a chance of catching him at home, except she felt sure he wouldn't want to talk to her. Not yet, if ever.

She listened to his curt message, followed by the beep.

"This is Teresa, and... I'm sorry." She nibbled on her lower lip. Confiding to the electronic silence was hard. "Maybe you won't believe me, but I want you to know that I really thought I was helping. I never wanted to put you on the spot, and I never, ever, thought any less of you because you have trouble reading. I'm just...incredibly insensitive, I guess. The thing is, you're so confident seeming and, oh—" she gave a small painful laugh "—such a catch, I never really believed that whether you could read or not mattered to you so much. I won't blame you if you can't forgive me, but—" she hesitated, then finished in a ragged whisper "—I do love you."

He didn't call back. She'd known he wouldn't. She had hurt him beyond forgiveness. Why should he take such a risk again? She'd blown it, big time. If only she could think of some way to prove she loved *and* respected him. But she couldn't.

She *was* a coward when she kept putting off telling the kids Joe wouldn't be around anymore. Normally they might have noticed how quiet she was or how puffy her eyes were mornings. But the horse was currently the center of attention; Mom took second place by twenty lengths. Nicole's new friend, Ariana, was over half the time, and Alan the rest of the time. Rosie was bathed and groomed until she gleamed like red-gold satin. Fortunately Nicole was reasonably generous in giving Mark and his friends rides on the mare. Apparently the Christmas spirit hadn't yet dimmed.

Teresa was grateful for work. She would have gone mad if she'd been home every day with nothing to do but clean house, watch the kids circle the pasture on the horse and brood.

How could she be so lonely so soon? She'd gone several days at a time before without seeing Joe. This shouldn't have been anything like losing Tom, who had been so big a part of her life. Months after his death, she still caught herself reaching for him in bed, turning to say something to him, putting off jobs around the house that had been his because they *were* his. As though, if she waited long enough, he would come back just to weed-whack the fence line.

So why was this as bad? It wasn't fair. How had Joe managed to inch his way into her family and her home and even her relationships with other people, to an extent that she hadn't realized?

Half the clients at the animal hospital chose that week to mention how highly they thought of the Hugheses. A few teased her or asked her to pass on a message to Joe. The Friday after Christmas, Eric asked if she had big plans that evening.

When she said, "No, how about you?" he raised his eyebrows.

"Joe busy tonight?"

She wanted to snap his head off, but of course it wasn't his fault that he'd asked the wrong question. "We're not seeing each other anymore," she said, hoping he'd let it go at that.

She suddenly knew what it felt like to be an animal on the examining table. One whose owner had just reported mysterious symptoms. Dr. Bergstrom was thinking hard. She half expected him to suggest some blood work.

But he surprised her with his tact. "I'm sorry," he said quietly, and she nodded. Not another word was said.

She hadn't been sleeping well, and she let herself into the house realizing that, to make matters worse, she hadn't planned anything for dinner. Any hope that Nicole had taken some initiative in the kitchen was squelched when Teresa sniffed. Floor wax. Somebody had mopped, but no meat was defrosting on the counter, the oven lights were off, and the house was quiet. Nicole was too interested in figuring out what combination of oats and alfalfa met Rosie's approval to give a care about earning her mother's.

Teresa was suddenly overwhelmingly weary. She opened the refrigerator door and gazed in. A moment later she closed it. Okay, they could eat out. Fast food sounded horrible. La Hacienda? She almost flinched, remembering that first date. Pizza was almost as bad. It was painful to remember Joe's patience with Nicole at her snottiest.

She could almost hear the soft rumble of his voice. *Your kids are okay. Takes more than that to scare me off.*

It had taken her own cruelty, Teresa thought. She gripped the edge of the counter and closed her eyes, letting the hurt wash over her in a wave that swelled and finally receded.

When she opened her eyes, she looked at the wall calendar. It was only the twenty-ninth of December. Five days since Joe had walked out. She felt as if it had been two weeks.

She was still sagged against the counter when the kids came in.

"What's wrong, Mom?" Nicole was more perceptive than her brother, who asked simultaneously, "What's for dinner?"

"I don't know what's for dinner," Teresa admitted. "I was just considering the options."

"You froze part of the lasagna you made for Christmas Eve," Nicole reminded her. "Why don't we have that? You can cook it in the microwave."

Christmas Eve. More pain. She forced a smile. "Good idea."

She got it out of the freezer and stuck the whole casserole dish in the microwave. "Do we have any French bread left?"

"I think so." Nicole was studying her with much the same expression Eric had worn.

Teresa tried a casual smile.

"Something's wrong, isn't it?" her daughter asked. "Did one of the cats die?"

"Nobody died." She busied herself getting margarine out of the fridge, pulling out the bread board, slicing the French bread.

"What, then? Come on, Mom, don't hold out on us."

Teresa laid down the knife and turned to face them. This was worse than performing her first surgery under the critical eye of the experienced vet who'd hired her right out of school.

"Well, you'll find out sooner or later. Joe...um..." *Get it over with,* she ordered herself. "Joe and I aren't seeing each other anymore."

"What do you mean?" Mark's chin thrust out. "Don't you *like* him?"

"Yeah." She compressed her lips. "I like him a lot."

Her son glared at her. "You said you'd marry him! You did! I asked you."

"Mark..." She reached out a hand. He backed up. After a moment her hand fell to her side. "I said I'd marry him if he asked. He hasn't asked."

Nicole frowned. "You mean, he doesn't like *you* anymore?"

Teresa sighed. "It's more complicated than that. I, uh, I did something dumb."

They spoke as one. "What?"

She didn't want to talk about it. But she couldn't claim it wasn't any of their business. It was. She'd encouraged them to like him, even love him. She'd involved Joe in their lives, knowing full well what she was doing. Now she owed them.

"Let's sit down."

They listened as she talked. A frown creased Mark's brow, the expression he got when he concentrated fiercely on some new problem. Neither said a word until she told them about the Christmas present.

Nicole jumped to her feet. "Jeez, Mom, how dumb can you be? How could you not know what that would feel like?"

"Believe it or not, I thought I was offering help." She squeezed shaking hands together.

"Help?" Nicole curled her mouth into that teenage expression of utter contempt. "You mean torture, don't you?"

Teresa's gaze fell from her daughter's glare. She couldn't argue, and she bowed her head. "So I'm dumb," she said bleakly.

"Joe doesn't like that word," her son piped up. "You shouldn't use it."

Just like that, she had tears in her eyes. "You're right," she said tremulously, reaching out to take his hand. "I shouldn't."

"I shouldn't, either!" Nicole wailed, sinking back into her chair.

"I didn't care if he couldn't read." Mark's voice was forlorn. "I thought maybe he'd be my dad."

"I'm sorry," Teresa whispered, tightening her grip on his hand.

Nicole hunched her shoulders. "I wouldn't have minded, either. He was really nice to me."

Mark glowered at his sister. "You just wanted him to marry Mom so you could see Alan all the time. You didn't care about Joe!"

"I did so!"

"Did not!"

"You don't know." She crossed her arms and turned her back. "You don't know anything!"

Teresa went to her, gently lifting her face. Nicole's cheeks were wet with tears. She sniffed. "He was nice even when I wasn't!"

Teresa used the hem of her sweatshirt to blot the tears. "He's not dead, you know."

Her daughter looked up with sudden hope. "You'll tell him you're sorry, won't you? I'll bet he'd believe you."

Teresa looked away. "I already told him. I left a message on his answering machine. I guess 'I'm sorry' isn't good enough."

Mark's eyes were wide with distress. "Do you think he'll forget all the things he promised me? Like...like riding on the logging truck?"

"I don't know," she told him sadly. "I don't think he'd forget, but it would be awkward for him to ask you somewhere, considering how things stand between him and me. Do you understand?"

"It's not fair!" Mark burst out. "I liked him!" And he stormed from the room.

Teresa took a step after him, then stopped. He'd reached an age where he didn't like her to see him crying. And what more could she say in comfort?

She turned to see Nicole watching her with a disconcertingly adult expression. "If you really love him, Mom, you ought to be able to think of some way to get him back."

"Unless—" it was hard to squeeze the words out of a tight throat "—he doesn't really love me."

"Yeah, but I'll bet he does. He was always hanging around here." She shrugged. "Uh, Mom, the microwave is beeping. Dinner's ready."

Most of the lasagna ended up back in the refrigerator. Mark wouldn't come to the table at all, and neither Teresa nor Nicole had much appetite.

Just before bedtime, Teresa dialed Joe's phone number. She could say, "I'm sorry," again. Beg. Cry.

Maybe tears would sway him. But when he answered the phone himself with a brusque "Yeah?" she chickened out. Quietly she set the receiver back in its cradle.

TERESA STARTED the washing machine, then paused in the back hall when she saw that the door stood open. It really needed replacing. It took a knack to close it, and the kids didn't bother.

But instead of pulling it shut, she stood in the open door, looking out at the pasture. Ariana and two other girls had ridden their horses over, and the four were conducting a mock horse show. The upper part of the pasture wasn't too muddy, and Nicole had already ridden bare a circle the size of a small arena. All four girls rode with backs straight and chins up, hands quiet and heels down. Then one of them said something and they all laughed. Next thing Teresa knew, one of the girls had risen to her knees on the broad back of her roan, and the horse show metamorphosed into a circus. Teresa wondered whether she ought to insist they keep their behinds on the horses' backs, then decided philosophically that the girls would just wait until she wasn't around. And they *were* all wearing helmets.

Teresa's gaze lingered on her daughter. Nicole was truly happy here. And not just because of Alan. She was thriving in school, in her dance classes, and with her new friends. She'd grabbed hold of this new life with both hands.

How ironic that Teresa was the one moping now. Every time she thought of Joe, every time her thoughts even skimmed near, something twisted painfully in her chest.

Well, she wasn't the only one suffering, unfortunately. Mark had become so quiet, so serious, so sad. He came home from school every afternoon and went straight to his room, where he'd shut himself in until dinnertime. Sometimes he didn't even stop by the refrigerator on his way, a true indicator of how unhappy he was. He'd decided he didn't want to play basketball, and she had a feeling he'd dreamed that Joe would coach his team.

It was worse knowing she hadn't hurt just herself, or even just herself and Joe. No, she'd undermined her once cheerful easygoing son's sense of security and optimism. She'd made wordless promises, then not kept them.

Now she tugged the door shut and returned to the living room, where she'd left the vacuum cleaner while she changed laundry loads. The Christmas tree was only a memory, although the sharp scent of fir needles still lingered.

She didn't want to vacuum. She didn't want to do anything. This lassitude caused by the weight of depression was familiar. After Tom's death, it had been a year or more before she got out of bed one morning and back into it that evening without once thinking of him, without cautiously examining how she felt and discovering the dull ache lodged behind her breastbone. A year! She closed her eyes against the sting of tears. A year. Could she bear it again?

What choice did she have? she asked herself caustically. Curl up in a ball and cry? Sulk in her room as Nicole had done? What worked best was to go on with life until she saw the pleasure in it again. And someday she would.

But please, God, not a year!

She turned on the vacuum cleaner and pushed it forward, around the coffee table, along the foot of the couch. She hadn't vacuumed *under* it since the carpet was laid, she realized.

Go on with life.

She turned off the vacuum cleaner, shoved the coffee table out of the way and pulled one end of the couch out. She went around, pulled out the other end—and saw the book.

Teresa sucked in her breath and stared at it, lying there facedown among a few dust balls, a red bow attached to a length of curling ribbon, a section of the newspaper folded open to show an unfinished crossword puzzle and three of her son's felt markers in green, brown and yellow.

Distantly she heard a moan and realized it came from her. She dropped to her knees and picked up the book, turning it slowly over. The yellow Post-it note still clung to the cover. *This comes wrapped with my help,* she'd written.

Help. *You mean torture, don't you?*

How arrogant she'd been! Had she really thought reading better would be so important to Joe? Or was it her own ego that had insisted he needed to achieve some standard she'd set? The truth was, Joe had accepted a limitation and made it irrelevant. He was unlikely to become more successful in his business just because he could read a little faster. His personal life certainly didn't demand it. Look how long she'd known him without noticing he didn't read! And although she enjoyed reading herself, she didn't actually get that much of it done. The previous month's professional journals still sat untouched on the end table. She'd read a grand total of *one* of the books she'd bought that night in Seattle. A few minutes at bedtime, while she ate her brown-bag lunch at work, sometimes while she was cooking dinner. Reading was hardly the center of her existence. She already knew that Joe was an intelligent man who followed the news and politics at least as well as she did.

So why had his reading been so important to her? Was she afraid of what her friends and family would think if they knew he read poorly? Had she been ashamed of him?

She remembered the moment he'd told Jordan and his wife. She'd tensed up, waited in agony for what they'd say. But what had she *felt?* Shame? Or fiercely protective of him?

She pictured telling her sisters, her parents, her other friends. She had to admit to herself that some of what she had felt—would feel—was ego. She'd always been competitive, driving herself to achieve the best grades. But mostly she didn't want to see Joe hurt.

And so, of course, *she* had hurt him.

Could he ever forgive her? She knew, gripping the book in her hands, that her ego and even the agonies she would suffer on his behalf were nothing compared to the emptiness she felt now. Compared to having Joe beside her when she woke up in the morning, having him across the dinner table, coaching Mark's soccer team, being able to reach for him at night. But would Joe believe her?

If only she could take this gift back, make it never have existed. Her instinct was to drop the book in the garbage can.

But that wouldn't change the past. What she wished most was that she could give him what she should have in the first place. A true gift, not a challenge or a reproach.

Tears ran freely down her cheeks. One landed on the cover of the book. She stared at it, seeing, instead, Joe's face as he opened the present. Disbelief first, then hurt, but longing had been there, too. Maybe not for this book in particular, but for what it represented, the world of ideas and experiences he could never tap.

In that instant, her love and aching sense of loss crystallized, and she knew what she could do for him. She wouldn't let herself wonder whether he would accept it. The gift was what mattered, and the generosity with which it was given.

She peeled the Post-it note off and crumpled it in her hand.

MAYBE HE'D BEEN A FOOL again, Joe thought, for the thousandth time. Teresa had told him that whether he could read or not didn't matter. Maybe he should have believed the words, instead of her actions. After all, she had never seen him struggle with a printed page, never seen his lips form words that weren't there, then his flush as he tried to figure out what he'd done wrong. She was inquisitive, exuberant. She didn't let herself admit to failure; she went after what she wanted. Her nature had made it inevitable that she'd try to undo his failure.

Did he want her to be different than she was?

He hunched his shoulders inside his parka and clapped the hard hat back on his head. No, he wanted Teresa Burkett just as she was. And he couldn't have her, because it was her nature to need more than he could give her. He'd understood that all along. If he'd been a fool, it wasn't when he walked out on Christmas Eve. More likely, it was when he'd arrived in the first place, convinced he'd found the kind of acceptance and need only a family offered.

"Hey, boss!" someone called.

"Yeah?" He strode from his pickup to where a cluster of men were staring up at a hemlock.

"This one's not tagged. Looks big enough."

Damn, that was a cold wind. The sun was high and frost still crackled on the ground. "Take it," he said.

Within minutes, a chain saw cut through the silence, and he stood well back watching when the tree went, vibrating the very earth when it hit and bounced.

He went back to the loader, where he'd been about to do a quick lube. He was finicky about maintaining expensive or dangerous equipment. On the loader, he did an inspection daily and greased some vulnerable parts, like the pump-drive-shaft joints. When the day was as cold as this, he repeated the lube job midshift if it was practical. Trouble was, he'd done this so many times it didn't keep his mind occupied. He could do the job with his brain in neutral.

As though she was standing next to him, he heard Teresa. *I never, ever, thought any less of you because you have trouble reading.* He would have given anything to believe her.

He'd replayed the phone message so damn many times he couldn't stop hearing her voice, trembling a little, so he knew she'd been crying. *I won't blame you if you can't forgive me, but I do love you.* Clamping his jaws shut, Joe stopped what he was doing for a moment, head bowed. In anguish, he thought, maybe she'd marry him if he asked her quickly, while she still felt guilty. At least that way he'd have her for a while before she decided again that he could be "helped" if he'd just try. A while was better than not at all, wasn't it?

Well, chances were it was too late now. Teresa hadn't called back or hunted him down the way she had the other time. She'd probably decided by now that he was the jerk, that he'd overreacted. Maybe she was even right.

He wondered what she'd told Mark and Nicole. Did they miss him at all? Joe figured the boy did. He'd responded so hungrily to any attention. He wanted a father.

Don't think about it, Joe told himself. *Why torment yourself?*

But he couldn't stop, not that day or any other day. Driving home at night was the worst, when it would have been so easy to go by her place, pet the dogs, step up on her front porch and knock. Say, "I was an idiot, and I miss you." His own house was too quiet, too big, too empty. Going to bed was almost as bad as passing her road. Lying in the dark, how could he not think about her? She'd been in this bed half a dozen times. Thinking about those times reminded him of the night when she teased him into finding a good spot to park. He remembered her breasts, pale in the moonlight, the squeeze of her muscles and the feel of her legs wrapped around him. Her amusement when he'd returned her panties, found under the bench seat.

He kept expecting it to get better. In time he'd quit thinking about her, wouldn't he? Two weeks passed. He saw her coming out of the grocery store, pushing a loaded cart. She was alone, unsmiling, beautiful even in denim overalls and a bright red flannel shirt. He could hardly breathe as he watched her transfer the bags to the trunk of her car, push the cart back in, then climb into her car. He couldn't get out of his truck he hurt so damn bad.

Rebecca had her baby in mid-January, which momentarily distracted him. She had a girl and they named her Katherine after Sam's mother. The kid was still red as a tomato, and already Sam doted on her. Under other circumstances, Joe would have found humor in watching this dark guarded man coo at his baby daughter.

Three weeks. At the Hughes family dinner, most of the family clustered around the baby. Alan, already blasé, talked about nothing but Nicole, with occasional asides about her mother or Mark. Joe had never envied anybody the way he did his nephew, who apparently half lived with the Burketts.

At three and a half weeks, he was near to cracking. If he had to read for her every night, wasn't that worth it? What was a little humiliation? But then he'd close his eyes and picture it, him sitting there at the kitchen table like one of the kids doing homework, reading aloud, following along as his finger moved on the page. But in this picture, he saw Mark listening open-mouthed. Hero worship wouldn't survive that kind of belittlement. Maybe even Teresa's love wouldn't. How could they help but feel incredulity and eventually scorn for someone so dumb?

He couldn't do it, couldn't pay her price. Anything else, but not this.

Seeing her only sharpened the pain, so Joe took to checking the parking lot carefully before he went into the store or post office. He didn't want to come face-to-face with her.

Instead, he ran into Dr. Eric Bergstrom, DVM. The vet been in White Horse three or four years. In that time, Joe and he had had a beer together a few times, even shot pool together once. Bergstrom was okay for a man with capital letters after his name.

Today he was frowning as he strode into the post office. When he saw Joe, he stopped dead. Then his mouth twisted with contempt and he shouldered past him.

Hell, Joe thought. Teresa must have talked to Bergstrom.

Head down, Joe crossed the sidewalk to his pickup. A hand on his shoulder suddenly jerked him around.

Eric Bergstrom glowered at him. "What happened with you and Teresa?"

Joe's emotions were so raw he roused to anger easily. "Is that any of your goddamn business?"

A different kind of man would have thrust his chin out and answered in kind. Bergstrom was too civilized for that. Too well educated.

He moderated his voice. "I don't like to see her unhappy. I thought maybe there was something I could do."

It hurt Joe to realize how much more Teresa had in common with her partner than she did with him. What if Bergstrom decided to console Teresa?

She'd be better off than she was with him. He swore under his breath, closed his eyes briefly and said in a defeated voice, "I'm dyslexic. Teresa decided to help me learn to read. I blew my top."

He waited for "That's all?" Or an incredulous "You can't read?"

Instead: "Ah." Bergstrom seemed to be thinking. After a while he said, "Teresa's gotten where she is by always pushing the limits. She doesn't like to think there's something she can't do."

"I know." Joe grimaced. "She doesn't belong with a man who accepts his limits."

A mother shepherding two small children passed them, and went into the post office. Bergstrom's steady gaze never left Joe's face.

"I'm not so sure about that," he said. "What goes on between a man and a woman doesn't have much to do with crap like that."

"Crap?" Joe echoed.

Teresa's partner slapped him on the shoulder. "Hey, I'm a vet, not a psychiatrist. All I know is, you gotta figure out what's important and what's not." With that, he turned and disappeared into the post office.

Good advice maybe, but Joe already knew what was important. Teresa. And it was pretty clear the only way he could make her happy was to learn to read, the one thing he'd failed at in his life. Failed at again and again. He couldn't give her what she wanted and needed. He'd never be her intellectual equal.

January twenty-fourth, one month to the day since he'd walked out on Teresa, happened to be a Friday. Joe had been avoiding the tavern both because he didn't feel sociable and because even there he was unavoidably reminded of her. But tonight he went and got drunk enough that one of his friends had to drive him home. He awoke late with a pounding headache and the realization that he'd have to get a lift back into town to get his pickup. He drank a cup of black coffee and called Lee, who did him the favor without asking any questions, though he was shaking his head when he left Joe in the parking lot of the tavern, otherwise empty but for Joe's blue Chevy truck. Joe felt like a teenager, except he didn't have youth to excuse his stupidity.

As he drove home, his mood was as black as an old-growth forest at night, where the ancient trees reared so high they choked out the moonlight. He stopped to get his mail from the box at the foot of his driveway. He never got much; even his bills went to the post-office box in town and were taken care of by his secretary. But today a small package lay on top of the junk mail. His name was printed in block letters on the front. The sender hadn't put a return address.

He drove up to the house, turned off the ignition and tore open the package. Inside was a small flat present wrapped in Christmas paper. Red ribbon looped several times around it, and the package even had a bow, though it was squished flat. He turned it over in his hand. A late Christmas present. But who the hell had sent it?

For some reason he was bent on getting the ribbon off without cutting it. That used up his patience. He ripped the paper off. Inside was an unlabeled cassette tape. He turned it over and over in his hands as if hoping some message would appear.

His heart had begun to thud so hard it was like a jackhammer in his ears. He turned the key so that the cassette player would work and shoved the tape in. For a second it ran in silence, and he gripped the steering wheel with fingers that were suddenly sweating.

A woman's voice said, "*One Man's Meat,* by E.B. White." He sat in a daze as Teresa read the thoughts of a man who saw the world clearly and with humor, a man who'd vowed to simplify his life.

Joe actually smiled a time or two, though he knew he would have to listen to it again, because right now he was hearing *her* message as much as E.B. White's. He knew without having read the title on the book she'd given him for Christmas that this was it, that now she was telling him reading was not the point of her gift. Sharing the riches of language and insight between the covers was the point. She'd found a way to do it that he could accept, a way that wasn't meant to be a prod or a lure.

The book was made up of short essays—newspaper pieces originally, he guessed. Joe had been listening for perhaps twenty minutes when she came to the end of one of them. Her voice subtly changed.

"To be continued—in person." The pause was long enough that he thought she was done. But she had one more thing to say. "Joe, if there's anybody around here who's a dummy, it's me. But I do love you."

The tape kept running, a faint whirring. Still gripping the steering wheel, he leaned his head back and closed his eyes. Emotions rolled over him in waves: pain, joy, relief, sexual hunger, anger—and a happiness that swamped the others.

He had to talk to her. His hand shook as he turned the key and the truck roared to life. He was halfway to her house when he remembered that this was Saturday and she'd be working. He drove to the animal hospital, instead, where he found her Volvo parked outside.

For the first time, he hesitated, looking at himself in the rearview mirror. Damn, he hadn't even shaved this morning! He rubbed a hand over the bristles, thought about going back home and knew he couldn't wait. She'd seen worse before. On a sudden impulse he hung the ribbon around his neck, the bow dangling like a pendant.

A perky blonde smiled at him from behind the counter. "How can I help you?"

"I'm looking for Dr. Burkett. Does she have a minute?"

"Oh, I'm sorry." The young woman looked regretful. "I'm afraid she was called out on an emergency. But I believe Dr. Bergstrom is in back. Would you like to speak to him?"

"Can you tell me where she is?"

Her smile didn't even falter. "I'm sorry, I can't. Are you sure you wouldn't like to speak to our other vet?"

He must look like a lunatic. Bloodshot eyes and a dark shadow on his jaw. "Yeah, okay," he said.

She used the intercom. A moment later, Bergstrom appeared behind her. His gaze dropped to the damn bow before returning to Joe's face.

"Joe! What's up?"

"Hi, Eric." He hesitated. Their talk had changed the footing between them, and he wasn't sure how he felt about that. How could they be friends? But, hell, if Teresa could love him, maybe he wasn't the pariah he'd believed himself to be all these years. "Uh, is Teresa due back anytime soon?"

Bergstrom's eyebrows lifted, but all he said was, "I don't know. She's out at Chuck Holland's farm. Heifer was having trouble delivering her calf. Could be a quickie or keep her there for two hours. That's why I came in. People had made appointments."

Joe glanced over his shoulder to see a woman with two kids and a cat carrier waiting beside a man holding a Pekingese. He knew both of them. They smiled with enough merriment to indicate they'd noticed the Christmas bow and his desperation. He nodded stiffly, the back of his neck flushing. By dinnertime, half the town would know he was looking for Teresa.

"Yeah, okay. Thanks," he muttered.

"You know where Holland's place is. Why don't you track her down there if it's urgent?"

"I might do that." He strode out, imagining the conversation that would start the minute the door shut.

Holland's dairy farm wasn't two miles out of town. Even two miles took long enough for Joe to come close to chickening out. Maybe he should wait until she got home tonight. But, of course, she'd know the minute she got back to the hospital that he was looking for her.

White Horse Animal Hospital was written on the side of the canopied pickup pulled close to a long barn. She was still here. If she had an arm deep inside the cow rearranging tangled calf legs, she might be less than glad to see him. Now he knew he wanted to chicken out.

But somehow his hands and feet weren't cooperating. In fact, he was getting out of the truck, pocketing the keys. He'd just take a look. Maybe he'd get lucky and she wouldn't notice him unless she was alone.

The barn was quiet and shadowy, the cement floor washed clean. Joe rounded a partition and saw her. Down at the end of a long aisle, she was leaning on some rails looking at something.

She didn't hear him coming. As he got closer, he saw the straw in her hair and that her sleeves were rolled up to bare hands and forearms red and sore from being scrubbed. But what he saw most was her smile, so tender he wanted it for himself. He knew what she must be looking at: a newborn calf with big brown eyes and absurdly long legs, alive thanks to her.

He guessed she thought he was Chuck, because she didn't turn her head when he stopped at her side, just murmured, "Look at her. I never get tired of this part of my job."

He did look, and saw a calf still damp from birth, rusty red and snowy white, already on its feet and suckling.

"I wouldn't get tired of it, either," he said, and she spun around.

"Joe!"

"I got your message."

Her mouth worked, but nothing came out. Her eyes, as brown and soft as the calf's, searched his face.

He kept his hands in his pockets and talked despite the lump in his throat. "I love you, too. But... have you really thought?"

Her breath escaped in a rush and tears welled in her eyes. "I've done nothing but think! Even Eric told me what an idiot I was! Do you have any idea how awful this last month has been?"

He balled his hands into fists. "If you marry me, you'll be stuck here. You'll spend the rest of your life in White Horse."

Her lips trembled as she smiled. "I can't think of anything that would make me happier."

"Are you sure?" He waited, rigid, braced for a rejection despite the certainty he saw in her eyes.

"Joe Hughes, I love you." Her voice broke. "And if you're asking me to marry you, I'll answer."

He still didn't let himself touch her. "I'm asking."

"Yes." Teresa threw herself at him and wound her arms around his neck. "Yes, yes, yes, yes..."

He could have listened forever if he hadn't needed so badly to kiss her. But that was just as sweet. He drowned in her kiss, in the certainty that this was right, that he could trust her.

They separated, looked at each other, kissed again. Soft nuzzling kisses, deep hungry ones. Their hands gripped each other fearfully.

One of those times when their mouths parted, she noticed the red bow. She fingered it, and new tears filled her eyes. "All I wanted for Christmas was you, and I drove you away."

"You've got me," he said, in a voice raw with need.

She pressed a kiss to his throat. "I think it's a matter of argument who has whom."

Joe had no intention of arguing. It didn't even bother him that she had *who* and *whom* down pat.

"Can we get out of here?" he asked.

Teresa's smile was as saucy and bold as he'd remembered it being. "Only if you know a good place to park."

"Oh, yeah." He grinned back at her. "My own driveway."

But he had to kiss her again first.

CHUCK HOLLAND had known the Hugheses for the past fifty years. He'd even asked Margaret Hughes to marry him back when she was Margaret Fitzgerald. He knew about her son Joe's problems, and he knew Joe was a fine boy.

But in all his days, he'd never expected to step into his own barn and find Joe Hughes passionately kissing the veterinarian. Of course, she was the first woman vet he'd ever known, which made the kissing acceptable. She was a pretty woman, too, almost as pretty as Margaret had been in her day. Capable, too, he'd decided after watching her work.

But the really strange part was the red ribbon around Joe Hughes's neck and the Christmas bow crushed in Dr. Teresa Burkett's hand. There was a story in that, he figured. But he didn't suppose it was meant for his ears.

Smiling, he quietly retreated. Not until he was out in the cold winter sunshine did he start whistling. He wasn't even surprised when the tune his lips shaped was a Christmas carol.